INTRIGUE

Books by Megan Fatheree

A ROYAL INTRIGUE
Intrigue

FOR SUCH A TIME
Dust to Dust
Beauty From Pain
A Time to Live

STAND-ALONE NOVELS
Codex

INTRIGUE

A Royal Intrigue | 1

MEGAN FATHEREE

ISBN: 9781735941110 (paperback)

For the dreamers.
For the ones who still believe in grand gestures and love at first sight.

Chapter 1

Jonathan exited the plane in a flurry of black suits and security safety phrases. The pomp and circumstance weren't strictly necessary, but not every day did a prince visit another country. Jonathan consented to arrive with all the ceremony, but he knew how to ditch his father's cronies when it came down to it.

Guillaume would have his back, should he need it. Jonathan was more than thankful that the ever-capable head of security left Vitromont Palace to look after the wayward crown prince. Jonathan wouldn't dare second-guess the skilled and trustworthy bodyguard.

No doubt one of the reasons that Jonathan's father insisted that he bring Guillaume along.

Once the men ushered Jonathan safely into the bullet-proof day limo, he finally relaxed. A sigh fell unbidden from his lips.

"Is it that bad already?" Guillaume asked from the seat beside Jonathan.

Jonathan huffed a laugh. "Are we all set for later? Everything prepared?"

"Simple." Guillaume flicked his fingers. "I pulled Adison and Ferrand to help. Just say the word."

Jonathan nodded. Giving Guillaume just enough leeway to be dangerous often worked the best. Although, Guillaume's strict adherence to security protocol sometimes made excursions too predictable. Just once, Jonathan would like a good surprise.

"How far to Margaret's home?" Jonathan watched the city pass by outside the heavily-tinted window.

Guillaume held up a finger, his other hand pressed to his ear. "What's the situation at the Magpie's Nest?" He listened to the response. "Good. Lion en route."

Jonathan leaned his head back. "Clear, then?"

"Except for some squabbling." Guillaume chuckled. "Margaret has always been the character. Are you sure about your accommodations?"

Jonathan nodded. "I'm here for her charity event. It only makes sense."

Margaret's home had excellent security. Jonathan had visited his cousin before. He didn't understand Guillaume's hesitance now, except perhaps a desire to avoid Margaret's over-the-top, flamboyant personality. Guillaume never had particularly liked the woman. Of course, Margaret never took security as seriously as Guillaume.

The ride to Margaret's house remained, blessedly, uneventful. By the time they reached the front gates, Jonathan's security had arrived to meet them. With the gates closed and the roof secured, the security team allowed Jonathan space to maneuver on his own.

The large double doors of Margaret's American chalet opened effortlessly. They closed behind him with a *clank*.

Margaret sailed down the stairs, draped in gossamer and scarves. "Jonathan, *darling*! How have you been?" She brushed a kiss through the air above each of his cheeks.

Jonathan chuckled as he returned the gesture. "I really can't complain, except to protest that you gave me so little advance notice about this charity event. Why all the secrecy, hm?"

"Don't dither over trivial issues." Margaret slid her arm through Jonathan's and tugged him toward the nearest archway.

"It's not so trivial." Jonathan laughed at her attempt to avoid the subject.

"In the grand scheme of things, my secrecy and tardiness are minute, insignificant details." Margaret shoved open the door to one of her favorite sun-rooms. "Have a seat, dear, and let's chat. It's been *so* long."

"Dear cousin." Jonathan sank into a chair and pressed his hand sarcastically over his heart. "Are you using a sovereign nation's only crown prince for a publicity stunt?"

Margaret's silence said more than her words.

A hearty laugh rumbled from Jonathan's chest. "You are! How terribly droll of you."

"It's not meant to be an insult or an amusement." Margaret pouted. "It's a very serious charitable cause."

"I would never deny that." Jonathan agreed. In any case, publicity stunt or no, she got him away from the palace for a bit. Running a country was not as glamorous as the media made it out to be. "I still find it highly amusing. Only a woman of your caliber could successfully execute such a plan."

Margaret laughed, a sophisticated, light sound she had no doubt been trained to make. Her fingers fluttered through the air. "Amusing or not, you're here now."

Jonathan could have sworn he detected a secondary meaning behind her words. An ulterior motive in her eyes. He made a point to never question his eccentric cousin Margaret, but on rare occasions like this he felt he must break his rules.

Jonathan sat forward in his seat. His eyes, narrowed now to show his seriousness, studied Margaret's gleeful countenance carefully. "Whatever it is you're planning, I won't be a part of it. I am not a man to be trifled with, cousin."

"What I'm planning?" Margaret tried to look appalled, but her eyes glittered with a barely-constrained mischief that Jonathan knew well. "I asked you here for a charity dinner. I was absurdly straightforward about it."

"Yes. Absurdly. Now tell me the real plan." Jonathan folded his arms, all business.

"Oh, the tea!" Margaret squealed, clapping her hands as one of her employees set a tray on the table.

"Don't think I'll forget about this just because there's tea." Jonathan reached for a biscuit and set it on a small China dish.

"Forget about what?" Margaret set about pouring the tea. Her flowing tunic sleeves fluttered with each little movement.

"Margaret…"

"Oh, heavens, Jean." She pronounced it like a French version of John. "Stop worrying and eat your biscuit. I swear, you take the fun out of everything."

"Which leads me to believe you have more planned than a charity ball."

"Shut it." Margaret set a cup of tea before him. "Drink up. Before it gets cold." But that gleam still hadn't left her eyes.

Jonathan's mind raced with possibilities. Despite his thorough knowledge of his cousin, he hadn't the foggiest idea what went on in her mind. She wasn't usually so close-mouthed. Her flamboyant personality didn't allow for secrets. The fact that she refused to speak a word about her plan kept him on edge.

Five minutes into tea-time, Jonathan couldn't stay silent any longer. "Maggie, *please.*"

"No. it's too amusing to watch you squirm." Margaret sipped her tea indifferently. "How is your family nowadays?"

Jonathan knew he deserved the payback after calling her out about the publicity stunt. He didn't like it, but he understood why she changed the subject. Diplomacy, in which Jonathan had been trained since birth, didn't allow him to argue with her.

A sigh slipped languorously past Jonathan's lips. "They are well. Frederick never misses the chance to have a bit of fun. You should have invited him in my stead."

"Mm." Margaret shook her head. "He's far too much of a libertine for anyone to take him seriously. Besides, everyone knows he's spending the month in Monaco. I'm sure casino atten-dance will increase with all those women pushing to get a look at him."

"If I were a lesser man, I might be insulted." Jonathan sipped his own tea.

"Don't fret your pretty little head." Margaret laughed. "All is as it should be. One prince to rule the nation, another to win the ladies' favor."

"Who says I can't be both?" Jonathan arched a brow, pleased when it elicited another of Margaret's giggles.

"True. True." Her eyes glittered again, far more perceptive than she let on. "Why shouldn't you be both?"

ೞೞೞ

"This is ridiculous." Alissa shook her head again.

She had a good life. A decent-paying job. Friends who took her creative insanity at face value. She didn't need a side-gig.

Especially not one with these crazy monochrome uniforms. It barely even fit.

"Come on, 'Lissa!" Violet pressed her palms together in a begging motion. "Please? For me? One night. You make extra money, some sweet tips if you're lucky, and my boss doesn't have to search for another part-timer."

"Do I have to?" Alissa wrinkled her nose.

Alissa loved her best friend to a fault, but sometimes Violet pushed the boundaries. Sometimes, Alissa questioned Violet's sanity. Like now. What in the world had Violet been thinking when she proposed this?

Violet flopped onto the couch and wrapped her arms around Alissa. "Pretty, pretty, *pretty* please?"

"What happens if I say no?" Alissa eyed Violet suspiciously.

Violet blinked big puppy eyes. "I already told my boss you would."

Alissa groaned. Violet knew—she *knew*—that Alissa hated to be a disappointment. By making a commitment on Alissa's behalf, Violet secured what she wanted. Even if Alissa wanted to say no. Even if waitressing wasn't her shtick. Even if this felt like a giant set-up.

"Fine."

Violet squealed and gave her friend a tight squeeze. "Best. Friend. Ever! Ugh, I love you so much!"

Alissa laughed. Violet always had been the outgoing one between the two of them. "Can I make a complaint about the uniform though?"

"You can try. Probably won't do any good." Violet let go and jumped to her feet. A miraculous record for the amount of time Violet could handle sitting still.

"They're hideous."

"They're standard issue."

Alissa shot Violet a knowing look. "Lapels this wide belong in the 80s, not on wait staff."

"If you squint, they're not bad." Violet shrugged her shoulders.

"And the shapeless skirt?" Alissa plucked at the material. It couldn't possibly be cotton. It might be denim. Either way, cheap at best.

Violet wrinkled her nose. "So it's not ideal. Four hours max and then you're out of there and a couple hundo richer."

Violet had a point. Alissa had never been averse to a little extra spending money. However, pushing her to this extreme felt a bit... desperate.

"Are you sure about this?"

Violet threw her hands up in exasperation. "Of *course* I'm sure! Don't be ridiculous, you rock that... outfit. Can it be called an outfit? Is 'uniform' more appropriate for the ensemble in question?"

"I'm not wearing this." If Violet kept rambling on, it would only serve to convince Alissa of the hideousness involved. "If he changes the uniforms to something professional, I may recon-sider." Alissa hastened toward the door to Violet's spare bedroom.

"Wait, wait, wait!" In a flash, Violet slid between Alissa and the door. Her hands gripped Alissa's shoulders. Intense eyes bore into Alissa's suspicious gaze. "If he changes the uniform, you'll do it?"

"I'll consider," Alissa confirmed.

"Give me twenty minutes." Violet's fingers fell away to whip her phone from her pocket.

Alissa didn't know what to expect. Violet had an aura about her, one that usually transformed based on the situation she found herself in. Not great when Alissa wanted to predict her best friend, but a genuine lifesaver when Violet needed to get something done. Or, in this case, convince someone of their own stupidity.

In the meantime, Alissa had every intention of burning the uniform. Right after she doused it in gasoline.

Alissa didn't fancy herself as picky when it came to fashion, but she drew the line here. She couldn't imagine how anyone worked for this company, wearing what could only be described as a reject of the twentieth century.

She had other complaints. Alissa didn't like the idea of kowtowing to large crowds of people. Once upon a time, she took a waitressing job, and it hadn't ended well. Ever since then, Alissa avoided the occupation like the plague itself. In Alissa's mind, waitressing sat on the same level as walking home alone in the dark. Stupid, unnecessary, and terrifying.

The only reason she entertained the thought now? Because Violet asked. Alissa would do anything for Violet.

Relief flooded Alissa as she slid into her own jeans. That thing they called a skirt should be ripped apart and drowned.

Perhaps a bit dramatic, but Alissa had her moments of drama.

A pattern of vibrations shimmied through the fabric of Alissa's jeans, which could only mean one thing. Sure enough, a quick peek at her phone showed a familiar number on the screen.

Alissa flopped onto the bed and swiped the green answer button. "Good afternoon, Miss Maggie."

"Must you insist on calling me by that name, dear?"

Alissa laughed. Leave it to Maggie to skip all the formalities and cut straight to the chase. Maggie did what Maggie wanted. Nothing more, nothing less. An eccentric woman with a mysterious silence around her origins. Alissa loved the intriguing aspect to Maggie's existence. It had always caught her curiosity.

"What can I do for you?" Alissa asked.

"It's been a while since we had a chat, the two of us." Maggie paused to bark an order at someone on her side of the line. "You should stop by tomorrow. I have that tea you so like and I'm looking forward to a look at your new manuscript."

"It's not finished yet." Alissa winced.

Her current manuscript needed hours upon hours of editing before it would be ready to see the light of day. Maggie always pushed her to show the "raw, unaltered talent" of the first draft. If Alissa hadn't agreed to it when they first met, she would reject the notion entirely. Instead, she found herself closing her eyes and hoping Maggie postponed their meeting.

"Nonsense. Whatever you have is fine. Creatives such as ourselves should share our work, don't you think?" Maggie giggled. "I have a wonderful piece of art I'd like you to inspect for me. Don't worry, darling, it won't hurt any more than a little prick of a needle."

Yeah, a needle opening a vein. Alissa bit back a whimper. "I guess you probably have a time you want to meet me?"

"Tomorrow, as I said. Come at two if you're free."

Of course she had free time, but for the first time since Alissa made a pact with Maggie, she didn't want to follow through. "I'll be there."

"Oh, Alissa darling!"

Alissa paused, her phone just shy of her ear. "Yes?"

"Don't be alarmed about security when you arrive. I've a guest and they're all unreservedly paranoid about something happening. I'll tell them you're allowed through."

"If it's too much trouble, we can postpone." Alissa crossed her fingers and prayed for help.

No such luck. "Of course it isn't any trouble. Don't be frightened of any of them, even if they act intimidating. They're all softhearted when you get to know them."

None of this sounded encouraging. Alissa didn't have a problem with the security at Maggie's house, but it made her feel squirmy. What if she couldn't keep her cool around the new insurgence of security? What if they thought she did something wrong? What if they arrested her?

Okay, so they probably wouldn't arrest her. Especially not without evidence. Alissa recognized illogical fears when they raised their heads.

"I'll see you tomorrow, then." *Please, God, let this meeting get canceled. I don't want to disappoint her.*

"Two o'clock. Don't forget!" A quick smack of Maggie's lips told Alissa she sent a kiss as her love.

The call ended.

Alissa set the phone on the bed and groaned out her frustration. She didn't have time to edit the single finished chapter of her next novel. Why did she have to make that stupid pact? Even fellow creatives weren't meant to see first drafts.

"'Lissa!" Violet skidded into the room and struck a triumphant pose. "Uniforms changed. Button-down white shirt and black skirt. No more lapels."

"Thank God." Alissa propped up on one elbow. "We have bigger issues now."

"We do?" Violet's arm, poised high in the air, slowly sank to her side. "What kind of issues? Did something happen that I don't know about?"

"Miss Maggie wants to have a meeting tomorrow."

"I don't see the dilemma." Violet shook her head, confused.

Alissa sat up and threw her hands in the air. "I only have one chapter and it's terrible!"

"Okay..."

"I can't show it to her, she's going to hate it. I have no muse!"

Violet rolled her eyes. Years of friendship gave Alissa and Violet the kind of relationship where they could be brutally honest. Violet didn't hold back this time, either.

"Look, muse is a myth. Your writing is good and Maggie isn't going to hold anything against you. She adores you. Besides, if you really don't want to show it to her, couldn't you just lie?"

"You know I'm a terrible liar." Alissa settled her thumb against her lips. "She'd see through me in a second."

"You'll figure it out." Violet threw the closet doors open. "For now, let's get you outfitted so we can go to work."

"No lapels? You're sure?"

"Yep."

At least one thing went well today. Small victories amounted to bigger accomplishments over time.

Alissa crawled from the bed and dug around for the items Violet described. Tonight may not be as bad as the last time. After all, these were elite-class philanthropists. How bad could they possibly be?

Chapter 2

The ballroom sparkled with crystal and lace. Champagne flowed freely. China plates shone from their pristine positions. The lavish atmosphere bespoke the caliber of guests that the fundraiser entertained.

Jonathan adjusted a cufflink and blew out a breath. Around him, his security huddled.

Guillaume peered out into the bustling ballroom, then tossed a look to Adison. "Check the exits and entrances again."

"Yes, sir." Adison dipped a bow and disappeared down the hall.

"Can we enter yet?" Jonathan resisted the urge to fiddle with his other cufflink. How did Margaret convince him to do this?

Markum, Jonathan's aide, snapped closed the cover of his tablet. "Three more minutes."

Of course, Jonathan knew the protocol. They would make their entrance after the majority of the crowd had already arrived. Once the crush ended, securing the area became easier. With minimal personnel, Jonathan understood the precaution. He didn't find pleasure in it, but he comprehended.

"All clear." Adison slipped back into the makeshift green room.

"Sixty seconds, then, your highness." Guillaume flashed a smirk. "No need to be nervous."

Jonathan shoved his hands into his suit pockets. "I'm not nervous."

"Cufflinks," Markum coughed.

"It's a habit."

"Leave him be, you'll only make it worse." Guillaume chuckled.

One of Margaret's security personnel poked his head through the door. He held out a set of in-ear communication devices. "These are issued by our side. Just for tonight, join us."

Guillaume tapped the piece already in his ear. "Margaret already connected us to your network."

"Really? Why didn't you say?"

"It's my job to be suspicious. I asked your boss not to tell you. You're all cleared now."

A disapproving frown manifested on the man's face before he disappeared.

"You don't trust Margaret's security?" Jonathan glanced to each of his people. "Why?"

"We'll discuss later." Guillaume opened the door.

Jonathan straightened his spine and planted a smile on his lips. Not that too many people took notice, but a few always approached to schmooze. They could, after all, easily recognize Jonathan's face. Even if he wanted, he couldn't hide his identity.

"Your highness!" A plump man, barely over five feet tall, took a step into Jonathan's personal space. A thick hand reached out. "Thank you for sparing us your precious time."

Jonathan pulled his fingers out of his pockets and shook the man's hand heartily. "For a good cause, I have no qualms clearing my schedule."

Only a half-lie. Coming here helped Jonathan's own need for space and time. Attending this party lent a convenient excuse, whether or not Jonathan believed in the cause.

"We greatly appreciate your interest in mental health. The board of directors looks forward to your speech on the matter."

"I hope to live up to expectations." Jonathan's meant for his congenial grin to put the man at ease. It didn't require the lofty laughter that followed.

"Your highness..." Markum leaned forward to whisper the words that would extract Jonathan from the awkward conversation.

Jonathan nodded at his aide. "If you'll excuse me, it seems I have a prior engagement."

"Of course, of course!"

Markum stepped to Jonathan's side and motioned toward the head table.

Jonathan fell in line three steps in front of Markum. No need to thank him. Markum's job entailed things of this sort. A constant eye on Jonathan's thoughts and emotions. A foolproof gauge as to when Jonathan had reached his limit.

Markum pulled Jonathan's chair from the table.

Jonathan unbuttoned his jacket and settled into the seat. A quick glance around the room revealed more than a dozen security personnel scattered throughout.

Father would be satisfied.

However, Jonathan was not. As much as his father cherished a secure location, Jonathan wanted one day to himself, no tag-a-longs.

Good luck with that.

Even if he wanted it, he could only get so close to alone. His position made a certain modicum of surveillance necessary.

"Must I sit here like a showpiece?" Jonathan folded his hands in his lap.

"Would you rather speak with the board of directors? The guests?" Markum gave a look borne from years at the Crown Prince's side.

"Is there anyone interesting in attendance?"

"An ambassador. A senator. A Federal Bureau of Investigation director." Markum checked his tablet. "A beauty queen, model, and actress?"

Not the kind of people Jonathan found particularly invigorating. He hadn't come for pleasure. Business took higher priority. He could make it through. For Margaret's sake.

"How long before dinner is served?"

"Five minutes. Twenty until your speech." Markum finally took his own seat. "We can make a fashionably early exit in an hour."

"So soon?" Jonathan expected as much in his own country, with his busy schedule. Here, on foreign soil, Jonathan thought Markum would surely force him to socialize for an extended amount of time. "Why are you being lenient?"

"Should I be a slave master instead?" Markum nudged his glasses up on his nose. "I thought your highness had plans later this evening. If that isn't the case, I could set a few meetings with the dignitaries—"

"That isn't necessary." The answer came too quickly, but Markum didn't need to continue that line of thought. Jonathan had no intention of staying any longer than he needed to stay.

Jonathan enjoyed a good party as much as the next man, but tonight something felt... off. He wanted nothing more than to flee.

What is this trepidation?

Nothing changed with the quick, silent question, either good or bad. It took every ounce of self-control in Jonathan's body to refrain from tapping his fingers. Something felt wrong.

A sea of wait staff descended on the room. Dinner found its way before each of the renowned guests.

Margaret waltzed into the ballroom fashionably late. She immediately took the place behind the podium. A smattering of applause sounded throughout the room, mostly from those who knew her from the board of directors.

"Treasured guests..." Margaret flashed her widest smile. "I'm so glad you've come this evening. Your concern about the mental health of this country's citizens moves me deeply. I am no expert on the matter, but my dear Michael loved these people more than any other, and so I aim to carry on his passion for such a noble cause."

This time, amidst the clinking of forks against china, the applause sounded more sincere.

"As I have not learned enough to present a promising plan on the subject, I would like to introduce you instead to my dear, dear cousin."

Jonathan choked on his stuffed mushroom. That was not in the plan. How dare Margaret skip across the schedule and blindside him like that? The tea in his glass slid smoothly down Jonathan's throat, thrown down in one gulp. He held the glass out to signal a waiter for a refill.

Margaret flung her arm toward Jonathan's general direction. "Ladies and gentlemen, His Royal Highness Jonathan Henry Christophe of the House of Manon, Crown Prince of Veldoria."

Applause erupted.

Despite his irritation, Jonathan rose to his feet. A single flick of his wrist buttoned his suit jacket. There would be plenty of time later to nitpick at Margaret about her lack of decorum. She should at least give him some warning before she changed the plan.

With the dignity and poise hammered into him since youth, Jonathan took his place behind the podium. Guillaume and Adison migrated closer, in case an issue were to arise. Markum, however, remained primly seated right where Jonathan left him. Self-assured rascal.

"Ladies and gentlemen, gracious hosts, it is an honor to receive such a chance to speak on a matter close to my heart. Mental health."

Jonathan knew the speech by heart. He practiced it on the plane and again at Margaret's. Speeches didn't take long to memorize, once he used the techniques he picked up over the years. People might think diplomacy came naturally to the Crown Prince. They would be wrong. It took ages to train it into his very pores.

As the rehearsed presentation flowed from Jonathan's lips, his eyes scoped the room. Listeners often revealed more about their interest by their unconscious signals. Tonight's guests seemed particularly intent on listening well.

The wait staff appeared again, silently slinking through the crowd. Dinner plates settled on carts and dessert plates found their way to the tables.

Jonathan couldn't help a peek at his own table.

The same woman who served dinner now cleared the dishes. She looked positively uninterested in anything going on in the room. Instead, her focus shifted to the leftover mushrooms as she set the plate on the cart. She shot a quick glance both directions before one of the mushrooms went directly into her mouth.

A grimace must have meant the woman didn't like something about the dish. Before Jonathan could register it, she grabbed his refilled tea glass and downed its entirety.

Jonathan had hardly paid attention to the woman before, when she served dinner. Now he wished he had asked questions. It would have been entertaining, at least.

Reluctantly, Jonathan forced his eyes away from the spritely woman to scan the other side of the crowd. Jonathan wished he hadn't written such a long speech. Why couldn't his words remain short and to the point?

An involuntary shift in his stature turned Jonathan back toward the tables the woman had been tasked to care for.

She carried herself with more self-possession than the other staff. As if she didn't belong here, but somewhere far nicer. Jonathan had never seen such demeanor, such confidence, on such a small woman before.

Jonathan's speech had finally neared its end when he noticed the woman's faltered step. Her hand flew to her mouth in a motion Jonathan recognized as nausea. The cart she steered clattered as her feet stumbled a second time.

Concern ratcheted through Jonathan's head and down to his heart. She seemed fine a moment ago. Something whispered in his head. Told him to check on her.

Jonathan ended his speech with a smile and an invitation for the guests to donate to the cause. He couldn't exit the stage fast enough.

Guillaume stepped to Jonathan's side in less than a second. "What's wrong? You seem upset."

"That girl." Jonathan pointed in her general direction. Even with Guillaume halfway in his path, he didn't stop his advance. "I want to make sure she's alright."

Jonathan spotted her again, taking yet another faltering step toward the kitchen doors.

Guillaume fell in line behind Jonathan, muttering something into his earpiece. It might have been a complaint, but Jonathan didn't care. Guillaume complained about too much.

Even with his height, Jonathan found it difficult to keep track of the waitress as the crowd surged to their feet. Mingling never felt like a worse idea to him.

"Your Highness!" The female voice broke through the crowd. In a flash, a slim, feminine body blocked Jonathan's march.

Jonathan shot a look over his shoulder, expecting Guillaume but finding Adison instead.

Adison gave a bow before he broke off in the direction Jonathan had been headed. Adison would see to the woman's well-being, and that's what mattered. Jonathan suddenly had another problem to solve.

"Lady Estrella. What are you doing here?" Jonathan reluctantly turned to the blonde woman before him.

Lady Estrella Hilmar had no reason to leave Veldoria. The last place on earth Jonathan expected to see her was before his very eyes. Of course, he should have expected as much. Their parents had been trying to arrange their marriage for years now. Finding Jonathan's location, for Estrella, must have been a piece of cake.

They had, of course, been friends since early childhood, but that's where it ended for Jonathan. Friendship. Though a marriage between the royal family and the Prime Minister's daughter seemed advantageous, Jonathan harbored no romantic feelings toward the woman.

However, he wouldn't abandon his friend. She didn't have many friends that would stay true to her. Jonathan intended to stay by her side regardless.

"Jean, don't be ridiculous." Estrella smoothed a hand down the side of her sequined gown. "Clearly I came because I missed you. What other reason would I have to attend such an event?"

"If you aren't here to make a donation, I don't think you have much else to say." Jonathan took a step to the side, intending to slip around her and flee.

Estrella wrapped a hand around his wrist. "Don't be this way, Jean. I thought you would be happy I came to see you. Daddy said not to, but I came anyway."

"Did you argue with your father again?" Jonathan sighed. "Estrella, when will you ever learn? Why are you really here?"

"I told you already, to see you. Shouldn't we present the front of a power couple?"

"I came here to get away from all that gossip. You know that."

Estrella dropped her fingers away from Jonathan's arm. "You came here to get away from me, didn't you? You're running away, too."

"No. It just so happens you're also at the center of those vicious rumors. So I suggest you go home. I won't stay away forever. You can last a week or two without me."

"If I try, who will put daddy in his place about the Anti-Monarchist bill? He's on the fence about it, you know."

"Your father will make the right decision for the country." Jonathan had full faith in that. Jonathan had known Prime

Minister Hilmar since his youth. Prime Minister Hilmar had never been anything if not a patriot. "I really must go, Estrella."

"Five minutes. That's all I ask. Introduce me to your eccentric cousin Margaret. You speak about her so often."

Jonathan wanted to say no, but he had never been able to resist the pleading look in Estrella's affection-starved brown eyes. "Alright. Five minutes, but then I have to go."

᎒Ꮳ

What was wrong with her?

Alissa left the cart in the kitchen and stumbled her way toward the bathroom in the back. She shouldn't have stolen a bite of food —or drink—but she couldn't help it. It all looked too good and she didn't eat before she came.

Now her stomach wanted her to pay the price. And why did the room keep spinning? That didn't make sense. Alissa had never been prone to dizzy spells.

Her legs gave out just before she rounded the corner to the bathroom. Alissa leaned her head against the cold wall and willed herself to calm down.

The hallway tipped and shifted. Colors skewed in front of her eyes, then righted themselves.

Another wave of nausea hit Alissa hard. She pulled herself closer to the corner.

"Is it satisfactory?"

Alissa paused, something inside screaming that danger stood nearby.

"Yes. It will do nicely. Be sure to wrap it up neatly for me." The second voice laughed.

An echoing chuckle sounded from the first voice.

Alissa dared to poke her head around the corner. It didn't help. She could only focus on so much at a time. Two men stood facing each other. One on his own, the other flanked by a third person.

She squinted to make out the first man again. Her fuzzy brain could only focus on his dark suit and a spirally band of plastic by his ear.

"If you need anything else from me, just call."

The second man accepted an envelope from the first. "If I need him out of the race for good? Will you help?"

"For the right price."

Nausea swept over Alissa yet again. Her palms slipped and hit the floor. Her shoulder and head collided with the wall.

"What was that?"

"I'll go check, sir."

Even if she had been coherent enough to register anything going on around her, Alissa couldn't have moved. Closing her eyes didn't do anything to help. Shoes thundered against the floor, then abruptly stopped.

Something landed on Alissa's shoulder, heavy and warm.

"Miss? Miss!"

Barely, Alissa managed to pry her eyes open. She wanted nothing more than to vomit. Maybe then the room would stop spinning and her head would stop floating.

The man in front of her pressed a hand to his ear. "Evacuate." The order was short and to the point, followed only by, "something's wrong."

Alissa groaned and closed her eyes again. "If you're not going to help, go away."

At least, that's what she meant to say. It came out as more of an unintelligible slur. Did her tongue decide to give up now, too?

The man pried open one of Alissa's eyes. "What's your name?"

She shook her head and immediately regretted it.

"I'm Adison Cebon. I'm going to touch your person, only because I don't think you can walk right now." Without any more warning, Adison scooped her off the floor and into his arms. With a determined stride, he set off down the hall.

A pair of men came rushing their direction. Both stopped when they saw the duo.

"Is he safe?" Adison asked.

"Yes. What's going on here?"

"Call an ambulance. And check glasses before they're washed. I want an explanation for her symptoms. If he noticed, it was obvious."

"Yes, sir." Both men hastened away.

Alissa groaned and rested her head on Adison's capable shoulder. "Who was worried?"

"Someone you'd never believe."

Alissa might have imagined those words, but she didn't care. They were the last thing she heard before the darkness swallowed her whole.

Chapter 3

"Alissa!" Violet launched herself into Alissa's arms as soon as the apartment door opened. "We thought you were dead!"

"We?" Alissa gripped Violet's arms to steady herself. The hospital may have discharged her, but that didn't mean she felt one-hundred-percent yet. Alissa needed sleep. Lots and lots of it.

"Yeah, Lucky Seven is here."

Alissa frowned at the familiar nickname. "You called my brother?"

"Of course I called your brother, I thought you died. Oh, hello. Who is this?" Violet must have finally noticed Adison.

Alissa turned to properly see him. "This is Adison. He was working security at the event and found me in the hall."

Cody, Alissa's older brother, jogged out of Alissa's bedroom. "What do you mean 'found you'? Are you okay? What happened?"

"It's nothing, Cody." *Dear God, let Cody stay calm.*

Alissa didn't want to argue with him. Cody took his job as Alissa's older brother *very* seriously. She couldn't remember a single time in her younger years when Cody had taken the opportunity to be lenient on anyone that hurt Alissa.

A sharp, canned ringtone caught Alissa's attention.

Every head in the room swiveled to stare at Adison.

Adison retrieved his phone from his inside jacket pocket and answered without preamble. "Yes, sir. Yes, I just dropped her at home. They said it was Ketamine."

"Ketamine?!" Cody pulled his sister closer to his side. "Somebody drugged you?"

Alissa wanted to yank her arm away from her brother, but she was too tired. Too tired to even answer Cody's question.

"Yes, sir. I'll wait until he arrives." Adison removed the phone from his ear.

Great. Just what Alissa needed. Another thing to worry about. "Who's coming?"

"Someone to drive me back. No need to worry. I'll be out of your space in a moment."

Cody wrapped an arm around Alissa's shoulders. "Can we revisit the part where someone mentioned Ketamine?"

"I think you should speak with Alissa about that." Aidson gave a small bow before he disappeared out the door.

Leave it all on her shoulders. Yeah, that was a brilliant idea. Props to security macho man. Alissa sighed.

"You were drugged?" Cody asked again.

Alissa nodded. This ranked low on her list of things she wanted to talk about. However, she probably needed to discuss it now to save a headache later.

"'Lissa?" Violet asked. "I need explanations. Who was that, really? Why were you drugged? Who dared to do this to *my* best friend? Do you have his address? Do I need to go punch him?"

"Queen Bee, take a chill pill." Cody directed the command at Violet as he led Alissa to a chair. "Sister dearest, I think it's best you start from the beginning."

Alissa sank into the offered chair and groaned. Truth be told, she didn't know when "the beginning" was. She didn't know how the drug got into her system or why someone would do that. She didn't know much about Adison or who he worked for, either.

"Earth to Alissa." Violet snapped her fingers before Alissa's eyes.

Alissa blinked. "Sorry."

Cody dropped onto the couch. "You're okay, right?"

His tone said more than the words themselves. Cody sounded exhausted. Utterly defeated. Like the life had left his soul.

Alissa never meant to make him feel that way. She didn't try to be a troublesome little sister. Even today hadn't been entirely her fault. The hospital assured Alissa she would be fine with some rest and the cops stressed the fact that Ketamine was a common date drug. Someone had definitely used it on purpose.

Who? And why? Alissa fretted over the answers. No matter the target, the intent harmed Alissa. What if it happened again?

"I vote we put Alissa to bed." Violet reached for Alissa's arm.

Cody frowned. "Shouldn't we get to the bottom of this first?"

Violet wrinkled her nose at him, clearly displeased. "What do you want to do, 'Lissa?"

"I have a meeting with Maggie tomorrow." Alissa looked up and batted her eyes. "I want to go to sleep. Sleep sounds good."

"Meeting with Maggie?" Cody scoffed. "That old bat?"

"Cody!" Both girls glared at him.

"Okay, alright, fine!" Cody threw his hands up in surrender. "Go to bed. We'll talk later."

"You're not staying, Lucky Seven." Violet pointed him to the door. "Come back during visiting hours."

"But visiting hours are so sporadic at your place."

"Maybe, but right now they're over. Get out."

"I don't want to."

"Guys." Alissa raised her hand like a kid in a classroom.

Violet planted her hands on her hips. "Who's the homeowner here? Oh, right, it's me. I said get lost, loser."

"Not a chance, bossy." Cody sprang to his feet and poked a finger at Violet's shoulder. "There's no guarantee when I'll be able to see you two again if I leave."

"Sounds good to me. I don't want to see your face anyway."

"Guys..." Alissa didn't like the drama unfolding here. Both Cody and Violet were tired and cranky, which always sent them down a path of destruction.

"Maybe you don't, but if you hang around my sister, you're going to see my face anyway."

"Not if I lock you out and tell Alissa not to let you back in." Violet stuck out her tongue.

Cody rolled his eyes. "Like you'd be able to convince her not to see her older brother. We're tight."

"Not as tight as she is with me."

"Guys!" Alissa shot to her feet. Why would they pull her into this ridiculous argument in the first place?

Violet and Cody both turned to stare at her. "What?"

"You know what? Never mind." Alissa brushed past them. "I'm going to bed. You two do whatever you two are going to do. I don't want to know about it. Just don't die."

What did it matter what they fought over? Right now, Alissa wanted nothing more than sleep. Lots of it. The hospital, the police investigation, and the aftereffects of getting drugged all worked together to provide a special kind of exhaustion.

"See what you did?" Violet hissed at Cody. "Now she's angry."

"Hey, that wasn't me. Get your facts straight."

Alissa slammed her door to drown out their bickering. She loved both of them, but their propensity for getting on each other's nerves irked her. Couldn't they put aside their differences for once?

Whatever.

Alissa pulled her blankets back and crawled into the bed. Her mattress never felt so pillowy, nor her sheets so soft.

Finally safe and uninterested in the questions swimming inside her head, Alissa closed her eyes. Sleep claimed her quickly and didn't let go.

ഇൽൽ

"Take this." Guillaume held a water bottle out to Jonathan.

Jonathan snatched it and downed a long drink. A morning run usually set his mind at ease. Today, it only brought more questions. He shoved a hand back through his sweaty hair, mostly to keep it from his face.

"I'm doing another lap." Jonathan handed the water back to Guillaume.

Guillaume stowed the bottle in a bag and slung the bag over his shoulders. "I'll join you."

"You don't have to."

"Use me as a sounding board."

Of course. Guillaume knew him too well. Jonathan always had too many curious thoughts. Guillaume knew how to set Jonathan's mind at ease, no matter the situation.

"Fine." Jonathan took off at a jog. He didn't want to overextend his muscles. If he jogged instead of running full-out, he could do more laps.

Guillaume fell into a rhythm beside Jonathan, the bag on his back jangling softly with each beat.

Jonathan focused on breathing as he tried to organize his thoughts. He came to this place to relax, not run into more trouble. Yet, trouble seemed to follow him in various ways. At least the fundraiser seemed successful.

"What happened to the waitress last night?" Might as well start there. No one gave him an update before Jonathan ultimately crashed due to jet-lag.

"Adison saw her to the hospital and then home. Apparently she ingested quite a bit of Ketamine."

"Ingested?"

"Yes." Guillaume didn't expound, Jonathan's first clue that the Head of Security had decided to hide something.

A flash of memory shot through Jonathan's conscience. A woman with absolutely no interest in being at the function, stealing food from a table. "She ate from our meal."

Guillaume chuckled. "You don't miss anything. We're checking into it."

"Was I the target?"

"It isn't clear yet. Like I said, we're investigating. The police are involved, which makes it a bit complicated."

"It could have been the Anti-Monarchists." Jonathan suggested. "It's the perfect opportunity to make a move, while I'm out of the country."

"I've already had the same thought. We have people looking into it. Don't concern yourself."

Jonathan shot a glare at Guillaume. "If this is Anti-Monar-chists, an innocent woman stepped into the line of fire. That is neither something I can forgive nor forget."

"Apologies, Your Highness." Guillaume paused his speech, but his gait never faltered. "Should I have Adison procure her medical records from her visit last night?"

"No. I think we've learned all we can about what happened."

Still, Jonathan's mind wasn't at ease. There should be more he could do. More to help or apologize. That woman didn't deserve what happened to her.

"Get me her information. I should at least know that much." Jonathan didn't wait for Guillaume's acknowledgment. He sped forward, sprinting the last lap in hopes of calming his conscience.

⁞⁝

Alissa pressed the buzzer button at the gate and waited. She would rather be anywhere but at Maggie's today. However, she made an appointment and she meant to keep it. No matter how she felt about it.

The gates clicked and opened, beckoning Alissa inside.

Alissa steered her car up the familiar drive. Something felt different today, like more eyes watched. It made sense, since Maggie made sure to remind Alissa that security had tightened. Whatever guest Maggie had stowed away in her house, Alissa's curiosity wanted to know more.

Even before Alissa put her car in park, two suit-clad men took a stance at the base of the walkway.

A quick look around didn't reveal any others, but Alissa had a feeling that was the point. Silent watchers, all. Even with

Maggie's reassurance that Alissa didn't need to be concerned, intimidation settled around Alissa's shoulders like a cloak.

Oh, well. She made a promise, so she should make good on it. Alissa opened her car door and stopped.

Both men centered their attention on her.

Alissa clutched her leather satchel to her chest. The fine gravel on the driveway crunched beneath her feet. She must look as petrified as she felt.

One of the men held out a hand to stop her. "Apologies, miss. We're going to have to check your bag."

The other held up a small, handheld metal detector. "Standard protocol. If you don't mind."

"Standard protocol is to search me?" Alissa didn't know which man to address first.

Who was this guest of Maggie's, anyway? Someone important if they merited this level of security, but still. A full-body search? After last night, Alissa didn't think she would emotionally survive it.

"Good heavens, boys, knock it off!" Maggie floated down the path in her usual gossamer dressing gown. "Alissa, darling, don't mind them. They aren't very good when it comes to manners. Is that any way to treat a guest?" Maggie swatted one of the men on the arm.

"Our orders are—"

"I know what your orders are. I'm overruling them." Maggie held out a hand toward Alissa. "Come in, come in. You look far too pale."

Alissa clung to Maggie's hand and side-stepped around the guards. "Last night didn't go so well."

Understatement of the century. Last night went horribly. Out of all the nights in Alissa's memory, last night stood out as the worst.

"Last night?" Maggie released Alissa's hand to throw open the grand double doors. "What happened last night? You didn't call to tell me. No, wait. Don't tell me yet. First, tea. That should help your countenance."

"What's wrong with my countenance?" Alissa pressed a hand to her cheek.

She looked okay when she left the apartment earlier. The last thing she wanted was to worry Maggie, so Alissa specifically made sure she looked like her normal self. Apparently she didn't do as good of a job as she thought.

Maggie led the way to her favorite parlor. "Alissa, dear. Next time you try to fool me, do a better job."

Typical Maggie. No explanation. No sympathy. Someone so blunt and so honest as Maggie always expected more than Alissa could give.

Alissa rolled her eyes. "I'm not trying to fool you, Miss Maggie. I'm going to tell you what happened."

"Oh, are you? That would be lovely." Maggie settled onto a bench and motioned Alissa to a chair. "You've brought your new manuscript?"

"I only have one chapter and it... isn't pretty." Alissa winced.

Extroverts like Maggie were great, as long as they didn't ask for things Alissa couldn't give. Unfortunately, Maggie had a propensity for stretching Alissa to her limits. One of the best and worst things about befriending the eccentric woman.

Maggie poured two cups of steaming tea.

Alissa inhaled the spicy aroma of the Oriental blend she liked. A smile lit her face. "You remembered."

"Of course I remembered. I have Cook bringing scones, as well." Maggie set down the teapot. An outstretched hand gave her final message loud and clear. She wanted to see the chapter.

Alissa blew out a breath. "Do you want to hear what happened to me last night first?"

"As long as we start somewhere." Maggie's hand fell back to her lap. "You seem quite shaken. Tell me what happened."

"I was waitressing for this charity event. Mental health, I think..."

"Oh, you were at the event! How quaint! I didn't see you, where were you?" Maggie smiled brightly.

The joviality oozing from Maggie grated on Alissa's nerves. Of course, she had yet to tell the woman what happened behind the scenes. Yet... How could Maggie look so happy about it?

"Like I said, I was a waitress." Alissa fiddled with her fingers. "I stole a bite or two of food from one of the tables. I shouldn't have, looking back. It was wrong, but I was bored and no one was going to eat it anyway."

"Oh, is that all? People do that all the time."

"It's not all." Alissa couldn't bring herself to look up. She didn't think it would be so hard to talk about what happened. "I started to feel bad shortly after. That's when things get fuzzy. I remember trying to make it to the bathroom and collapsing in the hall. Someone found me and took me to the hospital."

There had been something else, too. Something her drug-addled brain couldn't quite put a finger on. Alissa didn't bring it up simply because she couldn't remember what it was. Something else happened, but how did she make herself remember?

"The hospital? Food poisoning?" Maggie brushed her long, graying hair behind a shoulder. "It couldn't possibly be anything more sinister, could it?"

How did she tell Maggie that something much more sinister did indeed go on under the innocent surface? Alissa had no choice but to be honest.

"It was Ketamine. In something I ate."

Alissa didn't expound. Maggie would make her own assumptions, and they would be right. Alissa already did the math on how the Ketamine got into her system. Only one answer presented itself. An answer Alissa didn't like in the least.

Maggie sat silent for a long while. The cook came with a plate of scones and left again. Alissa didn't utter a word.

Finally, Maggie reached for a cranberry-orange scone, her movement too calm and controlled. "Whose table was it?"

"The speaker's table. I don't remember his name. I wasn't paying that much attention, I just wanted to finish and go home." A half-truth. Alissa's brain had been spinning, on overload. Even if she did hear the special speaker's name, she wouldn't remember it. "I didn't mean for anything like that to happen. I shouldn't... have done that."

If she had kept a bit more professionalism, none of that would have happened. She would have been fine. The intended target hadn't been Alissa. Right?

Maggie's long fingers wrapped around Alissa's fidgeting hands. "Don't apologize for something you have no control over. Some terrible person did this, and I will do everything in my power to find them."

"Really?" Alissa hated that tears pressed against her eyes. She didn't want to cry in front of Maggie. But, in contrast to the argument between Cody and Violet last night, these were words Alissa desperately needed to hear.

Maggie nodded. "Of course. You're not at fault. Why would you do such a thing to yourself?"

"I'm glad you believe me." Alissa's relief knew no bounds. She had heard horror stories about people who doubted women with similar stories. Thank God that Maggie wasn't an accuser of that type.

"Of course I believe you. Who was it that took you to the hospital? Do you remember a name?"

"I—"

The parlor door flung open.

Alissa snapped her mouth shut. A quick dash of her fingers against her cheeks dispelled her tears.

Maggie stood to her feet, chin high. "Jean! What are you doing here? Weren't you at an appointment?"

"I came back to clean up after my run." This new voice rang deep and projected through the room with an air of authority. "One of the team said you had a guest that didn't pass security."

"Alissa doesn't need to go through security. We've been friends for years. Don't be ridiculous."

Alissa didn't want to turn around. She didn't want to face Maggie's celebrity guest. All the fun of the mystery left the instant someone spilled the information. Besides, he sounded... upset. Alissa didn't like to upset people. Especially when she didn't know them. First impressions made up ninety percent of a profile of what other people thought about her. Botching a first impression meant giving the wrong filter to look through later.

"They're the rules, Margaret." The man sighed heavily. "Why can't you see it's for the better?"

"Of course I don't agree with the rules when Alissa and I have had consistent meetings every week for years." Maggie folded her arms with her own huff. "Respect the home you reside within, Jonathan."

"As you should respect your guests, *dear* cousin."

Whoever Jonathan was, he sounded less pleased now than he had earlier. Alissa winced and slid her eyes closed. She should say or do something to quiet this controversy, but she didn't know what to do.

Thankfully, yet another voice interrupted them all. "Sir."

Alissa frowned. She knew that voice. Had heard it all too recently. Why couldn't she place it?

In the end, her curiosity got the better of her timidity. Alissa spun in her seat and took a good long look at the owner of the voice.

"Adison?"

Everyone froze. Maggie blinked so fast her lashes could cool down the room.

Adison grinned sheepishly. "Hello again."

"You know her?"

For the first time, Alissa gathered enough courage to look at Maggie's guest. He towered over Maggie's height, though Adison seemed of a similar stature. Dark hair wisped in perfectly disheveled waves against the man's forehead. Dark, intelligent eyes stared back at her.

Alissa shied away. "I know Adison, yes. He and I... we met."

"When?"

"Jonathan, be cordial!" Maggie folded her arms, all aflutter. "Have you any idea what this poor child went through?"

"If someone would explain, perhaps I would know." Jonathan shot a glare at Adison. "Who is she? You've not been here long enough to garner a date."

"She..." Adison cleared his throat, "is the woman from last night."

It might have been Alissa's imagination, but she thought she saw recognition and then terror cross over Jonathan's face. In the same instant, his expression turned stoic. As if he reined in his emotions and hid them beneath the mask. Then he smiled. A smile that didn't reach his eyes but bared his perfect teeth.

"You were there last night?" Alissa rose to her feet, as well. Sitting left her at a disadvantage when everyone else stood.

Jonathan's smile faltered, for a split second. "Yes."

"I don't remember seeing you." Alissa didn't mean to sound rude. If he had been at the fundraiser, she couldn't place him. Simple as that.

Mentally, Alissa flipped through the tables she served the night before. Other faces stood out in her head, but she didn't think she ever saw Jonathan.

Alissa gave him another once-over before she shook her head. "I don't think you were there."

Adison's snort sounded like a chuckle, but he quickly covered it with a cough.

Maggie didn't waste her efforts concealing her own peals of laughter. She threw her head back and let it ring against the ceiling.

Jonathan's lip curled in a soft sneer. "Who are you to say whether I was in attendance or not? Do I not seem trustworthy?"

"I wouldn't know, I just met you." Alissa shrugged a shoulder. Something about the way he bristled made her not want to play nice. Something that didn't happen often. Alissa prided herself in her agreeable personality.

"Oh! Apologies for not making proper introductions." Maggie rounded the table. Her stance, directly in the middle between Jonathan and Alissa, seemed too calm. "Jonathan, you've heard me speak of Alissa. Alissa, this is Jonathan. My guest."

Of course. The weekend couldn't possibly get worse. As long as Alissa had already insulted Maggie's guest, she figured she might as well keep it up. Consistency also meant a lot to her.

Alissa extended a hand. "It's nice to meet you." She expected a brush off. Or, perhaps, a handshake.

A spark of mischief flitted through Jonathan's eyes. He reached a hand to grasp Alissa's, but what happened next surprised Alissa. Instead of shaking her hand, he gently turned it palm-down. With incredible ease, Jonathan bent his tall stature down and brushed his lips to Alissa's knuckles.

"The pleasure is mine, I'm sure."

Alissa inhaled sharply and snatched her hand away. What kind of crazy psychopath did Maggie let into the house? This was a whole new level of insane. Who kissed a woman's hand in this day and age?

Alissa's confused stare turned to Maggie.

Maggie shrugged. "Enough, Jonathan. You're frightening the poor thing."

"I'm not scared." Alissa shook her head. Quite the opposite, actually. Part of her wanted him to do it again so she could try to figure him out.

Jonathan grinned. This time it reached his eyes. Alissa found she liked his real smile a lot better than the fake one he offered first.

"Ah, now I see the real you." Alissa pushed her hair off her shoulder. "You're happier than you'd like me to think."

"And you're quite jovial for a woman who endured what happened last night." Jonathan's hands folded behind his back, giving him a regal bearing.

Alissa shrugged her shoulders. "I can't mope about it forever. It's in the past. I'm moving on."

Only half of those were lies. Alissa didn't want to think about it, but not because she'd moved on. Not even because she planned to move on. It hurt her head and her heart to remember her own helplessness.

A thought occurred to her, then. Alissa narrowed her eyes at Jonathan. "How do you know what happened last night? I just told Maggie."

"I already discussed this with you. I was there." Jonathan motioned to the security guard next to him. "Adison works for my detail. He's the one who found you in the hall."

"Yeah. Good timing, by the way." Alissa flashed Adison a bright smile. She hadn't been coherent enough to thank him properly the night before. No one expected her to put on social graces so soon after what happened.

Adison saluted with two fingers. "Now that it's all straightened out, I have places to be. Oh, Guillaume said to tell you not to leave without him." He patted Jonathan's shoulder before he high-tailed it out the door.

"Who's Guillaume?" Alissa asked.

Maggie wrapped an arm around Alissa's shoulders. "It's better you don't know everything, dear. Jonathan is a very auspicious character in the grand plotline of life."

Jonathan's shocked face mirrored Alissa's. Maggie had a way with odd metaphors, but this one took the cake. Alissa made a mental note to use it for the next eccentric character she created.

"In any case, I'm sorry for your inconvenience last night." Jonathan's smile disappeared for good this time. Alissa found she missed it. "My team is looking into it, so you shouldn't worry too much. We'll get to the bottom of it."

"That's another thing. Why on earth do you have a team? And what's with the mass amount of men in black suits around here?"

"I think we should let Jonathan leave now, Alissa. He has an appointment." Maggie pulled Alissa back toward the table. "Go on, Jonathan. Alissa and I will chat a while longer."

Jonathan looked like he wanted to say something, but he didn't. Instead, he dipped a slight, curt bow toward Alissa. "I hope to see you again soon."

Alissa couldn't form coherent sentences about that, so she nodded. "Okay."

There were a thousand things she wanted to know as Jonathan strode from the room. A thousand more she asked herself once the door shut. Still, Alissa had no choice but to sit back down to tea. Her questions could wait. As long as her curiosity didn't get the better of her yet again.

Chapter 4

Jonathan tapped his fingers on the table. What had he been thinking? What possessed him to do that? He didn't usually kiss a woman's hand or outright *flirt* with her.

"Why does she make me like that?"

"Who? Like what?" Estrella looked up from her menu. "Should I be jealous?"

Jonathan wrinkled his nose. Estrella, like both sets of their parents, assumed she and Jonathan would wed some day. He hadn't meant to ask the question aloud, especially in her presence.

"You shouldn't be jealous." Because Jonathan had no plans to *ever* ask for her hand in marriage.

Estrella set the menu aside and folded her perfectly manicured fingers on the table. "She seems to trouble you."

Jonathan opened his mouth to protest. He couldn't, because Estrella had a point. Alissa did trouble him. In more ways than one.

The whole debacle at the fundraiser still boiled his blood. With no leads that panned out, Jonathan's concern for all parties involved only escalated. What if the culprit tried something more sinister next time?

Jonathan already felt responsibility for the girl who went to the hospital because of him. How much more responsibility would he feel if she had been truly hurt?

"Jean?" Estrella tapped a hand against his to garner his attention. "What's wrong?"

"It's nothing." Jonathan pulled away from her touch. "Have you decided what you'd like to eat?"

"I think salad today. Maybe tomorrow we can have steak."

"This will be our last appointment in the States."

Estrella's menu clattered to the table. "What? Why?"

Jonathan refrained from rolling his eyes. Drama had always been Estrella's weak point as a businesswoman. Apparently that translated to her personal life as well.

"We have no reason to see each other." Jonathan scanned his menu again. "I came here to escape Veldoria for a while. To escape confusing responsibilities. You only remind me of them."

Estrella's lips twitched in an unamused sneer. She obviously knew better than to ask whether that meant a breakup or not. She and Jonathan held a tentative friendship. Topics of romance balanced on an even thinner thread.

"I won't force you back to Veldoria." Jonathan also didn't like threatening people. Unfortunately, few passive measures could change Estrella's mind. When the situation called for it, Jonathan could use his authority to get his way. "Instead, I hope you have a wonderful time on your vacation."

"It seems you and your rebel brother have more similarities than I thought," Estrella scoffed.

"Do not insult Frederick. His life doesn't hold the heavier burdens of my own."

How dare Estrella bring Frederick into this as if Frederick's lifestyle could be made into an insult? Jonathan often wished for the freedom his younger brother enjoyed. Frederick still had maturing to do, that's all.

Frederick didn't have the weight of an entire country on his back. He played as he wished without the fear that he would ruin lives over something trivial. Besides, where diplomacy came through much learning for Jonathan, it came naturally to Frederick. Jonathan had always been a little jealous of that.

Despite all that, Frederick never did anything wrong or illegal. He and Jonathan got along splendidly. Estrella didn't have the right to make Frederick out to be some kind of criminal.

A waiter came to take their order.

Jonathan muttered something that sounded like a food order. Because it would be impolite to both Estrella and her father if Jonathan stood up and walked away in the middle of this luncheon. Still, Jonathan couldn't focus enough to make his order coherent.

"You do realize that your parents expect our union?" Estrella seemed to have cooled down some, but not enough. "Our mothers meet weekly. How are you going to break it to them if we aren't together?"

"Our love lives have nothing to do with them."

Their mothers had been friends for years. A trifle such as their children going separate ways wouldn't ruin the women.

"Perhaps not." Estrella flipped her perfect blonde braid over her shoulder. "But it is the nation's business. Everything you do has the potential to influence or harm Veldoria as a whole."

"You think I don't know that?" Jonathan's fingers twitched in his lap. He gripped his napkin to keep them steady. "The truth is, Estrella, I think you would make an excellent queen. You're intelligent, elegant, and you carry yourself in a classic manner befitting royalty."

Estrella splayed her hands before her. "Then I don't see why you insist on fighting it so hard."

"Because I don't think you would make a good wife. Not to me." When everything boiled down, that was the reason at the root of it. Jonathan pondered long and hard to come to that conclusion.

"Me? A bad wife?" A humorless laugh spilled from Estrella's lips. "Oh, this will be priceless. Why not?"

Jonathan blew out a heavy breath. He hadn't come here to argue with her. Lunch with Estrella had always been one of his favorite pastimes. Today, something in the air sparked differently. Perhaps because of the foreign soil beneath their feet. Or, perhaps, because Jonathan saw things as they were for the first time in a long time.

A cute brunette skipped through his imagination again. Jonathan squeezed his eyes shut and willed all thoughts of her to go away. He didn't need that complication right now.

When he finally had himself under control, Jonathan leveled his most stoic gaze at his lifelong friend. "I don't love you, Estrella, and I don't think you love me, either."

"What are you talking about? Of course I do."

Jonathan shook his head. "You're infatuated with the glamour and the aristocracy of the position. I don't think you and I are a good match romantically."

"How can you be so cold about it?" Estrella's lips pursed into a pout.

Jonathan didn't have an answer that would satisfy her. Estrella didn't listen well, something that recently became more of a fault than a blessing.

"Why are you so sure you love me?"

This time, Estrella fell silent. There must not be an advantageous answer to the question. If there were, Estrella wouldn't overlook it. She saw everything too meticulously.

The silence only thickened as the waiter returned with their food. Neither Jonathan nor Estrella wanted a witness to their ill fate. That's how rumors began.

Once the waiter disappeared, Estrella looked up. "Do you really have to ask that?"

"Yes." Jonathan refused to back down. If he gave Estrella even an inch, she would take it and run a mile.

Estrella's face fell. "There's really nothing between us? You think that?"

Once again, Jonathan let her draw her own conclusions. The more words he spouted, the more Estrella would find to manipulate. He couldn't let her get a foothold. Not if he wanted a clean break, romantically speaking.

"Thirteen years, we've known each other. You're going to throw all that away on a whim?" Estrella stabbed her steak with a fork. "Does our friendship mean that little to you?"

"On the contrary. Our friendship means that *much* to me." Jonathan twirled his pasta around his own fork. "I wouldn't go to such lengths to protect our friendship if it meant nothing."

"This is you protecting our friendship?" Estrella sniffed derogatorily. "Thank you so much for your *great* kindness."

Jonathan didn't take her words to heart. Estrella set her dreams on the plans her parents set for her. Marrying the future king had always been one of those plans. Of course she would be angry when he explained it simply wouldn't happen. He expected as much.

Still, the irritated hush around them hurt Jonathan's heart. Estrella had always been one of his best friends. He thought she would understand his need to keep her close as such. Surely she would come around to his way of seeing things, once she calmed down. Estrella had always been a hothead. It would be okay once she processed the news thoroughly.

Jonathan wanted to believe everything he told himself, but when he and Estrella parted ways, she still seemed far too annoyed. Walking away without apologizing to her was one of the hardest things he'd ever done, but Jonathan did it. For the sake of his future.

Chapter 5

"Do we have to?" Alissa pouted at Violet, hoping it would get her out of everything.

Violet smacked a hand against the back of Alissa's head. "Snap out of it. You're the one who agreed to do this when you moved in."

"I feel dizzy. Maybe the drugs haven't completely worn off yet..."

"Shut it. It's been five days, you're fine." Violet thrust Alissa's tennis shoes toward her. "Put them on and let's go."

Alissa wrinkled her nose in disdain. In all fairness, she had promised Violet when they moved in together that she would go jogging whenever Violet wanted. Alissa hadn't expected it to be today. Jogging didn't sound fun in the least.

Not that Alissa couldn't jog, she just didn't want to. Violet didn't have an issue getting all hot and sweaty and sticky, but Alissa would rather not. Even with Violet's assurances that a quick shower would take care of all the sweat and dirt.

"Put the shoes on and let's get going." Violet dropped the shoes into Alissa's lap. "Get to it."

Alissa glared at her best friend. Some days she regretted the decision to let Violet into her life. But, what was she supposed to do when she had known the girl since preschool? They were sworn besties for life now. Alissa couldn't get rid of Violet if she tried.

With a disgruntled huff, Alissa pulled the shoes onto her feet. "Fine. I'm putting them on. See? Happy?"

"Very." Violet looped her arm through Alissa's. "You're finally doing what you promised. That makes me super happy. And proud. My little Alissa, all grown up and adulting. It's touching."

"Not as touching as you think."

Alissa hated how easily Violet talked her into this. No point resisting if Violet could talk her down. Alissa almost always gave in to Violet's begging, so why did she try to say no in the first place?

Alissa rolled her eyes at herself. Maybe she should grow a stronger backbone, but seeing Violet happy and content was all Alissa could ask for in this world.

Violet grabbed Alissa's hand and tugged her out of the apartment.

Alissa and Violet's apartment sat less than two blocks from a large park. As far as Alissa knew, that was also part of Violet's evil plan to get Alissa to jog. However, the trees stood tall and pretty, and the running paths clear and tranquil. The park, itself, brought Alissa a sense of peace.

Which is how Alissa found herself wheezing at Violet's side. Turns out, the park putting Alissa in a good mood might also have been part of Violet's scheme.

Even though Alissa meant to refuse to move faster than a brisk walk, somewhere along the way Violet started jogging in earnest. Not wanting to be left behind, Alissa fell in step. Unfortunately, as she already attempted to point out to Violet, jogging wasn't her thing.

"Vi? Can we... slow down... or something?" Alissa winced at the pain in her side. If they kept this up much longer, she would die. She just knew it.

"You're doing so well, though." Violet tossed a precursory glance to Alissa. "You're keeping up."

"I'm in pain."

"Probably not breathing right. Exhale when your left foot hits the ground."

"Nope. Can't do it."

Alissa stuttered to a stop. Doubling over, she pressed her palms against her thighs. Catching her breath seemed harder than she thought it would. Then again, who wouldn't be in this state after their best friend talked them into a torture session?

Violet made a U-turn and returned to Alissa. "Hey, what's wrong?"

"You're trying to kill me, that's what!" Alissa pressed her fingers to her aching side.

"I didn't think you were in that much pain. You should have said something."

"I did!"

"Is everything alright?" A new voice, this one deep and accented, broke into the conversation.

A voice that seemed all too familiar. Jonathan.

Oh, good Lord, no.

Alissa squeezed her eyes shut. "Violet, please tell me that isn't who I think it is."

"Who? I see no flaws with this guy. You know him?" Violet didn't wait for an answer. She stepped around Alissa, no doubt with her brilliant smile in place. "I'm sorry, do we know you?"

"I believe you met one of my employees a few nights ago. Adison Cebon."

"*That* Adison?" Violet didn't bother to try to be quiet. Quiet wasn't her style.

"The same."

Alissa couldn't believe what she heard. Why, out of all the places in the universe, did he have to show up here? Today? At this moment? She looked terrible, she knew. No makeup, hair a mess, sweating and gasping for breath...

Alissa squatted down, wrapped her arms atop her knees, and buried her head inside them.

Behind her, Violet scuffed a foot against the cement. "What's your interest in us now? That incident is behind us."

"I'm concerned about your friend."

Another scuffle of feet shifted the atmosphere. Violet's silence worried Alissa, but she refused to look up or move. Maybe if she stayed still long enough, she'd turn invisible.

A large, warm hand landed on Alissa's shoulder. "Excuse me, miss, but are you alright?"

"I'm fine, go away," Alissa muttered into her knees.

The hand didn't move. "You don't seem fine. Are you in pain?"

"Not anymore." Why did she even bother to answer? The more she spoke, the longer he would stay. At this point, Alissa was only ninety percent sure he knew her identity. Might as well keep that ten percent of hope.

"Which means you were." A sigh tousled the hair bunched up in a ponytail atop Alissa's head. "I would feel much better if you looked at me. I might even consider leaving you alone."

The thought was tempting, to say the least. Alissa didn't want him to bother her anymore, but she wasn't sure she wanted him to see her in this natural state, either. Not that it mattered. She didn't like him or anything.

Okay, so she liked him a little. For inexplicable reasons.

That still didn't mean she wanted to show him her bare face and messy hair. A girl had her pride, and Alissa didn't want to lose hers in a moment of weakness. Besides, what good would come from looking up at him?

"No."

"Alissa. Please. I'm concerned about your well-being. Again. This time, at least, allow me the chance to see you're doing well before I go."

Dang it, he made a good argument. Since Adison worked for him, Alissa would wager money Jonathan had been the one to send him to check on her. Which meant he had, indeed, been worried about her in some fashion. Alissa worked her teeth over her bottom lip once. She could say no again, or she could get it over with and never see him again.

One inch at a time, Alissa lifted her face back into the sunlight. To her dismay, even on an early morning run, Jonathan looked the part of a dapper gentleman. Stylishly unkempt hair, a gray Calvin Klein sweatshirt, a sparkle in his eyes. She should have expected as much, having seen his return from exercising last time.

A corner of Jonathan's lips tilted up in a half-grin that could have melted any female in the vicinity. Alissa liked to think she wasn't as weak as all that.

A sharp draft soared by Alissa's ear and whipped loose strands of hair into her face.

A tree behind Jonathan splintered.

Violet shrieked.

A loud *pop* filled the air around them.

The whole world went topsy-turvy and then came back into focus. Alissa blinked, unsure what just happened. She found herself pinned against the ground, Jonathan crouched above her.

A quick perusal confirmed their location. Jonathan had rolled them both into the bushes at the side of the trail.

"What's wrong?" Alissa pushed up on her elbows.

"Shh." Jonathan held a finger to his lips. "Be quiet. I think someone tried to shoot me."

Or me. Alissa wrinkled her brow. What could anyone possibly gain from shooting either of them? She wasn't that famous of an author. In fact, her first book sold less than a hundred copies. Big disappointment after all the hard work she poured into it.

"Wait, what about Violet?" Alissa scrambled around to look out on the path.

Jonathan wrapped a hand around her arm and pulled her back to the ground. "Don't worry about your friend. Guillaume has things under control, I'm certain."

"She could be hurt." Alissa craned her neck to look out again.

"She wasn't the target." Jonathan used his free hand to turn Alissa's face back toward himself. "Hold still."

"Why?" Alissa didn't know why she asked. She had no intentions of disobeying the order.

Jonathan released her face and instead reached his fingers upward. A single finger tucked Alissa's wayward hair behind her ear. A thumb stroked along the delicate flesh there.

"Ow!" Alissa smacked his hand away. "That stings. What are you doing?"

Jonathan showed her his fingertips, covered in a red stain. "I think the bullet grazed it. We'll have to get you treated once we're out of here."

"I'm beginning to think next to you is a very dangerous place to be." Of course, Alissa didn't mean to sound unkind. Her words came out sharper than she intended. After two separate injuries in the span of a week, her mood soured.

Jonathan took it well, as far as she could tell. He helped her sit up and get her feet under her, but neither dared to stand from the bushes that hid them.

After the first and only shot, the trail had fallen much too silent. A knot of pure dread tightened in Alissa's stomach. The eerie silence weighed her shoulders down.

Jonathan wrapped his hand around her wrist and changed his stance. "We should be prepared to move quickly."

"I can't. That's what got us into this position in the first place." Alissa rolled her eyes. To think, five minutes ago she had been complaining at Violet for making her run. Ironic that her least favorite activity might be what eventually saved her life.

Jonathan chuckled, a pleasantly low sound that Alissa wouldn't mind hearing again. "You'll be fine. Guillaume will have called backup. We'll be out of here in no time, minimal running necessary."

"You say that now..." Alissa didn't know why she felt a need to argue with Jonathan. He saved her life, as far as she could tell. There should be some level of respect for that.

Maybe her nerves were getting the better of her. After all, it wasn't every day that someone happened to be in the middle of this kind of situation. Her mental state was stable, but probably deteriorating fast. Self-diagnosis, of course.

Jonathan turned his attention to her, looking down with an expression Alissa had never seen before. "I mean it."

For some reason, Alissa believed every word he said. Stupid of her, but she wouldn't question it right now. Later, she could reevaluate her decision-making paradigm. Right now, as long as Jonathan got her out of this, she would be grateful.

The calm, steady hum of an engine conflicted with the squeal of tires.

Alissa flinched. "What's that?"

"The cavalry." Jonathan parted a pair of branches to look out.

Alissa, nosy as always, peered over his shoulder.

A sleek black car sailed down the running path. It pealed to a stop in front of the bushes. Two men jumped out, guns drawn and eyes alert.

The whole thing might have concerned Alissa, but she recognized the one closest to her as Adison. No need to be frightened of him, of all people.

After a quick scan of the area, Adison opened the back door to the car.

Jonathan's hand tightened on Alissa's wrist. A few long strides launched him into the car. The momentum pulled Alissa in behind him.

She hit the leather seat with a thud. Adison slammed the door shut.

Seconds later, the car engine revved. The driver sped in reverse, back toward the road.

It took a moment to catch her breath, but Alissa had questions that needed to be asked. "What about Violet?"

"She's with Guillaume, she'll be fine." Jonathan glanced out the back window.

"Stop saying that!" Alissa folded her arms. "I don't even know who this person is. What's so great about Guillaume?"

What if Violet had been hurt? What if someone took a second shot and that bullet hit Violet instead of its intended target? Violet's scream didn't give Alissa a warm, fuzzy feeling.

"Guillaume is my head of security." Jonathan raised his brows as if daring Alissa to talk back to him. "Is that a sufficient explanation?"

It sounded like the safest place Violet could be, but it only brought more questions to Alissa's mind. At the very least, it relieved Alissa that Violet was—most likely—safe and sound.

Which left plenty of head-space free for interrogation purposes. "Why do you have so much security, anyway?"

It might have been her imagination, but Alissa didn't think so. Jonathan's whole body tensed. Alissa didn't know what she said wrong, but Jonathan's whole posture screamed discomfort. Why would an innocent question like that make him uncomfortable, unless he had dark secrets?

When Jonathan finally answered, it wasn't at all what Alissa expected. "Because I am a very important individual to many, many people. My safety is imperative to their everyday lives."

The vague, roundabout answer only spurred Alissa's desire to know more. When Maggie introduced them, Jonathan never volunteered any information about himself. Even though he seemed to know everything about Alissa, he apparently set the "personal life" topic in as strictly off-limits.

It made Alissa want to dig deeper. "Why?"

A sharp, chipper ringtone pierced the silence between them.

Adison turned in his seat. "It's Guillaume, sir." He extended his hand, the phone securely tucked into it.

Jonathan took the device and slid the green answer button. "Speak."

Alissa slid across the seat and pressed her ear to the outside of the phone. A shocked glance from Jonathan did little to deter her.

"...are under express orders to deliver you straight back to the Magpie's Nest." This voice didn't sound familiar, but Alissa already knew who it was. Mr. Head-of-Security.

Jonathan nudged his shoulder against Alissa's, clearly trying to push her away.

Alissa didn't budge.

Jonathan sighed. "And the girl?"

"She's fine. We'll return shortly and—" Guillaume's voice cut off as scattered shouts from Violet echoed like static. "I'm sorry, sir, but the young lady would like to speak to her friend."

Alissa snatched the phone before Jonathan could react. "Violet? Vi, are you okay?"

"You should ask! Are *you* okay? Seriously, I thought you died or something. I've never seen anyone shield you so fast. If you know this guy, he's a keeper. I mean it."

Violet was fine. She wouldn't ramble like that if she had been hurt. In fact, the advice to Alissa meant Violet didn't feel affected at all by any of this. Lucky duck.

"You didn't get hurt?" Alissa asked again.

Violet laughed. "No. The projectile missed me and hit the tree. Plus, this Guillaume guy tackled me. Except for some scrapes on my hands, I'm fine."

Thank God. Alissa finally breathed a sigh of relief. "You're going the same place we are?"

"Heck yeah. I'm not about to let some stranger abduct you without tagging along. That's just the kind of friend I am. See you soon, I'm getting glared at."

Alissa reluctantly handed the phone back to Jonathan. Until she saw Violet in person, there was nothing else she could do. Except to ride the wave this whole happenstance rolled her way. If she hung in there, this would all be over soon. She would never have to see the dangerous man beside her again.

So why did that make her heart sink in sadness?

Chapter 6

Alissa hadn't said a word since they left the park. Jonathan couldn't help but glance at her in concern from time to time.

He wanted to explain to her about the threats and the precautions taken to avoid them. But, if he explained, would Alissa look at him differently? If he told her, he would begin to wonder if she liked him for status and money. Not that she didn't like him now. Jonathan couldn't tell if she liked him or not. That was the issue.

No one had ever failed to react to Jonathan in one of two drastic ways: elated, over-exaggerated happiness or unadulterated disdain.

Alissa hung somewhere between. An odd sort of indifference that kept Jonathan on his toes. Perhaps, for one of the first times in his life, someone saw him as a person. Not a figurehead.

Part of him wanted to keep this woman close. She called to some protective part of him. Another part of him demanded he push her far away. Staying close to him seemed to be dangerous for Alissa's health and well-being.

So large a decision required more pondering.

Jonathan didn't miss the worry emanating from the front seat. Adison kept looking over his shoulder at Alissa. Jonathan couldn't blame him. Somewhere between the park and their current location, Alissa's skin had gone from pale to ghostly.

He could tell the exact moment reality set in. Her fingers began to shake, stifled only by their grip on each other.

"Adison," Jonathan tried his best to keep his composure, but Alissa's distress also distressed him. "Call ahead and have tea and blankets prepared. Also a first aide kit."

"Yes, sir." Adison reached for his phone too quickly. As if he'd been waiting for such an instruction.

"And tell Markum to cancel my schedule for the rest of the day."

"Yes, sir."

Curious Alissa didn't blink or ask questions. A sure sign that something had gone wrong. Jonathan didn't know what to do. How did he keep her from panicking or shutting down?

Alissa ran her shivering fingers over her hair. Her entire body crumpled over, her elbows on her knees and her head in her hands.

"What's our ETA?" Jonathan directed his question to the driver, but Adison answered.

"Three minutes."

"Make it two." Jonathan wrapped an arm around Alissa's shoulders. "Alissa, look at me, hm?"

Hair tumbled against Jonathan's cheek as Alissa shook her head. "I'm going to puke. And don't speak in that tone. How are you so calm? Someone shot at me!"

"It's because you've been shot at that I'm behaving so calmly." At least he had her talking. For a moment, Jonathan had feared that Alissa would pass out. She still didn't seem particularly coherent.

"That doesn't make sense."

"What if you're going into shock? Would my panic help matters?"

Alissa moved one finger away from her eye so she could peek up at Jonathan. "Violet would panic with me."

"I don't know if you've noticed, but I am not Violet."

What a sporadic thing to say. Jonathan remained much relieved that he and Violet were different people. The short moment he spent in Violet's company made him wary to cross her path again.

Alissa sighed. "Still nauseous. Not helping."

Jonathan repressed his chuckle. If he laughed now, Alissa would truly hate him forever. However, something about the sincerity of every word she spoke made Jonathan want to smile. It was refreshing, at the very least, for someone to speak so openly and honestly to him. Most would consider it out of turn to mention such things before their future king.

You should tell her before you fall any harder.

Jonathan shook his head to dispel the thought. "Will you be alright?"

"That's a complicated question." Alissa pressed her fingers over her eyes again.

Somehow, Jonathan knew he'd been shut out. Whatever went on in that head of hers, Alissa didn't want him to know any more. Not knowing her inner thoughts irritated Jonathan more than he thought it would.

He barely knew this girl. Jonathan rolled his eyes. Once a royal, always a royal. Trying to take on this woman's troubles as well as his own didn't seem like a smart idea.

Too late, he realized. Jonathan felt a sense of responsibility toward her, more dangerous than anything else he could feel.

The car pulled to a stop in front of Margaret's chalet.

Adison opened Alissa's door and reached to help her out.

Jonathan waved him off. "Alissa, let's go inside now." He nudged her toward the open portal.

Alissa's movements seemed sluggish to Jonathan. He didn't expect her to be steady in this situation, but he hadn't expected her to shake like a leaf in the wind.

Step by fragile step, Jonathan assisted Alissa up the path and through the front doors.

Margaret shot forward out of the midst of a half-dozen security personnel. "Alissa! Oh, darling girl, whatever happened? Are you alright?"

"She'll be fine," Jonathan assured.

"I didn't ask you." Margaret shoved him out of the way and wrapped her own arms around Alissa's shoulders. "You must be exhausted after such an ordeal. I have a spare bedroom. You must rest."

"Treat her injuries first." Jonathan wasn't about to let Margaret take this over. Margaret hadn't been the one by Alissa's side when a bullet grazed her. If the shot had been more accurate, it might have killed Alissa. Jonathan's stomach churned at the reminder.

"Injuries?" Margaret shrieked.

Jonathan winced at the sound. "Perhaps I should tend to her instead."

"Nonsense! Someone bring the first aide kit, would you?" Margaret took Alissa's hand in hers. "Let's move you to the sitting room."

Jonathan didn't like the way Margaret whisked Alissa away, but he didn't have a choice. In this situation, he should wait for Guillaume's arrival and receive a complete briefing on the details.

For the first time in his life, Jonathan resented his ever-present duty to protocol.

The front doors banged against the wall.

Shadowed by Guillaume, Violet stormed in. "Where is she?"

Jonathan took Violet's outburst in stride. She must be quite upset over the events of the morning. Coolly, he folded his hands behind his back. "I'll tell you, if you make me a promise."

"Well, this could be interesting. I'll hear you out." Violet crossed her arms, whether in intrigue or annoyance, Jonathan couldn't tell.

"Don't scold her too much. Be gentle with her, and tell me how she is once you've spoken to her. I'm asking this as a favor."

Jonathan held his breath. Violet didn't have a certain pattern she followed. So far as Jonathan could tell, no matter the situation, her emotions got the better of her. He hoped that this time she would see the light in his request.

Violet arched her brows. "I was right. Interesting. Fine, I'll be your spy for today. Point me in Alissa's direction."

Even though Violet agreed too readily, Jonathan motioned a hand toward the sitting room. He got what he wanted, so he would give Violet her request, as well. He didn't expect the firecracker of a woman to step into his personal space.

"Let's be very clear. I'm not doing this for you. I'm doing this because Alissa clearly likes you and I think you two look cute together." Violet stabbed a finger against his chest. "The second you break her heart, I break every bone in your body. *Capisce?*"

"I understand."

"I'm glad we understand each other." Violet flipped her hair and marched down the hall.

Jonathan had half a mind to tell her that threats didn't work against him, but what fun would that be? Let Violet think that she won this round. He had never sparred with a woman's best friend before. It seemed a vital part of gaining Alissa's affections.

Strange, that Alissa's affections were his first thought. However, Jonathan didn't mind it. The truth had never bothered him. One couldn't cover the truth, no matter how hard they tried. Thus, for the first time, Jonathan let himself wonder what it might be like to love and be loved by such a woman as Alissa.

"Your highness."

Jonathan snapped his attention to Guillaume.

Guillaume motioned to the stairs. "This way, please."

With a single glance back toward the sitting room, Jonathan marched up the stairs. They had a battle plan to hash out. For everyone's sake.

Jonathan and Guillaume settled themselves in the upstairs office, a space Margaret gave Jonathan use of for private matters.

Guillaume didn't waste time. "It's the Anti-Monarchists. The reception and now this. I'm sure of it."

"Do you have proof?" Jonathan sank into the chair behind the desk. It lent a modicum of stability to his frazzled nerves.

Guillaume took a stance in front of the desk, hands folded before his torso. "Not yet. I have reliable information that the Anti-Monarchists intended to use your highness to bring down your father."

"It wouldn't have worked. Even if father stepped down, Frederick is in line after me." Beyond that, there were several viable options for the next king. Overthrowing a monarchy? Not as easy as one might think.

"It seems they've become stronger. My spies aren't high enough in their organization to give more information than this." Guillaume sighed. "I should have placed them sooner. Apologies, majesty."

"You couldn't have known. Factions like this are cunning." Jonathan steepled his fingers against his lips. "The close attacks are disconcerting. How did they find my schedule?"

"I'll look into it immediately," Guillaume assured.

Jonathan nodded. Outwardly, he could keep calm. Inwardly, he wanted nothing more than to flee. If he left, wouldn't the innocent victims of today's shooting go back to their own quiet lives? It might be best for everyone, but Jonathan had learned years ago that it was better to face a problem head-on. Unemotionally.

Jonathan didn't know if he could do that this time. The Anti-Monarchist regime toyed with innocent bystanders too many times already. What if they didn't stop there? Jonathan's best course of action would be to stay far away from the girls.

Unless the Anti-Monarchists already thought that the women had some relation to the royal family. What a complete mess.

"Assign someone to Alissa. Since she's been at the center of both attacks, I feel it necessary." Something about both attacks put Jonathan on edge. An empty puzzle piece, a vital piece of information, must be missing. Sadly, Jonathan couldn't decipher what it might be.

"Yes, sir. I'll assign Adison, if you're alright lending him out."

"Lend him. I trust Adison's discretion." Jonathan couldn't think of a more capable man on the detail. Former Black Forces and more vigilant than any other member of Jonathan's security team.

No one could provide a better shield for Alissa on such short notice.

"Your highness, if I may..." Guillaume shifted on his feet. "Is it wise to provide this woman security? Anyone looking on may take it the wrong way. In my personal opinion, it's safer to leave her alone."

"This isn't logic, it's intuition. Assign Adison to watch her." Jonathan didn't exactly know why he felt the need to lend a bodyguard to Alissa, but his instinct rarely steered him wrongly.

A strange sense of foreboding settled in Jonathan's bones. One that warned him this could be a long, dangerous ride.

⋈⋉

"His interest is fading." Estrella folded one long, lean leg over the other. "It's time to step up our game."

From the dim confines on the other side of the limousine, a haughty chortle resonated. "*Our* game? I'm not invested in this like you are. Nor do I prefer to become involved in others' personal business."

"Jonathan is everyone's personal business. He'll be king soon."

"I wasn't talking about your prince. I was speaking of you, my dear." A flimsy orange circle glowed through the dark. A puff of rancid smoke billowed through the midst of the vehicle. "If you can't even catch him properly, how do you expect me to help?"

"There's another woman. I can see it in his eyes."

"Hardly evidence."

"He was preoccupied with her during our entire luncheon. You said you would help me."

His sigh sent another puff of smoke wafting in Estrella's direction. "What do you want me to do? Do you have her number?"

"Of course not."

"Name?"

"Don't be ridiculous."

"Then perhaps you have a plan to confirm your suspicions."

Estrella sneered at the man's derogatory tone. "I wouldn't ask for your help if you weren't a professional. I'll take care of things on my end, so you just find the girl and make sure she and Jonathan never see each other again."

"I don't think you're in a position to threaten me, *my lady*." Every trace of sarcasm had left his tone. In its place sat nothing but cold, hard fury.

"You are in no position to refuse me, either," Estrella scoffed. "If you think for one moment that your groundless threats frighten me, you are a fool. You can't touch me."

"If you believe that, you don't understand how I work."

"You need me."

"I need no one, least of all you. You are simply... the easiest means to achieve the end I desire."

"As you are the same in my eyes." Estrella leaned forward in her seat. "So let's use each other to the end, shall we? Find the girl and I'll make sure to follow through on our deal. Back out now and... well, I'd hate for daddy to learn what you're up to on Veldorian soil."

"Your father can't do anything to me, either." The man drew another long drag from his cigar.

"Perhaps not, but he does have the king's ear. I'd hate for you to be blacklisted from the country." Estrella let her smile shine bright in the darkness. He thought he could play her? Unlikely.

Silence met her declaration like the calm before a storm. Another puff of smoke swirled in the air.

"It seems we understand each other, then," the man deadpanned. A rap of knuckles against something hard probably meant he knocked on the divider. "It's time for you to get off, Lady Estrella. I'll contact you when I've located the woman in question."

"I look forward to your call." Estrella knocked on her own side window. The security guard pulled the door open.

Estrella didn't bother with goodbyes. Both she and her companion knew the other didn't care one way or another. Theirs wasn't that kind of relationship.

Chapter 7

Alissa hiked her bag onto her shoulder and stepped out onto the sunny sidewalk. Writing in a coffee shop gave good vibes, but it provided more distractions than she hoped for. She should have gotten more done. However, the steady stream of rich and semi-famous venturing in and out of the restaurant across the street seemed more entertaining than her characters. Even with muse, she couldn't seem to focus.

A familiar black car pulled to a stop on the opposite side of the street.

Oh, good Lord, please no.

After almost a week of not seeing Jonathan, Alissa had finally come to terms with the fact that they weren't meant to be in each other's lives. Apparently she had been wrong.

Sure enough, a tall, handsome foreigner stepped out of the car and shoved his hands into his pockets.

Alissa spun around, back toward the coffee shop doors. Why did her heart decide to start fluttering every time Jonathan came around? Unfair.

Don't look this way, don't look this way, don't look this way...

"Alissa?"

Alissa stopped in her track and squeezed her eyes shut. *He could be talking to anyone. There must be thousands of Alissa's out there.*

A long bout of silence nearly convinced Alissa to believe her own justification.

"Ms. Alissa Cassidy?" His voice resounded so closely Alissa could feel his presence.

Great. No hiding now. Which left only one course of action. Denial.

Alissa took a breath and swiveled to face him. She threw her most brilliant smile on her lips. "Jonathan! What a complete surprise!" Even to her own ears, it sounded too cheery.

An amused grin tugged at the corners of Jonathan's mouth. "Considering I didn't seek you out on purpose, I would hope it comes as a surprise." He bent forward, far enough to catch her gaze with his. "I don't need to be concerned that you're stalking me, do I?"

Alissa shook her head. "Oh, no. No, no no. I'm definitely not a stalker." She didn't mean to run into him anywhere. How could such a large city seem so small?

"You've come out for coffee?" Jonathan straightened again.

Alissa blew out a shaky breath. Why did he make her nervous? "I've been here a while. I was just leaving. What about you? What are you doing here?"

"I've been forced to attend a luncheon I had no intention of attending. My... *friend*, Markum, is persistent about it. Some government official." Jonathan rolled his eyes, the first time Alissa saw him break his stiff persona.

"If you don't want to go, why are you doing it?" That seemed like an idiotic idea to Alissa, but, hey, who was she to judge the situation? She didn't even know what Jonathan did for a living.

"I have reasons, but I don't like any of them."

A mischievous idea formed in Alissa's head, fueled by Jonathan's disappointment. It posed risks, but Alissa could never stand to see someone being forced into something they didn't want to do.

Alissa bent sideways to look around Jonathan. No Guillaume or Adison in sight. She righted herself. "What if I could get you out of it?"

Jonathan blinked. "Is that possible?"

"Everything is possible, silly." Alissa giggled. "Come in for some coffee. Leave the lunatics behind."

"Lunatics?" Jonathan peered over his shoulder at his assigned security detail. "I suppose you're not so far off. Give me a moment. Don't go anywhere."

Alissa wanted to admit that wouldn't be possible, but instead she gave her standard answer to such a statement. "You have sixty seconds."

"I will only need forty." Jonathan glanced both directions down the street, then jogged back to his car.

Alissa didn't know what he said to the men, but not one of them argued with him. Did they look displeased? Yes. However, they allowed Jonathan to return across the street.

Jonathan tugged open the coffee shop door. "After you, my lady."

Alissa couldn't help but grin. Not only was Jonathan a consummate gentleman, but the way he called her *my lady* felt... nice. With a new skip in her step, Alissa entered the coffee shop. Again. The odd look that the barista on duty gave didn't phase her.

Jonathan joined her at the counter. "What is this plan of yours, anyway?"

"Well, it starts with ordering a cup of coffee. Your buddies are still watching." Alissa perused the menu, even though she knew it by heart. It might give Jonathan more time to make a decision.

"They aren't my... *buddies*." Jonathan cleared his throat. "After you."

Alissa took that at face value and ordered a tea instead of coffee this time around.

Jonathan, to her surprise, ordered a macchiato and handed over his card.

"You don't have to pay for it. I would have paid." Alissa didn't mean to pout, but it happened that way. She couldn't help it. Not that she didn't enjoy being taken care of, but not many people did it without asking five times.

Jonathan shook his head. "Absolutely not. You're helping me already and I have more money than I know what to do with. Allow me this, at least."

Alissa threw her hands up in surrender. "I won't question it."

"Good." Jonathan motioned toward a table nearby. "Shall we?"

As if on instinct, Alissa followed his directive. Interesting. He held himself with the bearing of someone in charge, and she listened. What a peculiar development.

Alissa seated herself where she could see out the windows and across the street. "Okay, just act natural."

"Who's acting unnatural?" Jonathan settled onto the chair opposite her. "Is your plan so scandalous that you must be nervous?"

"No. I just... feel like we're doing something wrong." In all actuality, they probably could have fired the security detail for the day. Instead, Alissa wanted to seem adventurous. Not a typical reaction for her, but she would roll with it. "You aren't going to get in trouble for this, are you?"

"The worst I can receive is a scolding from Father."

"Oh. That's a relief."

"Not if you know my father."

Alissa's response died on her lips as the barista set their drinks on the table before them.

Jonathan offered a tight-lipped smile to the young man. "Thank you kindly."

The barista nodded and disappeared back behind the counter. Not the most friendly fellow, but not all baristas had the ability to be friendly.

"I assure you, nothing too terrible will happen, even after we ditch them." Jonathan wrapped a hand around his mug to lift it to his lips. "I've never used that word in such a context before. I quite like it."

"I'm glad American colloquialisms can entertain you." Alissa rolled her eyes, but Jonathan's genuine smile was worth letting it slide this time. "If you're interested in getting away, listen up. I'm going down the back hall to the bathroom. Wait a few minutes, then come check on me."

Alissa rose before Jonathan had time to ask questions. They stood on her turf now. She wanted to get every ounce of satisfaction she could. Besides, it wasn't like Jonathan didn't keep secrets from her. He still hadn't explained why someone shot at them.

If Alissa believed in revenge, even a little, this could be counted in that category.

The back hallway provided a hint of quiet in the otherwise bustling shop. A long, thick wall muffled the outside noises and provided a straight path to the restrooms. Alissa didn't travel far. She had no real intention of going to the bathroom. In the grand scheme of sneaking away, this seemed the best ruse.

Five minutes ticked by in unbearably slow seconds. The catchy pop song floating its way in from the front changed two times. A single ant scurried its way up the opposite wall.

Finally, when Alissa thought she might burst from tension, Jonathan took a step into the hall.

Alissa grabbed the sleeve of his jacket and yanked.

Jonathan stumbled closer.

"This way." Alissa pushed open the back door and peeked out like a meerkat from its hole. Without any security presence in sight, she felt it safe to pull Jonathan outside behind her.

Jonathan remained strangely silent, but at this point Alissa didn't mind. It felt like an adventure or a spy novel. Both of which she had always wanted to experience.

The tricky part came next. Walking away without anyone noticing. Jonathan's security didn't seem shabby. They probably figured out that their charge had disappeared by now. Going the opposite direction and getting out of sight might be the best idea at this juncture.

"Be extra quiet," Alissa instructed Jonathan. Not that she expected him to listen, but it seemed more spy-like if she said it that way.

A quick glance back at Jonathan revealed that amused grin again. Alissa liked his real smile, so different from the one he put on for others. It made him appear... softer.

"Lead the way," Jonathan coaxed with a wave of his hand.

Alissa crept around the corner of the neighboring building. Her back hugged the wall. The tips of her toes found purchase against the slanted sidewalk.

A twig snapped and clattered against the concrete.

Alissa froze.

Jonathan glanced over his shoulder.

Two bodyguards rounded the corner of the cafe. One started toward Jonathan and Alissa.

Jonathan grabbed Alissa's hand inside his own. "Run." He took off down the sidewalk.

A squeal jumped from Alissa's throat. Fantastic. Again. Why did she always have to run when around this guy? Jonathan didn't give her any choice in the matter. Besides, she heard the guards' footsteps pounding the pavement behind them.

Jonathan carted her across the street and around corners. Even out of breath, Alissa didn't dare stop lest she stumble and fall. She had a niggling suspicion that this wasn't the first time Jonathan ran away from his security detail.

Jonathan spun into an alley and tugged Alissa in behind him. A quick set of footwork landed both of them, crouched, on the far side of a dumpster.

Alissa wrinkled her nose, but she was too busy gasping for breath to scold Jonathan for doing this to her. Jonathan didn't seem too out of breath to her. Unfair.

The guards stopped at the entrance to the alley, then moved on. Almost as if this had been planned.

"Okay, spill the tea." Alissa ran her fingers back through her hair to push it away from her face. "Why do you have super-glue guards and how often do you run away from them?"

Jonathan turned his attention to Alissa, smiling like a Cheshire cat. "Oh, I haven't done this to them in years. I had forgotten how exhilarating it is. Are you alright?"

"Yeah, sure, whatever." Alissa flicked her wrist. "You didn't answer my first question."

"It's complicated." Jonathan stood up and held out his hand. "Shall we? They'll have gotten far enough away by now. Do you have a car or are we walking?"

"I walked from home." Alissa shrugged a shoulder. "Now that we ditched them, what do you want to do?"

"See the sights, I suppose." Jonathan suddenly seemed at a loss. "I hadn't thought that far. Where were you going before I interrupted you?"

"There's an independent bookstore two blocks from the coffee shop. I like to spend time there some afternoons." An easy answer, thank God. For some reason, Alissa's wits disappeared around this tall, handsome person. When did she turn into such a pushover?

"Let's go there, then." Jonathan held his hand closer to her. "Come on, get up."

Against her better judgment, Alissa settled her hand back in his. Carefully, she rose to her feet and pulled her hair behind her shoulders. "Your espionage skills impress me."

"As do yours." Jonathan shot Alissa a wink. "Lead the way, my lady. I fear I need a guide in this unfamiliar city."

Alissa rolled her eyes. "Let's not wax poetic. I'm immune to many things, but not that."

Oh, gosh, had she flirted again? This felt like flirting. At this point, Alissa didn't know what her problem was, only that she had a long way to go to fix it. Lord help her if Jonathan ever met her parents. Alissa had never had a boyfriend before. Her dad was liable to go overboard in his interrogation.

He is not your boyfriend, you twit! Alissa winced at her own inner voice.

Jonathan equaled danger. She already established that fact. Therefore, dating him would be a very, *very* bad idea. But, a part of her sincerely wanted to date him anyway.

"Are you alright?" Jonathan's gentle prodding brought Alissa back into reality.

"Hm? Oh. Yes. Thank you for asking." Alissa ripped her hand from his as if she had been scalded. "Let's get going, then."

Jonathan's face fell, concern and questions filling his gaze.

Every instinct in Alissa's body wanted to explain, but she knew it was a bad idea. She would enjoy today, taking it at face value. A very brief rendezvous with a very attractive stranger. After that, she would cut herself off from him. Or so she told herself.

INTRIGUE

Chapter 8

Jonathan watched Alissa pluck yet another book from the shelf. He didn't know what he did wrong, but she closed herself off since the alleyway earlier. Perhaps he had come on a bit strong, but he thought he handled all of this rather well, all things considered.

Pages crinkled as Alissa flipped through them. Nothing new there. Most bookish persons in Jonathan's acquaintance skimmed through their books before they bought them. The reluctant sigh and the way Alissa shoved the volume back on the shelf tipped him off.

Clearly, Jonathan did something to vex her. Again.

If he could discern his sin, Jonathan would gladly apologize for it. However, he couldn't think of a single thing he did wrong this time. It was her idea to escape security. Her idea to come to this quaint little bookshoppe. Did Jonathan say something wrong?

A brief moment of diplomatic debate later, Jonathan settled on clearing his throat to ever so gently garner Alissa's attention.

She spun on him like a fidgety tigress. "Did you need something?"

Even if her words were meant to push him away, the silent challenge behind them only reeled Jonathan further into the web of affection. "Are you cross with me?"

"Me? Cross? No, why would I be?" Alissa's smile felt forced to Jonathan.

"My apologies." What in the world had he done to upset her so badly? In a vain attempt to make up for his perceived transgressions, Jonathan tugged the small stack of books out of Alissa's hands. "I'll purchase these for you. Any others you would like, as well."

Alissa's eyelashes fluttered in surprise. "You will?"

Desperate to take advantage of the momentary let down of Alissa's guard, Jonathan nodded. "Of course."

"As many as I want?"

"Within reason."

In a split second, relief turned to concern. The glitter in Alissa's eyes bespoke another plan of ill intentions. Jonathan didn't think Alissa would hurt his person, but his bank account? She had no qualms about denting it sizeably. A fact he quickly confirmed.

In only twenty minutes, an entire cardboard box of books appeared in Jonathan's arms. He had no idea how it got there, or when, or what kind of books sat within. He only knew Alissa smiled again and his credit card had noticeably less balance left upon it.

Jonathan didn't give Alissa a chance to argue over who would carry the books. He hefted the box into his arms. "Let's go."

"You're going to carry that to my apartment?" Alissa's voice squeaked.

Jonathan bit back his chuckle. So easy, to fluster this woman. "Is there a law that says I'm not allowed to do so?"

"No." Alissa shrugged her shoulders. "I just thought... you know... it might be heavy... or something."

"Precisely why I insist on carrying the books. They are heavy." Jonathan jerked his chin toward the door. "Shall we?"

Alissa gave an indignant huff, but she didn't argue. A win, in Jonathan's eyes. In all his years, he never had so much trouble wooing a woman. Not that he tried to woo women often, but as far as he remembered, the few he charmed had been much more willing.

You absolute dolt. What are you thinking of right now?

Jonathan couldn't afford to think of Alissa as a woman. Not in that way. Too many obstacles stood between them if he decided to go down that path. Yet, he couldn't help but want to know her better. Alissa had a sort of magnetic pull Jonathan rarely encountered.

"I don't live far," Alissa announced for the umpteenth time.

Jonathan laughed, this time. "I'm alright, if you're worrying. I've transported heavier burdens than a small library."

"Sorry." Alissa turned to walk backwards, supposedly so they could chat more easily. "I didn't really intend to buy that many books, but... you offered. I got a little crazy."

"Understandable. Please watch where you're walking. I'll feel better about it if you do so."

Alissa rolled her eyes, but spun to face forward. "You're quite the mystery man, Jonathan."

Sadly, Jonathan didn't know how to interpret that. Good? Bad? Indifferent? "I'm not sure what you're getting at."

"I think it's dangerous to be around you. Bullets and drugs? Not my speed." The look Alissa shot over her shoulder reflected pain and confusion.

The simple agony of it made Jonathan's heart ache. "It isn't always like that. I am sorry to have dragged you into such gruesome activities."

"It's not like we can do anything about that now." Alissa shrugged, but Jonathan saw her whole posture go rigid.

Finally, a spark of understanding flickered. It had never been about liking him or disliking him. He didn't understand why that gave him such relief, but it did. A light at the end of a long, lonely tunnel grew a bit brighter.

"This is me." Alissa hitched a thumb toward a glass door. "Let me grab the mail if Vi hasn't, then I'll be up. Second floor, third door on the right."

Of course, Jonathan already knew that, but he didn't want to seem creepy. Jonathan hadn't meant to take note of her address from the dossier, but circumstances had demanded a watcher for Alissa. It hadn't been his fault, entirely, that said watcher so happened to work for the monarchy.

Jonathan took the stairs two at a time. The little apartment complex was... quaint. Considering he was more than used to the larger, more bustling metropolis of Capitol City, a two-story building had little impact.

Alissa followed him, empty-handed.

"No mail?"

"Vi probably grabbed it already." Alissa shrugged.

Her indifference put an end to the conversation. Diplomatic as he was, Jonathan didn't know how to revive a dead dialogue.

Alissa silently unlocked the apartment door and stepped inside. "Vi, I'm home!"

Since she didn't tell him to stay out, Jonathan crossed the threshold as well.

Alissa disappeared through one bedroom door, then came back out and poked her head inside the other. "Strange..."

"Is she not here?" Jonathan didn't like the spider-leg sensation that crawled up his spine.

"She probably ran to the grocery store or something. The mail's here, so she's been here at some point." Alissa grabbed the stack from the table. "You can put the books by the couch."

Lest Alissa resort to anger again, Jonathan obeyed and settled the box in the desired location.

A sharp intake of breath from Alissa drew his full attention.

Alissa's hands settled in the air near her face, palms outward as if she dropped an object or surrendered. The paleness of her face indicated either shock or fear. Jonathan didn't know which to pick.

Five long strides carried Jonathan to Alissa's side. Asking her wouldn't do any good, judging by her trembling fingers and frozen stature. Jonathan turned his gaze down to the table.

His heart skipped a beat.

Jonathan reached into his jacket to pull out his cell phone. A quick unlock and two taps later, it rang through.

"Adison, come up here now." Jonathan wasted no time assessing the situation and making a plan. "And call the police."

He didn't need to hear an answer to know Adison would follow through.

"I'm... I'm okay..." Alissa nodded as if to assure herself that the lie was true.

"You're not. No one would be after that." Jonathan jabbed a finger at the photograph on full display.

It would have been enough that the picture seemed to be taken with a long-distance lens. Like someone watched from afar. More disturbing even than that was the missing face, violently scratched out from Alissa's person. A threat if Jonathan ever saw one.

Touching without gloves would put his fingerprints on the evidence. Jonathan looked around for something to handle the photograph or envelope. A few tissues did the trick.

Carefully, Jonathan snagged a corner of the torn envelope and turned it over. Only Alissa's name, and no return address. Which meant they knew where she lived. Had been here.

Adison barreled through the open door and stopped short. "What happened?"

Jonathan dropped the envelope and held out a hand. "Keys."

Obediently, Adison dug his car keys out of his pocket and tossed them to Jonathan.

Jonathan snagged Alissa's hand and tugged her out the door.

"We should wait for the cops." Alissa unfroze long enough to glance over her shoulder.

"No."

Jonathan didn't like to play the brute, but right now Alissa's safety was his number one concern. At the apartment, she was vulnerable and open. She would be safer under the careful scrutiny of trained security, especially since Jonathan had a hunch about this threat.

Adison would take care of the details with the police and Violet. When the authorities needed Alissa's statement, they could come to Margaret's. For now, that seemed safest.

The lack of resistance on Alissa's part denoted the level of her fear. Jonathan tucked her securely into the passenger side of the car. In under a minute, they took off down the street.

One thing Jonathan learned a long time ago: the faster the target got to a safe place, the better. He couldn't worry about

Alissa going into shock or breaking down. Not until he had her tucked away.

The Anti-Monarchists were known to be ruthless. This was a whole new level of cruelty, even for their twisted schemes.

Jonathan didn't care how fast he sped. Sometimes diplomatic immunity had its advantages. Besides, the faster he drove, the faster they got to safety.

By the time Jonathan raced up Margaret's driveway, his entire security detail had emerged in full force. Adison must have called ahead and warned Guillaume. Guillaume would most certainly give Jonathan an earful later.

Gravel crunched and sputtered as the brakes caught. One of the guards pulled open Jonathan's door.

Jonathan jogged around the front of the vehicle and pulled open Alissa's door himself. Even when he took her hand in his, Alissa didn't startle out of her daze. That meant one of two things. Either she felt comfortable around Jonathan, or she had retreated into her own head again.

Jonathan sincerely hoped for the former.

Guillaume met them at the door.

With a learned reflex, Jonathan held up a hand to stop Guillaume from saying anything. "Later."

Even though Guillaume didn't protest vocally, Jonathan saw the displeasure in his expression. Later would come sooner than Jonathan prepared for.

It didn't matter. For now, Jonathan needed only to discover the truth behind all the incidences surrounding Alissa. At this stage, coincidence had long past flown out the window. Someone had deliberately made Alissa a target. The fault probably lied with none other than Jonathan.

Alissa held it together until the moment they stepped into the family room. There, she tugged her shoulders out of Jonathan's grasp.

"This is crazy." Alissa's fingers ran through her hair and gripped as if she might pull out the strands. "I'm insane. Or dreaming. Right? Things like this don't happen in real life."

"It appears that by spending time with you, I've put you in a rather dangerous position. My enemies seem to have earmarked you as a weakness." Jonathan hated to admit it, but he had always been brutally honest.

Alissa took a wary step away from him. "That's why you should stay away from me. If you're not around, they'll let it go. Whoever they are. And don't tell me, because I don't want to hear that you head up the foreign mafia or something."

"I assure you, I do not." Jonathan wanted to say he understood. That this whole ordeal would be too much for anyone to handle alone. He knew because he had been there. But he didn't know if that would help. Instead, he stuck to business. "Is there somewhere else we can go for now?"

"We? Oh, no, no, no." Alissa released her head to wag a finger in Jonathan's direction. "There is no *we* right now. Not even close."

"I beg to differ. Staying away from you did nothing to dissuade them, so the better option is to stay beside you. One watchman won't be enough if they've truly set their mind to this. Like it or not, you've acquired my personal attention for the foreseeable future."

"Who are they anyway?" Alissa folded her arms. A defensive gesture that shouldn't have amused Jonathan, but did.

Jonathan shrugged a shoulder. "That's a story we don't have time for right now. There must be another safe haven for you. We need to leave before they trail us."

"Wait, what? Trail us? What on God's green earth are you talking about? Why does it sound like you've done this before?"

"Because I have." Jonathan's phone trilled in his pocket. He pulled it out only to see Adison's name flashing on the screen. "One moment, I should take this." Despite Alissa's indignant huff, Jonathan slid the green button. "Yes?"

"There are two officers headed your way now to retrieve statements. If we cooperate, it shouldn't take long."

"We will cooperate to our utmost. Guillaume will tell you our location as soon as we know it."

"Understood." The line clicked.

Typical Adison, never one for formalities. He did his job, he did it well, and he did everything in his own way. It didn't bother Jonathan. In fact, Adison happened to be one of his most trusted allies because of it.

"What if I don't want to go anywhere with you?" Alissa spat.

Jonathan slid the phone back into his jacket pocket. "I think you'll change your mind after you think about it. Let's take a break and speak with the officers, then we'll discuss our next move."

"Oh, for Pete's sake. This isn't a spy novel!" Alissa threw her hands up in surrender. "I'm a normal American citizen. I work part-time jobs and chase my dream. How did I get mixed up with someone as confusing and hazardous as you? Is this an alternate reality?"

"I can assure you, this is very, very real." It was the only affirmation he could offer.

Alissa still looked pale to him, worse than before. It must be quite shocking to receive such a threat directly. Especially when she hadn't been dealing with such things her entire life, as Jonathan had.

"Have a seat. I'm begging you." Jonathan motioned her toward a chair.

"I'm fine." The words sounded weak and fragile. Despite all her bravado, Alissa sank onto the chair as if her legs couldn't hold her anymore.

With a heavy heart, Jonathan watched her fingers tremble. Once more, he had brought fear into her life. What kind of future king would he be if he couldn't even protect one woman? How did anyone expect him to protect an entire nation?

A rap of knuckles on the door brought Jonathan's attention around to Guillaume.

Guillaume allowed two police officers into the room. "They've come for a statement." An arch of Guillaume's eyebrows denoted unanswered questions on his part.

Jonathan shrugged a shoulder at his head of security. "We'll discuss this in a moment. Officers, please come in. Have a seat. Can we get you anything? Water? Coffee?"

"No. Thank you." The first officer loomed large in the room, with broad shoulders and a thick build.

The second, dwarfed by his partner, gave the ornate living space a once-over. "Fancy digs you got here."

"Oh, they aren't mine. They belong to my cousin." Jonathan motioned them to have a seat.

"Right." The second officer cleared his throat. "Well, then. I'm officer Jenkins and this is my partner, Wilko."

"Thank you for responding so quickly." *You choose now to be a diplomat?* Jonathan wanted to roll his eyes at his own courtesy. Ironically, his manners and training wouldn't let him.

"Uh... yeah." Wilko scratched at the back of his neck. "We have some questions for miss... Cassidy? Alissa Cassidy?"

Alissa raised her eyes and offered a tight smile. "That's me."

"The one the letter was addressed to, yes?"

"Yep." Alissa tucked her hair behind one ear. "Ask away, I'll answer anything."

"Let's start with you giving us the story. What happened this afternoon?"

Alissa blew out a breath. "I was out most of the day, and when I got home there was that letter sitting in the mail. Not much to the story. It had my name on it, so I opened it. You know the rest."

"What time was this, approximately?" Wilko scribbled something on a notepad.

"Um... I don't know. Less than an hour ago."

One hour. Time that ticked by like a bomb, waiting to expose both Jonathan and Alissa to more dangers. He needed to get her out of there before someone decided to lay siege to Margaret's house or something. At this point, he couldn't exclude any possibility.

Jenkins shifted in his seat, narrowing his eyes in intent concentration. "Do you have any enemies or upset ex-boyfriends or anything? Any idea who would do this kind of thing?"

"I don't." Alissa shot a look to Jonathan, then pasted her attention back on the policemen. "I don't know who would do this."

It wasn't a lie, Jonathan realized. She really didn't know, since he refused to tell her. Maybe he should let her in on the secret, if only to make her see how dangerous the situation had become.

"You were with her?" Wilko turned to Jonathan.

Jonathan nodded his head. "Yes. Since noontime."

"You're not from around here, are you?" Jenkins must be referring to Jonathan's accent. Which Jonathan didn't mind, in all honesty.

"I am not."

"Where are you from, then?"

The suspicion in Wilko's voice made Jonathan chuckle. "Gentlemen, I think you have the wrong impression of me. I am not the stranger you seek. In fact, if you continue this line of questioning, I may have to claim my diplomatic immunity."

Alissa's frantic giggle rang sharply through the room. She leaned a fraction closer to Jonathan. "You have diplomatic immunity? What kind of weirdo are you?"

"The best kind." Jonathan gave her a wink and stood to his feet. "If you will excuse us, I believe we answered everything you need. You can contact us any time in the future."

Jonathan held a hand out to Alissa, pleased and relieved when she settled her palm against his. Together, the two evacuated the room. Suspicious policemen were the least of Jonathan's worries right now. The Anti-Monarchists could very well be on the move and he had no knowledge of it. He and Alissa needed to escape immediately.

"Your highness." Guillaume jogged Jonathan's direction and held out a phone. "It's your mother. Urgent."

Jonathan released Alissa to snatch the phone. His mother never used the term *urgent* unless she meant it. Something must have happened at home, or she wouldn't have interrupted Jonathan's vacation. Not that it was turning out to be a very relaxing one.

"Mother?"

"Jean, thank heavens. I couldn't reach your phone and when Guillaume mentioned the police... Oh, never mind. That's not why I called. Your brother..." Her voice broke.

Jonathan's mother never cried. Which meant...

"Mum, what's wrong? What happened to Frederick?" A panic settled in Jonathan's gut. He had always liked his little brother. Despite their differences, he never wanted anything bad to happen to Frederick.

"There was a motorcycle accident. Or, what they're calling an accident. Jean, I don't think it was. He's not critical, but he is unconscious..."

"Do I need to come home?" Jonathan didn't know what he feared worse. Going home and leaving Alissa on her own, or staying with Alissa and leaving his brother.

The queen sniffed. "No. No, don't you dare. It might be what they want, and we can't chance that. I'll keep you updated on your brother as soon as they fly him home from Monaco. Call him once he's awake, will you? This self-destruction has to stop."

"I'm certain Frederick isn't trying to upset you, mother. He can't help such an incident."

"Frederick?" A female voice floated melodiously from the front door. "What happened to Frederick?"

For the first time in a decade, Jonathan fought the urge to curse. Of all the people to arrive at this exact moment, it had to be the one he wanted the least to see. One look at Alissa's brow, wrinkled in confusion, made Jonathan's decision for him. He couldn't let anyone in this room assume anything.

"I'll call you back later, mother." Jonathan hung up before his mother could argue the fact. "Estrella, who let you in here?"

"Don't look so distraught. I came to see Margaret, thinking you would be out." Estrella shrugged a delicate shoulder. "It's coincidence that I've run into you, as per your instructions."

Estrella didn't understand the spirit of the law. The woman had always been insanely literal. Jonathan didn't know why he expected anything else now.

"I didn't ask who you came to see, I asked how you got in. We are under a strict lock-down." Jonathan did his best to keep his voice level. Reaching back for Alissa's hand would have helped if she responded.

Of course, Estrella's sudden and untimely arrival probably sent Alissa into shock again. As if the day hadn't been eventful enough.

"The front gate allowed me in." Estrella hooked a thumb over her shoulder to denote the direction she came from.

Though Estrella's chocolate eyes bespoke confusion, Jonathan knew her well enough to understand her acting skills. She may seem sincere, but Jonathan refused to take Estrella at her word. Not because he didn't trust her, but because Alissa didn't trust him. He had a need to prove himself. If he couldn't prove himself to one woman, how would he ever prove himself to a country?

Alissa shifted behind Jonathan, pressing closer. No doubt she sensed the sudden tension in the room.

"Do you plan to stay here?" Jonathan kept his voice gentle. Estrella had always angered easily.

Estrella shrugged her shoulders. "If you're in lock-down, do I have a choice?"

"If you're staying, we're leaving." Jonathan didn't bother to ask for Alissa's hand this time. He laced his fingers around hers as if his life depended on it. If he didn't hold onto something, he might spiral into a mental breakdown. Could anything else go wrong? "Guillaume!"

Guillaume stepped from the shadows and dipped his head in a half-bow. "Yes, sir?"

"We shouldn't stay here. Let's leave now." Like a small boy, Jonathan wanted to beg Guillaume to take them somewhere safer than here. To hide them until the danger passed. He wouldn't, because that wasn't something a prince should do.

Guillaume looked relieved rather than cross. He pressed a finger to his ear and rapidly issued instructions. Within seconds, Guillaume held the front door open and motioned Jonathan out.

Alissa didn't speak a word until Guillaume shut them securely in the waiting car. Then, she only asked one question. A question Jonathan knew he couldn't avoid, no matter how hard he tried.

"Who's that woman?"

Chapter 9

There were so many questions she could have asked. Why did she choose that one? Alissa winced internally. Why did it bother her?

The woman seemed vaguely familiar, as if their paths had crossed before. That didn't seem possible, but the impossible oftentimes happened. The impact that the woman's presence had on Jonathan bothered Alissa more.

Which led Alissa to yet another question. Had Guillaume called Jonathan 'your highness'? And what about the diplomatic immunity that Jonathan claimed to have? It all added up to a solid theory. A deduction that Alissa hesitated to believe. Things like this didn't happen in her normal, everyday life.

"That's Estrella." Jonathan sighed, garnering Alissa's attention once more. "To be more precise, Lady Estrella Hilmar. She and I are childhood friends."

Yeah, totally sounded like it. Except Jonathan's statement left a lot unsaid. His tone came across gentle, yet upset. Did something happen between the two of them? An ex, maybe?

Alissa, you idiot, you really have to stop watching television dramas. He's not even interested.

"Is there someplace we can go that isn't in the city?" Jonathan turned his body to face Alissa's side of the car. "Somewhere you feel most at home."

An idea sprang to mind, but Alissa didn't want to put Jonathan in that kind of situation. Yet, he had asked first. Should she tell him? Or should she claim not to have anywhere to go? What crazy scheme would he drag her into if she said no? In the end, self-preservation won out.

"There is a place, but... I'm not sure you want to go there." *Please, God, let him say no.*

Jonathan shrugged a shoulder. "Do I have much choice in the matter? Right now, we need security, not etiquette. Tell Guillaume the address."

How did she tactfully tell him that "security" might be the least of his worries? What words could she use to make her point? "No, I don't think you understand. You *really* don't want to go there with me."

Jonathan folded his arms, the first time Alissa had seen the petulant gesture from the noble diplomat. "Why wouldn't I?"

Alissa took a deep breath. Only one way to get through to him on this one. Though... she didn't like it.

Alissa squeezed her eyes shut. "Because I've never brought a guy home to my parents before and they'll probably interrogate you like the KGB or something."

"You do realize it isn't called the KGB anymore, don't you?"

"Of course I know that, just go with my analogy!" Alissa's eyes shot open as the car raced forward. Her arms reached out to brace against the seat and the door. "Seriously, do your drivers have a slow mode?"

"When not under emergency protocol, yes. In this instance, the quicker we leave, the better."

"What about Maggie and... that other chick?" Alissa tossed what she hoped wasn't a glare back at the house.

Jonathan's chuckle indicated that she failed to stop her scowl. "My security will put Estrella on the first flight back to Veldoria.

As for Margaret... she's more than capable of taking care of herself. Anyone trying to cross her should think twice."

"Then wouldn't we have been safer staying with her?"

"We're the ones putting her in danger. If we vacate the premises, she'll be fine." Jonathan settled back in his seat. As if the whole world hadn't turned topsy-turvy on them.

Alissa shook her head. What kind of weirdo was he? How could he be so calm in this kind of situation? If she thought about it much more, she might go insane, so how did he manage to sit back and relax? Alissa refused to act like a bitter ex-girlfriend.

"Guillaume called you *your highness*." Okay, fine, that sounded a little too sarcastic. Not that she harbored any ill feelings, but she needed to know for sure.

Jonathan merely nodded once. "Is there a question in there?"

"There's an interesting explanation that I would love to hear from you." In a long, detailed monologue, preferably. Alissa still couldn't quite wrap her brain around the one word that wanted to lodge into her psyche. *Prince.*

"Guillaume wouldn't have called me 'highness' if I didn't hold a title, now would he?"

"Still doesn't give me an explanation. Expound."

For a brief moment, Jonathan's and Alissa's eyes met. His, guarded and calculating. Hers, reflecting the same.

The first to look away was Jonathan. "Promise me that you won't tell anyone or go loony over it."

"I'm not that dramatic." Lie of the century, but Alissa had no intentions of spilling Jonathan's secrets. "Tell me."

"My full title is His Royal Highness, Jonathan Henry Christophe of the House of Manon. Crown Prince of the Kingdom of Veldoria." Jonathan flinched as if he expected a blow.

Alissa took everything in stride, as much as she could. Her brain didn't want to wrap around that title. Pieces of it stuck out. Like, Jonathan had two middle names. HRH applied in this circumstance. *And he's a crown prince.* Which meant one day he would inherit an entire country. Jonathan would be a king, and yet here he sat beside insignificant Alissa Cassidy.

Yeah, I really shouldn't bring him home. But she wanted to. That was the issue.

"Alissa." Jonathan reached out for her hand. "This doesn't change anything between us. Does it?"

Alissa wanted to say that it changed everything, but in the long run, wasn't it just a job? Besides, one look at Jonathan's tortured expression had her shaking her head. He looked so afraid that Alissa might run away from him. Alissa wanted to sit down and have a few choice words with whoever had hurt Jonathan over this issue.

Why did she want to act like his girlfriend? He hadn't even stated intentions! What kind of hopeless romantic behaved this way?

Alissa blew out a breath and gently tugged her hand from Jonathan's. "It's a lot to take in."

"I should have told you from the beginning, that night at the auction. I shouldn't have sent Adison to check on you when I was the one who saw it first."

Alissa blinked. She had always assumed Adison ran into her on accident. He had been sent? In hindsight, it made sense.

"You saw what, exactly?" she asked.

Jonathan retracted his hand with a sigh of his own. "You seemed tipsy. You had taken food and drink from my table, so I was concerned. Since there shouldn't have been alcohol and you covered your mouth as if you were ill. I felt a small responsibility if you suffered from food poisoning or the like."

"I don't know what would have happened if Adison didn't find me."

"All you have to say is thank you. Nothing happened because we took you to the hospital posthaste. Don't worry about the could-have-beens."

"That's really not what I'm worried about right now." Alissa shot Jonathan a wry smirk. "My brain is still processing the whole future king... thing."

"It shouldn't concern you so much, either." A small, humorless laugh fell from Jonathan's lips. "I'm like any other man. With a bit more power."

From the front seat, Guillaume cleared his throat. "I'm sorry to interrupt you two lovebirds—"

"We're not lovebirds." Jonathan and Alissa answered in unison, both sounding equally panicked.

"Yes, of course. I hate to interrupt, but if you could both buckle your seat-belts a bit tighter, it appears we have a car trailing us."

"We've got a what now?" Alissa tried not to panic again. How bad could one day get? When would the chaos end?

"Highness, if you don't mind." Guillaume reached a hand under his jacket and retrieved a gun, which he settled on his lap.

Jonathan reached over and tugged Alissa down against the seat, far enough that neither of their heads reached above the leather back. "We stay like this until it's all clear. We don't know what kind of weapons they have or what their plan is."

"Is this really necessary? Don't people usually just out-ma-neuver them on the highway? No muss, no fuss."

"Perhaps, in movies and dramas. I am a crown prince. It is imperative that I remain alive."

"So why am I down here?" If his life was so important, why did he keep dragging her along into it?

Jonathan shook his head, a movement that made him seem annoyed. "Because they know hurting you would hurt me. I'm not void of compassion."

An interesting way to state that. Alissa couldn't argue with it, but it intrigued her. Why would hurting her, hurt him? That made no sense. They'd only known each other a few weeks. Strange how time flew. It felt like she had known him for far longer.

The car took a corner at too sharp a turn.

Alissa braced against the back of the front seat to steady herself. Jonathan shifted his hunched stance. "Are you alright?"

"I would be better if people would stop following us." She didn't want to admit how this situation frightened her. Alissa wrote about villains and absurd situations, but she didn't live them. Not until recently.

"Wouldn't we all?" Jonathan's muttered statement almost died before it reached Alissa's ears. Thankfully, they were in tight confines. She caught it before the tone fell flat.

Guillaume turned in his seat. "We seem to have lost them."

"You know, you're really calm and indifferent." Alissa wrinkled her nose at Guillaume.

Guillaume shrugged. "It's my job to be calm as head of security."

"That only explains half of my concerns." Alissa shot him a tight smile, meant to be more sarcastic than friendly.

Jonathan tipped his head back and bellowed. "She certainly has your number, doesn't she?"

Guillaume sighed. "I don't mean to be indifferent. It's the only way I can think logically and keep everyone safe. I care, believe me. I practically helped raise the insolent prince over there." Guillaume hooked a thumb in Jonathan's direction.

"Insolent?" That was a new one. Alissa had yet to hear anyone truly describe Jonathan, as a person. She understood the dilemma of choosing words to do him justice, but *insolent*? Guillaume now had her full attention.

"He used to try to skip out on his studies to visit the security recruitment center. He claimed he wanted to be a royal guard."

"Yes, well, you always kicked me back to the study rooms, though you were much more lenient toward Frederick."

Guillaume rolled his eyes and faced forward again.

This time, Alissa laughed. She didn't know why the thought of small Jonathan trying to train with adult guards tickled her. It was an honest profession. It just didn't seem to fit Jonathan, the calm royal. Alissa couldn't picture him in any sort of fight.

"Is it really that funny?" Jonathan asked.

Alissa shrugged her shoulders. "I'm not sure what's funny or not today. It's been super stressful. It's better that I laugh than cry."

So she told herself. Alissa didn't want to look back on the events of the afternoon. The morning had gone so well. What changed between her date with Jonathan and returning to her apartment?

Wait, date? Did she really just think that? It hadn't been a date. No matter how she looked at it. She helped him escape his security for a few hours. Which, in hindsight, might have been a bad idea and slightly illegal.

"I'm sorry to interrupt, but if you don't mind, we need an address." Guillaume turned a kind gaze to Alissa.

"Oh. Yeah." Alissa rattled the address off without even thinking about it. She never needed to think about it before she said it or wrote it, that's how well she knew it.

The car fell silent after that, everyone lost in their own thoughts. The city lights faded and disappeared behind them. The stillness of country highway overtook the bustle of traffic.

Somewhere along the way, Alissa dozed off, lulled by the rocking of the vehicle and the odd sense of safety engulfing her.

Chapter 10

Somewhere in the countryside, far from the reaches of the treacherous city, Jonathan and his entourage found themselves creeping up a gravel-paved driveway. Solar-powered garden lights lit the sides of the path at intermittent points.

"This is the correct address?" Jonathan glanced at the still-sleeping Alissa. She didn't seem the type to trap or trick them.

Guillaume made a noise that Jonathan took as an affirmative.

"Who lives here?" Jonathan leaned forward to peer out the windshield.

Guillaume shrugged a shoulder. "I didn't have time or resources to find out. It seems secluded, which could be to our advantage."

Jonathan ventured another glance at the sleeping Alissa. It must be someplace she trusted if she could so easily rest.

"It isn't her parent's home... is it?" Jonathan gulped at the frightening thought.

As a Veldorian, the importance of meeting a woman's parents meant more to him than it might to other men. His country viewed it differently than most western cultures. Meeting the parents didn't happen if you didn't plan to marry the woman.

An interesting turn of events. With what Jonathan had seen so far, he wouldn't mind marrying Alissa. Kings had wed for less.

No, no. Don't go down that path. You've caused her enough suffering. Jonathan sighed.

Even if he wanted to marry her, Alissa would never say yes to such a ridiculous plan. Would she? A stupid idea, even if she would. He barely knew her. Yet... there remained the unmistakable pull begging Jonathan to stay by her side.

The driveway culminated in a circular path in front of a two-story farmhouse. The car rolled to a stop.

Jonathan reached for Alissa's shoulder, then withdrew his hand. Should he wake her or let her sleep? It had been a long day for her.

"Your highness?" Guillaume queried from the front seat.

Jonathan retreated from Alissa and reached for the handle of his door.

Guillaume shot out of the car faster than Jonathan could. Jonathan so rarely opened his own door that he didn't blame Guillaume for overreacting.

In lieu of helping the prince, Guillaume pulled open Alissa's door.

Jonathan rounded the back of the car just as Guillaume bent to retrieve the sleeping woman. "I'll do it."

Guillaume arched his eyebrows, but straightened and took a step away.

Jonathan bent to peer inside the dimly lit vehicle. Alissa slept so peacefully, her lips slightly parted and her lashes long against her cheeks.

Pull yourself together. Jonathan rolled his eyes at himself. This may not even be her parents' residence. Stupid old traditions were no excuse for Jonathan's rapid heartbeat and matrimonial thoughts.

With a sigh, Jonathan wrapped one arm around Alissa's waist. He tucked the other arm beneath her knees. Hefting her out of the car didn't take as much effort as he thought it might. She barely stirred.

Guillaume shut the door and waited. He knew better than to try to dissuade Jonathan from anything he set his mind to do. A long history of arguments attested to that fact.

With only the solar powered lights along the driveway to guide him, Jonathan headed for the front porch. Guillaume and the driver fell in line behind him. As good security personnel should.

The night was eerily silent, strangely dark. Jonathan hadn't been outside the city in so long, he hardly remembered the look of stars in the sky. They didn't light as much as storybooks and ancient folk tales would have people believe.

Without a free hand, Jonathan looked to Guillaume to wake the residents here.

The doorbell rang loud and clear in the still air. Guillaume waited a minute, than rang the bell again.

Alissa whined and nestled her head closer against Jonathan's shoulder. No doubt to escape the noise.

A light flicked on inside the house.

The door opened.

The man peering out appeared no older than Jonathan's own father. His hair grew salt-and-pepper around his ears and dark like Alissa's on the top of his head. The man lent a glance to Guillaume first, then studied Jonathan from head to foot. His eyes lingered on the sleeping girl in Jonathan's arms.

"Honey!" The man called over his shoulder. "Make some coffee and bring my shotgun."

Both security guards stepped closer to Jonathan.

Jonathan gulped.

The man shoved open the screen door. "Come in. Let's have a chat."

Since it seemed unlikely that either Guillaume or the driver would make way for Jonathan to enter the house under threat of a shotgun, Jonathan took the initiative on his own.

The man moved aside to allow Jonathan inside the front hall. "Let's take her to her room."

"You must be her father. It's my pleasure to meet you, Mr. Cassidy."

Alissa's father raised a brow in suspicion. "Can't say the same yet."

"If you'll point me in the correct direction." Jonathan figured it might be best to change the subject. American customs and Veldorian traditions varied greatly. He hated to think he would break some unspoken taboo.

Mr. Cassidy motioned toward the stairs at the end of the hall. "Follow me."

Jonathan shot a look over his shoulder at Guillaume. "Stay here," he hissed. The last thing he needed to do was to frighten Alissa's father.

Guillaume didn't look happy, but he did as Jonathan ordered.

Jonathan trailed Mr. Cassidy up the stairs and down the hall. Through a door on his right.

"Lay her here. She'll probably sleep until morning." Mr. Cassidy pulled down the blankets.

Jonathan didn't dare try to make conversation. Alissa's father seemed put out enough without Jonathan adding fuel to the fire. Instead, Jonathan laid Alissa gently on the bed and stepped away. He shouldn't give Mr. Cassidy any more wrong impressions.

Mr. Cassidy pulled the covers over his daughter and pressed a kiss to her forehead. Then he turned to Jonathan. "Downstairs. Let's go."

Jonathan didn't understand the level of his own fear. Perhaps he feared Alissa's father because the man asked for his shotgun. Or, perhaps, Jonathan feared Mr. Cassidy because, in some deep part of himself, Jonathan wanted the man to approve of him. The second option concerned Jonathan more. Because that option meant that, for some reason, he had legitimate feelings for Alissa. If that were the truth, Jonathan didn't think he could let her go. Not ever.

That didn't bode well for anyone involved.

Downstairs, Guillaume waited in the same place that Jonathan left him. The driver had disappeared, which meant Guillaume had sent him to check the property. Fair enough.

"What's all the commotion?" A female voice asked from the top of the stairs.

All three men in the hall turned to look.

Mrs. Cassidy was as beautiful as her daughter. Chocolate hair framed her face in a trendy bob hairstyle. Even without makeup, her skin fairly glowed. The woman didn't look a day over thirty-five, yet Jonathan knew better.

Jonathan dipped his head in a slight bow.

Mrs. Cassidy smiled. "I'll make some coffee." She descended the stairs and disappeared through a doorway.

Mr. Cassidy shot Jonathan a disapproving look. "Might as well come sit down. I have questions."

Of course he did. Any father in his right mind would have questions about Jonathan's sudden appearance. As much as Jonathan wanted sleep, clearing the air seemed more important.

Mr. Cassidy led Jonathan and Guillaume through the same doorway his wife had disappeared through.

Jonathan found himself in a large, quaint kitchen. White and blue gave it an airy look, even with the darkness outside the windows.

Mr. Cassidy took up residence at a small table in the corner. He motioned for Jonathan to join him. Of course, Guillaume took the seat beside Jonathan, his eyes still wary and his stance still stiff.

"Who's he?" Mr. Cassidy jutted his chin toward Guillaume.

Jonathan took each moment in stride. It was the only way he would ever get through this. "My bodyguard." A simplified answer, but hopefully acceptable.

"And the other guy?"

"My driver." Honesty. Always the best policy. Or so Jonathan told himself.

"They don't even have coffee yet," Mrs. Cassidy piped up from the other side of the room. "Why are you interrogating him?"

"He showed up carrying your daughter. Don't you want to know who he is and what he does?"

Mrs. Cassidy carried two mugs of coffee to the table. She gave one to Guillaume and one to Jonathan. "There are nicer ways to ask."

Jonathan couldn't help but smile at the exchange. "You want to know my intentions with your daughter."

Mr. Cassidy's attention snapped back to Jonathan. "Exactly. I see you're a smart one. What do you do for a living?"

"My intentions are very clear, sir." Jonathan avoided the last question altogether. "I've been attempting to provide some help in your daughter's current situation, but I will admit to using that as an excuse. Where I'm from, men simply don't meet a woman's parents. Not unless he has every intention of marrying her."

Guillaume choked on his coffee.

Jonathan reached a hand over to slap Guillaume on the back. No doubt Jonathan's parents would hear about this in the morning. At this juncture, he didn't care.

Mr. Cassidy stared, wide-eyed. "You... um... What *do* you do for a living?"

"I'm a kind of... public relations expert." Jonathan feared he would give the man a coronary if he mentioned the words *Crown Prince.*

"That's vague."

Mrs. Cassidy slammed a third mug onto the table. Coffee spilled over the rim. "Let him have one win, dear. He seems nice enough. Don't scare him away."

Mr. Cassidy opened his mouth to protest.

Mrs. Cassidy narrowed her eyes. "Alissa doesn't bring boys home." She turned a smile to Jonathan and Guillaume. "You said Alissa's in a situation. What kind of situation?"

"I think it's best she tell you herself." Jonathan sincerely hoped they listened to his advice.

As much as he wanted to tell them everything, it wasn't his place. This was Alissa's fight as much as it was his. She may not know about the Anti-Monarchists, but she had become their target. Jonathan thought it best she explain in her own way, so her parents would listen better.

"At least tell me why you brought her here."

Jonathan could live with that. He smiled wanly. "She needed a safe place to stay. She couldn't think of anywhere safer than with you."

Chapter 11

A beam of sunlight through the blinds spread warmth across Alissa's cheek. She reached her arms above her head and stretched. After an exhausting evening, she couldn't imagine a more perfect way to wake up.

"I'm not saying you never talk to me anymore, but, uh, who's the guy downstairs?"

Alissa sat bolt upright. What day was this? Where was she? How did she get here? A quick perusal of the room revealed all familiar items. Her room at home. Which meant... Oh no.

Cody snapped his fingers to garner her attention. "Yo, little sis. You've got some 'splaining to do."

"Not now, Cody." Alissa flung her blankets aside and scrambled to her feet.

Jonathan definitely came with her, which meant he was the 'guy' Cody had referenced. Which meant Jonathan must be alone with her parents. Alissa didn't like the logical conclusion to all this. She needed to intervene. Jonathan didn't know the fate that awaited him.

Cody darted in front of the door and spread his arms wide. "You're not going anywhere until you explain."

"I don't have time. Move." Alissa planted her hands against Cody's side and shoved.

Cody barely budged. "Let's think through this logically. Last time I saw you, you had that security guy with you. The one Vi was making eyes at. Now you've got... who? Some schmuck from IT?"

"First of all, I don't have an IT guy." Alissa took a step back and folded her own arms. "Secondly, it's a long story and *logically* I need to save him from mom and dad first."

"Okay, but I liked the last guy. He saved your life."

"That is no reason for me to date anyone. Move it, Codester!" Alissa shoved at his chest this time.

"Right. I get that. But who's this guy? What's he got to offer? Did he save your life?"

"Yes. He did."

"Really? Are the two guys connected?"

Alissa huffed. "The first guy works for this guy."

"So this guy... runs the hotel?"

Why does this dork think that? Alissa wracked her brain, finally coming to the realization she had told Cody that Adison worked hotel security. "Yeah, sure, okay. We'll go with that."

"That's not a yes."

"I don't care. Just get out of the way." Alissa waited three seconds for Cody to move. When he didn't, she dodged right, then lunged around his other side when he made a move to stop her. "Sorry, Codes!"

Barefoot, hair a mess, Alissa raced her way downstairs and followed the sound of low voices. *Good Lord, don't let my dad wig Jonathan out.*

Alissa didn't analyze the reasons she cared whether or not the two got along. Being a romantic meant when she fell, she fell hard. Alissa always had a difficult time owning up to that.

She found her dad in the living room, relaxed in his favorite chair. Across from him, Jonathan sat prim and proper at the center of the couch.

Alissa marched to Jonathan's side first. "Are you okay? You're not hurt? He didn't shoot at you, right?" She took Jonathan's face in her hands to inspect it, then moved to his shoulders. Arms. Hands.

"Is this worry? Over little old me?"

Alissa looked up to see a smirk on Jonathan's lips and a mischievous glint in his eyes. She dropped his hand and rolled her eyes. "You're fine."

"I don't shoot people without a reason, Alissa. You know that." Her dad stood and held his arms open. "Come give me a proper hug."

Alissa didn't hesitate to enter her father's arms. It had always been one of her favorite places. The embrace lingered as if her father didn't want to let go. Quite frankly, Alissa didn't want to let go, either.

"Aw, how sweet. Now, someone explain the guy on the couch."

Alissa wrinkled her nose. Of course Cody followed her and ruined the moment.

"I think everyone has an explanation to make." Alissa's dad motioned Cody to the love seat. "Let's all hash this out together."

As much as Alissa wanted to point out that she would rather not, she couldn't say no to her dad. In a matter of moments, Alissa found herself seated beside Jonathan. At some point, she realized there were juice and snacks on the coffee table. She didn't have the appetite for any of it.

"Jonathan and I were talking last night, and it seems Alissa is in some sort of predicament." Her dad leveled his gaze at her. "Care to explain?"

"Predicament?" Alissa smiled too brightly. "Oh, you mean that? It was... nothing."

The dual glare coming from Cody and her father made Alissa reevaluate her ability to lie. A look over her shoulder at Jonathan showed much the same disapproval.

"Okay, fine! So it was something!" Alissa threw her hands up in defeat.

"A missive so vicious can hardly be described so trivially." Jonathan's little interjection didn't help matters.

Alissa shot Jonathan a glare. "Hey, you. With the posture and the vocabulary. Shut up and let me tell it my way."

Jonathan raised a hand and motioned for her to continue.

Alissa took a deep breath. "Apparently someone wants me dead or something. There was a stalker-y picture and scratches. Gorey details, really. I'll be fine."

"Fine? *Fine*?!" Cody gaped at Alissa like she had lost her mind. "What about stalker-y messages is fine? You can't go back there. I forbid it."

"Okay, nice try, but seriously, you can't tell me what to do."

"I concur," Jonathan opened his big fat mouth again. "Having dealt with such matters before, I think it best if Alissa stays here for the time being."

"I'm sorry, but as your father I have to agree with this boy." Alissa's dad shrugged a shoulder. "Stick around for a while. Just until things cool down."

"My people are attempting to locate the culprit. It shouldn't be long."

Alissa couldn't believe what she was hearing. "It wasn't that big of a deal!"

"Then why did you almost faint straightaway?" Jonathan reached out a hand to rest it on Alissa's shoulder. "I don't mean to be overbearing. Allow me to offer advice as someone who knows how to handle these things."

Cody glared at Jonathan's hand.

Alissa's dad folded his arms across his chest. "I thought you said you worked in PR."

"PR, my foot," Alissa snorted. "He's a prince. Real, live, genuine. A crown prince, even."

"Alissa!" Jonathan cried.

Alissa turned and stuck her tongue out at him. "What? You can tell my secrets but I can't tell yours?"

"Mine are a little larger than yours, don't you think?"

"So, when you say prince..." Cody leaned his elbows forward against his knees. "Do you mean 'future ruler of a country'?"

Alissa nodded. "Fun, right?"

"And you want to marry our daughter?"

Alissa froze. What had her dad just asked? What kind of question was that?

Jonathan cleared his throat beside her, as if the question caught him off guard too. But not like it surprised him. Which meant those two had talked. And... Jonathan had professed love?

"We're not even dating." Alissa gaped at Jonathan.

Jonathan folded his hands neatly in his lap. "A crown prince doesn't have much extra time for things like dating. I'm a man who goes after what I like."

"Okay, sure, but marriage? Already?"

Jonathan leaned in closer. "I like you."

"We're not dating!"

"You two do realize I'm sitting right here?" Alissa's dad glowered. "Flirting is now forbidden."

"Okay, that's not fair, daddy." Alissa turned around to redirect her ire.

Cody shot a hand in the air. "I agree with dad's decision. Really, you two disgust me."

Alissa frowned at him. "That's because you can't catch a decent girl to save your life."

"I could, but I choose not to. Get your facts straight."

"Get your head straight. This isn't a love triangle, you're just a spectator, so stay out of this." Alissa shifted in her seat to face her dad. "What if this flirting turns into something more? What if I really start to like him?"

It was probably too late for what-ifs. Alissa already liked him, despite her own denial. Jonathan took everything she shot at him with a gentleness she didn't know a guy could possess. Even though she told herself he was bad for her, Alissa wanted to know more about him. If that wasn't a crush, at the very least, she didn't know what it was.

"Do you realize the logical end to all this, Alissa?" Her dad didn't loosen his stance. "If you two become something, you'll have to move out of the country. Leave us all behind. It's an all-in or all-out kind of thing. You can't do this on a whim."

Jonathan cleared his throat before Alissa had a chance to refute. "I have a proposition to make."

Alissa flopped back on the couch. "Go ahead."

"Give me one month. I will remain by your side for one month, and if you don't have feelings for me by the end of that month, I will never see you again."

The room fell silent. No one dared move as they processed the offer.

Alissa spoke first, soft and timid. "What if I only like you because I have a hero complex?"

"I don't think that's the case, and if it were, I believe you are intelligent enough to sort that out by the end of one month."

The exact deadline of one month niggled at the back of Alissa's mind. It seemed definite, as if he knew something she didn't. On the other hand, it was one month that she would have him alongside her, even if she never saw him again afterward. The offer was too tempting to pass up, but...

"If you're going to date me, you should ask my dad's permission."

"If he says yes?"

Alissa nibbled at the corner of her lip. "Then I think we should give it a shot."

A smile lit upon Jonathan's face. He reached out to take Alissa's hand in his. "Thank you."

"Why are you looking at me like that?" Alissa eyed Jonathan suspiciously.

"Yeah, why are you looking at her like that?" Cody mimicked.

Their father cleared his throat. "Jonathan and I already had a chat last night. He asked my permission then."

"And you gave it?" Once again, Alissa didn't know quite how to process this information. How much preparation did Jonathan put into this?

Her dad shrugged. "He seems like a genuine guy and he made a good argument. At the very least, he's attentive. Besides, I won't be far away."

Alissa didn't doubt that, but she never expected Jonathan to win her father's permission so quickly. A glance to her brother revealed a glare that said Cody expected explanations. Alissa knew less than he did. What the heck happened while she was asleep last night anyway?

Chapter 12

"What do you mean you lost them?" Deadly calm laced through the question gave away every malicious intent.

The henchmen cowered, their limbs shaking with anticipation of the horror to come. No one dared utter an apology. It would only fuel the flames of The Boss' anger.

"If you lost them, find them again. You know what's riding on this." A flicker of orange flared, then dimmed again when The Boss pulled the cigar away from his lips.

One brave subordinate dared to speak up. "It's not that easy, sir."

An icy chill radiated from The Boss' stare. "Why not?"

"They escaped before we had eyes on them and we don't have access to any CCTVs and..."

"I'll get you access." The Boss stood to pace the floor behind his desk. "You just work on trailing them. Do what you can for now. I'll have the cameras in a few hours. What about the business from overseas?"

"All the loose ends are cleared up. There shouldn't be a problem with anything."

"All the loose ends except one. Cut it properly. I don't give second chances." The Boss brushed a hand through the air dismissively. "Go now. Before I change my mind."

The henchmen scrambled out the door as fast as their feet would allow.

The Boss sank into his plush desk chair and extinguished the cigar. He wouldn't let one little slip-up cost him everything. He would get what he worked so hard for, and no one would stand in the way of that. Especially not *them.*

೩೦೦೮

"I'm sorry I'm late. I wanted to be positive that no one followed me." Adison dipped a bow to Jonathan and a friendly nod to Guillaume.

Adison was too good at his job. No one would dare follow him, especially if they knew the areas of his expertise.

Jonathan held back his grin. "Were you followed?"

"For about two hours."

"By whom?" Guillaume's stance didn't change, but his tone turned serious.

Adison shrugged. "Lady Alissa's plucky friend."

"She could call Alissa if she wanted her location. It wouldn't be hard." Jonathan rolled his eyes. "I'm glad you're here now. Guillaume will give you orders."

Jonathan and Guillaume had discussed the best course of action the night before. Adison would shadow Alissa, on a semi-permanent basis until they got to the bottom of the malicious threats in the mail. Jonathan trusted Adison with Alissa's life.

"Where are you off to?" Adison asked, directing his question to Jonathan.

Jonathan couldn't help but smile a little wider. "I have something of a date to attend to."

Adison raised his brows. "A date?"

"Yes. It seems Alissa's family is having a small party. I've been invited to attend."

"That's a terrible idea," Guillaume muttered.

Both Jonathan and Adison froze to look at Guillaume. Guillaume didn't state his opinion often, but when he did he meant every word.

Jonathan gulped. "May I... ask why?"

"If it's a family gathering, most of the family will be there."

Adison nodded as if he understood.

Jonathan still didn't grasp the situation. What did that have to do with anything? "Pardon?"

"You're the new boyfriend." Guillaume shrugged. "I'm fairly certain they'll attack."

"Oh, is that all?" Jonathan clapped a hand against Guillaume's shoulder. "That's why I have you."

"It's not that kind of attack." Guillaume shrugged off Jonathan's hand. "I'm sorry, highness, but you're on your own this time."

"What?" Jonathan glanced between the two bodyguards. Both gave him the same look of sympathy. Jonathan didn't understand why they were acting like this might be the last time they saw him. "It's only her family."

"Highness, forgive my saying so," Guillaume winced, "but you're quite naive in these matters."

Adison nodded his agreement. "It's adorable. And dangerous."

"You're both being ridiculous." Jonathan rolled his eyes.

How bad could it be? He had dealt with larger crowds and tougher audiences. He could handle a small family gathering. Diplomacy would do the trick, certainly.

"If he isn't going to listen, you should let him do as he wishes."
Adison stepped aside and motioned sarcastically toward the door.

Jonathan hesitated. Neither Adison nor Guillaume had reason
to lie to him or purposely make him nervous. They would both
understand that Jonathan's anxiety had already mounted. Though
they weren't in Veldoria, the traditions of his people bore deep
into Jonathan's bones. To meet Alissa's family, in Veldoria, would
mean that Jonathan intended to marry her without any dubiety.

It didn't explain the warnings from Guillaume and Adison. In
America, the Veldorian traditions didn't count and weren't
common knowledge. Why did both men think Jonathan bit off
more than he could chew?

"Tell me. What's so wrong about meeting her family?"

Guillaume grinned. "From what we've gathered, you are her
first and only boyfriend."

Jonathan nodded. "Your point?"

"Her family won't see you as a royal," Adison volunteered. "To
them, you are simply a man who happens to be dating their most
precious Alissa."

"I still don't see where you're going with this insinuation."

"Your highness..." Guillaume cleared his throat. "Don't be too
shocked when the interrogation begins."

"Interrogation?" Please. It couldn't be as bad as all that. Alissa's
family had been kind to him so far. The others would accept him
as well. Jonathan checked his watch. "I'll be late. We should go."

The two security members took a step back to allow Jonathan
to go first. Jonathan didn't like the grave expression on either of
their faces, but it was too late to back out now.

Guillaume climbed into the car after Jonathan had safely tucked
himself in the back. He didn't say another word about the family

gathering, but the sighs and mutterings that came from his general direction didn't sound pleasant.

The location given for the family gathering led Jonathan and Guillaume to a local community center. Jonathan had visited many similar buildings, small and rectangular with a kitchen at one end. However, it would be his first time entering for a personal occasion. Usually, he cut ribbons, shook hands, and left fashionably early.

"I'll wait here." Guillaume wouldn't take no for an answer, once his mind had been made up. Jonathan knew that well.

Jonathan wouldn't complain about the distance that Guillaume established. He should, of course, take care of things here on his own. Judging by the make and model of the vehicles already parked, Alissa's family maintained a standard middle-class income on all fronts. To throw them into the world of security protocols and royalty may be more culture shock than Jonathan wished to inflict on anyone.

With more trepidation than he had felt in years, Jonathan stood from the car and started toward the gathering. He could do this. He had charmed much larger audiences. One family couldn't be as hard as Guillaume would have him think.

Jonathan stepped through the door to the din of conversation and laughter. It echoed off the ceiling and bounced off the concrete floor. Even with the volume, warmth and friendliness permeated the atmosphere.

On instinct, Jonathan scanned the crowd for Alissa. He found her perched at a table in the far corner with a small gaggle of older women. Like a moth to flame, Jonathan couldn't resist the pull.

As inconspicuously as possible, Jonathan skirted his way around the room.

Alissa caught sight of him as he picked his way between two nearby tables. She stood from her seat, her fingers drumming nervously against her legs. "Hi."

Every woman around her followed Alissa's gaze.

Jonathan couldn't help the stupid grin that crossed his face. Just seeing Alissa made him want to smile. He stopped by Alissa's side, cautious not to reach out and touch her even though he wanted to. "That's the fewest amount of words you've ever said to me."

"Don't get used to it, I'm just not over the shock of this whole relationship." Alissa winced as the words left her lips. As if she didn't intend to say that out loud.

"Oh, this is the boy?" One of the women rose from the table and held out her hand. "I'm Lucille. Aunt Lucy to you. You must be Jonathan."

"So Alissa has told you of me." Jonathan shook the woman's hand. "It's a pleasure to meet you."

"Don't bet on that." Lucille motioned to the other two women at the table. "My sisters. Doris and Carol."

"A pleasure." Jonathan smiled at each.

Neither smiled back.

Alissa wrapped an arm around the crook of Jonathan's elbow. "Don't let them railroad you."

Jonathan was about to ask what Alissa meant when Lucille motioned him to the only available seat left. Across the table from Alissa.

"Sit down. Let's have a chat."

Jonathan glanced down at Alissa, but she had already released him to take her own place. A shrill warning bell signaled in the back of Jonathan's mind, but he ignored it.

Doris posed the first question. "So, you have the hots for our little girl?"

Alissa swatted at the woman's shoulder. "Why would you ask that?"

"I don't mince words. You just stay silent and let us have a talk." Doris turned back to Jonathan. "What kind of a toy do you think she is, yanking her around like this?"

"Aunt Doris!"

"Pardon?" Jonathan blinked. Who in the world was this woman? What had Alissa told her to make her think that? "I believe you're mistaken. My care for Alissa is genuine."

"So you say." Doris reached for her tea and took a sip.

Lucille rolled her eyes. "Don't mind her. Tell us how you met Alissa. She's a bit hush-hush about the details."

"I do believe we first met at my cousin's home." Jonathan didn't mind that question. Everything had been above-board. He didn't see a reason to lie or omit anything.

"Alissa said it was a gala," Carol finally spoke up.

Alissa pressed her lips together and shut her eyes.

Jonathan blew out a breath. Of course. "We didn't meet that night, but I saw her, yes."

"Don't give us that love at first sight crap." Doris folded her arms and glared. "I don't believe in it and neither should you. It's all a myth."

"I will admit at that time it was only concern." Jonathan did his best to keep a light, diplomatic smile. "I believe the first time I considered it attraction was at a small coffee shop." And running down a few alleys afterward, but he wouldn't say that out loud. It sounded unscrupulous.

Carol tipped her head in a bird-like gesture. "Why were you concerned about her? Did something happen?"

Alissa widened her eyes and shook her head, so slight that Jonathan almost missed it. However, he agreed. It wouldn't be wise to tell these aunts.

"She seemed lightheaded. I was afraid she might faint or fall." Jonathan shrugged a shoulder noncommittally.

Doris snorted. "That's a load of bull."

"Aunt Doris, would you stop?" Alissa folded her own arms in an imitation of the older woman's body language. "Just because you don't believe it, doesn't mean there aren't gentlemen in the world."

"Keep telling yourself that, sweetheart." Doris winked at her niece.

Lucille waved a hand to silence both of them. "Your accent is unique. Whereabouts are you from?"

"I hail from Veldoria." Jonathan didn't mind letting the cat out of the bag. None of them would guess that they were talking to a crown prince. Jonathan liked it that way. For now.

"Never heard of it," Doris interjected.

Lucille rolled her eyes again. "Doris, do you have to be such a Debbie Downer? The boy is telling us he's foreign. Let him get a word in edgewise."

"I don't like him."

"Doesn't matter. Alissa does." Lucille smiled at Jonathan. "So sorry about her. You said Veldoria? That's in Europe, right?"

"Yes, it is." Jonathan wasn't sure what to say that wouldn't get him in trouble with one or another of the aunts. "A beautiful country. Very lush and green."

"How long have you known Alissa?" Carol asked.

Jonathan smiled wryly. "Not long enough. About a month? That seems accurate."

Alissa nodded. "We've gotten to know each other well over the past several weeks. I told you, Jonathan is very nice."

"Every boy seems nice at first." Doris again.

Lucille raised a hand as if she wanted to smack her sister. "Carol, reach over there and whack her a good one."

"She'll hit me back." Carol shook her head.

Lucille scrunched her nose. "Fine. I'll just beat her later."

"Are any of you ladies married?" Jonathan ventured to ask.

Alissa's sympathetic expression should have given him a clue how the next hour would go. One by one, Lucille, Doris, and Carol went on about their significant others. Lucille spoke on her husband and how they had grown apart but were too comfortable with each other to break up or divorce. Doris ranted on about her previous two husbands and didn't have anything better to say about her current husband. Only quiet, reserved Carol spoke about a loving relationship.

Jonathan could have done without all the drama, but it passed the time to hear their stories. Made him understand them a little better.

Just when he thought he would never get out of the conversation, Alissa rose and circled the table.

She took Jonathan's hand and gave a tug. "If you'll excuse us, there are other people to talk to."

Jonathan took the opportunity to get away. To the complete opposite side of the room. Alissa's hand always felt small in his, but somehow it felt surer today. Warmer.

"I'm sorry about my aunts. They're always like this." Alissa laughed.

Jonathan missed seeing her so light-hearted. "I think I did well. Aunt Doris doesn't seem to like me much."

"Aunt Doris doesn't like anybody." Alissa looked down to her feet. "Thanks again for putting up with them. I know it's a lot."

Jonathan reached out with his free hand. Tucking his fingers beneath her chin, Jonathan lifted Alissa's gaze. "It's nothing much. You've met Margaret. She isn't the looniest relative of mine. Nothing to concern yourself with, as I have no intention of ever breaking things off with you."

Alissa smiled, somewhat bashfully. "Can you read me that easily?"

"You're an open book." Jonathan couldn't lie about that. Alissa had a way of expressing everything she thought through her face. Endearing, and completely helpful when he wasn't sure what went wrong. "But I like it that way."

Alissa gave Jonathan's hand a squeeze. "Thanks."

"Stop thanking me, it's unnecessary."

"Sir."

Jonathan and Alissa both turned at the sound of the familiar voice.

Guillaume held out a phone. "It's your mother."

His mother. A small part of Jonathan panicked. His mother didn't interrupt things like this without a purpose. Something had happened.

Alissa squeezed Jonathan's hand again. "You should take it."

"I won't be long," Jonathan promised. He kissed the back of Alissa's hand, snatched the phone from Guillaume, and stepped outside. "Mother?"

"Jonathan. We found the footage of your brother's accident."

"How is Frederick? Has he woken yet?" Jonathan didn't want to believe the worst, but something in his mother's tone sounded grim.

"No. He hasn't. But, Jonathan..." His mother released a heavy sigh, as if the weight of the world rested on her shoulders. "It's time to come home."

Chapter 13

Alissa always enjoyed her family's gatherings. They provided entertainment, if nothing else. Jonathan had held his own with her three outlandish great-aunts, which spoke volumes for his sincerity. Not just anyone would sit there and take all that insanity. Especially not if they didn't mean what they said about the girl in question.

For a brief moment, Alissa allowed herself to believe that Jonathan really could harbor some kind of feelings toward her. She couldn't help but smile.

Alissa didn't realize how long she had been lost in her own head. People had started to exit, some gracefully and some without so much as a goodbye. That was family, a little eclectic and very unpredictable.

The doors opened again, silhouetting three familiar men in the dwindling daylight.

Alissa wrapped her arms protectively around her torso. As far as she knew, Guillaume and Adison weren't supposed to come in unless something happened. As much as she didn't want to look at Jonathan's face, Alissa pushed through the dread.

Jonathan's lips settled in a thin, grim line. His long legs and sure strides ate up the space between the door and Alissa.

Alissa shrank back. "Something's wrong."

"I'll drive you home, we can speak in the car." Jonathan reached out a hand. He left it settled in the air between them, an open invitation to accept or reject the offer.

Alissa couldn't say no. Even though she knew nothing good would come out of it. Even though she knew something terrible must have happened. If she felt this bad, he must feel so much worse. She settled her fingers inside Jonathan's and gave a reassuring squeeze.

Jonathan tugged her closer and wrapped his arms around her. "I'm sorry, Alissa."

Alissa didn't ask why he apologized. He would tell her in his own time. Even in the short time they had known each other, she learned that about him. This relationship had started too quickly, but somehow it felt right. Like destiny. That scared Alissa more than anything else.

"Sir." Guillaume cleared his throat. To garner Jonathan's attention, Alissa wagered.

With a world-weary sigh, Jonathan took a step back. No words passed between Jonathan and Alissa, nor Guillaume and Adison. Alissa could practically feel the stares boring into the back of her head. She would explain to her family later.

Jonathan helped Alissa into the vehicle, then rounded the rear fender to take his own seat on the other side of the car.

Alissa waited only until all four doors had closed. "What's going on? You seem upset."

"Guillaume, take us back to the house, please." Jonathan leaned back in his seat.

Alissa turned to face him. "Putting it off won't make it any better. Tell me what's going on. What did your mom say?"

"I don't know how I'm going to keep my promise to you, but I will."

"Okay. That's... cryptic. Go on."

"I've been called back home. I think I have to go." Jonathan looked out the window, as if it shamed him.

Alissa hesitated to reach out a hand, but in the end she placed it against his shoulder. "There must be a reason. I don't think you would take off like this without a reason. Did I... do something? Say something?"

Jonathan reached up a hand to press it on top of hers. "It has nothing to do with you. It's because of some things happening in Veldoria. I must take care of them."

"Like what?"

"Like my brother's accident." Jonathan turned a tortured gaze to Alissa. "It wasn't a simple accident."

Alissa wanted nothing more than to comfort Jonathan, but she didn't know how. So she sufficed with, "Is he okay?"

"He hasn't woken yet. There aren't any signs of brain damage, so the doctors don't know what to think about it. I should be there in case something happens again. And I must address my people."

For the first time, Alissa realized that Jonathan didn't belong to only one or two people. He had an entire country to lead. People depended on him to ensure their own survival. What must that feel like? Could his shoulders handle such weight?

"Then you should go."

"I promised you a month."

"I can't keep you from your country, even if I wanted to."

"It isn't fair to you." Jonathan tucked her fingers in his. "I'll find some way to come back. It shouldn't take long. I'll leave Adison to watch over you, just in case."

"I really can take care of myself, you know. I've been doing it for a long time."

"It will make me feel better."

Alissa conceded with a nod. Even if she refused, she had a gut feeling that Jonathan would leave someone behind to watch her, anyway. "What about all those guys you left behind at Maggie's?"

"They will follow me to Veldoria. Guillaume will call them."

"And this relationship you want to build?"

A soft smile played on Jonathan's tense face. "Technology. We can phone one another, or video call. Whatever it is the kids do nowadays."

"Are you saying we're old?"

Finally, Jonathan relaxed. A laugh rang loud in the car. "I suppose that's what I implied. I did not mean it that way."

"People do long distance relationships all the time. We'll be fine." Alissa smiled like she believed it. In reality, she didn't know if it would work. Their romance had barely started to blossom. What if time and distance killed the first blooms of love? "When do you leave?"

"We shouldn't delay. The sooner I leave, the sooner I can come back." Jonathan held out his free hand. "Your phone, madam."

Alissa didn't understand the change in subject, but she went along with it. Easy enough, to hand her phone over to Jonathan.

Jonathan shook his head at her. "Unlock it, please."

"What are you even doing?" Alissa reached out one finger to punch in the PIN.

"We don't have each other's contact information. I'm giving you mine..." Jonathan dialed a number. A buzzing vibration came from his pocket. "...and stealing yours, as well. You'd best save this and answer when I call, hm?"

Alissa snatched her phone away from him. "You could have just asked."

"What fun is that? It seems you trust me more than you think you do." Jonathan winked playfully.

Alissa rolled her eyes. "Just you wait. If you keep pushing it, I may not save the number."

"Then let me save it for you." Jonathan reached out for the phone.

Alissa yanked her hand away, the phone safely tucked inside her fingers. "Nope. Not gonna happen."

"Please save it. It will make me feel immensely better knowing you have a hot-line directly to me."

Alissa couldn't help but laugh at Jonathan's pout. As mature as he seemed most of the time, it appeared he could also be childish. She had to admit, it was adorable.

"Fine, I'll save it, but I'm not guaranteeing what title I'm going to save it under. Don't make me be mean."

"Whatever you decide to call me in your contacts, I think I can handle it. You have no idea what I've been called by the press. Savages, the lot of them." Jonathan turned his attention to his phone.

Alissa peered over his shoulder to see him saving the number that most recently dialed his. "What's my name in your phone?"

Jonathan turned it so she couldn't see. "It doesn't matter, does it? You won't tell me, either."

Alissa wrinkled her nose. She didn't like how his logic always made sense. There were some people who needed to learn how to lose once in a while. Jonathan's name sat at the top of that list.

Adison turned his head to shoot information over his shoulder. "The plane will be waiting in an hour. You should leave as soon as you drop Alissa at her home."

"Tell them we'll be there." Jonathan didn't sound pleased, but he didn't necessarily sound upset either.

Alissa recognized the tone. The one he used to placate strangers. She heard it before, when he gave his speech. How difficult must it be for him to hide his feelings all the time? Especially since Jonathan seemed like a fun person, in general.

The rest of the ride home didn't take long. A godsend, that no one spoke a word. The awkwardness hung like a heavy, wet blanket. After all, how did one comfort a newly formed couple who had to leave each other so suddenly? No one knew how long they might be apart.

Guillaume pulled to a stop at the front porch. "Please say your goodbyes."

"I'll walk her to the door." Jonathan didn't leave room for argument.

Adison stepped out of the vehicle, but made no move to open doors or go inside. Alissa assumed he stood there solely for security purposes. As if there was anything around here that might attack.

Jonathan helped Alissa out of the car, then tucked her arm around his own. "I am truly sorry that this happened."

"Is it the Anti-Monarchists that you mentioned before?" Alissa couldn't help her curiosity. Curiosity comprised a large part of her personality. To take it away would be to change a deep-rooted part of herself.

Jonathan nodded solemnly. "We believe so. No one is certain what their plan seems to be, but it's assumed that they want Frederick dead. He's an easier target than I am. I'll have to be present for the investigation. I don't know how long it will take."

"You'll call when you get back to Veldoria?" Alissa alighted on the porch's top step and turned to face him.

Jonathan didn't release her arm. "I'll text between meetings and call when I can. Don't lose Adison, he's one of my greatest assets. If I didn't think you needed him, I wouldn't leave him here."

"I'll take good care of him. Feed him three times a day, make sure he doesn't catch a cold." Alissa giggled despite the ache pressing on her heart. "You don't have to worry."

"I'll worry, anyway. I don't think I can be apart from you without feeling concern." Jonathan clucked his tongue. "What kind of bewitching magic do you carry?"

Alissa shrugged. "It's a secret."

"Your highness," Guillaume called from the car.

Jonathan waved a hand at him. "It appears my time is up. Take care of yourself. Eat well, don't fret, and for heaven's sake stay out of dangerous situations."

"What dangerous situations will there be if you're not here?" Alissa forced a smile for Jonathan's benefit.

Jonathan took Alissa's face in his hands and leaned forward. Gently, slowly, he pressed a kiss to her forehead. "I'll be in touch. I promise. And I *will* come back to you."

"You'd better. I'd like to get to know you a lot better."

"Until next time." Jonathan released her, but even to Alissa it seemed reluctant.

She could relate. Alissa didn't say it out loud, and she tried not to show it, but her heart beat an irregular rhythm. Her chest ached. What kind of reaction was this? A goodbye? Or something more?

Even as Alissa watched Jonathan and Guillaume drive away, she couldn't quite understand the emotions coursing through her head and heart. Would absence make their hearts grow fonder? Or would it split them apart before they'd even begun?

⁚⁚

"He's returned to his kingdom." The Boss sat back in his chair, fully relaxed despite the situation he found himself in.

"You move quickly. I should have paid you instead of making a deal."

The Boss snorted. "This time, it wasn't my doing. I merely made mention of it to someone who had a need. I've resolved your problem, now leave me to resolve my own."

"I wish you luck with everything. It won't be easy."

"I never thought it would be. The end result will be worth all the effort. I hope we won't have reason to speak again."

The call ended.

The Boss leaned his head back and closed his eyes. Everything had gone so perfectly up to now. Why did they have to ruin his plans with one single mistake? How could his subordinates *lose* them? He thought he hired more competent workers than that.

It shouldn't be long now. It had been a week. Even idiots could find her by now. He should get a phone call or visit at any time.

The Boss reached for his cigar and placed it between his lips. Imported always satisfied more than some cheap replica. Of course, he had to be careful where he imported it from. He didn't want a scandal to start. Which is why he always took care of loose ends.

The door opened and closed. Rapid footsteps clicked and clacked their way toward The Boss' chair.

"Sir." His henchman skidded to a stop, huffing and puffing. "We found them."

"Proceed with the original plan." The Boss took a long pull of his cigar. "None of this can lead back to me. Understood?"

"Yes, sir." The henchman dipped his head in a small gesture of respect. "We'll take of it."

"Do it properly this time. No more mistakes."

The tone, alone, had the henchman cowering in fear. "Yes, sir. Trust us. We'll finish the job."

Chapter 14

Jonathan exited the elevator into the nearly empty hallway of the Royal University Hospital. Of course, no one would be in this wing. Only palace personnel, the royal family, and a few select doctors and nurses were allowed entrance. Jonathan knew he wouldn't run into his mother or father. They both had prior engagements. Hence his presence. Someone had to come when the hospital called.

His phone trilled in his pocket. Jonathan checked the time and winced. He answered without looking at the number. "Apologies. Something urgent came up."

"It was a long shot, anyway." Alissa sighed on the other end. "I was hoping you had a minute. I'm bored and there's nothing to do."

"Again, my sincerest apologies. Frederick regained consciousness. Do you mind very much if I call you back after he and I have spoken?"

"He's up? That's great!"

Jonathan couldn't help but smile at the 180-degree turn-around in Alissa's demeanor. Frederick's wakefulness moved Jonathan one step closer to going back to Alissa's side. "I promise I will call before the evening is out. Alright?"

"Okay, fine. You'd better remember though." A pause. "I miss you."

"And I, you. Be well today."

"You too."

The phone call didn't last long, but it lifted Jonathan's spirits tremendously. One week had flown by, but at least for now, he and Alissa seemed to be doing alright. At the very least, she seemed safe now that he had distanced himself from her.

"Your highness." Guillaume leaned around Jonathan's shoulder to motion him forward.

Jonathan chuckled. "Yes, thank you, Guillaume."

Jonathan silenced his phone and put it away. He didn't need to be told to proceed. The phone call with Alissa had been a momentary distraction, but Jonathan knew the reason for this visit.

A nurse wandered out from behind the station. Spotting Jonathan, she immediately dipped a bow. "Your Highness!"

"I hear my brother has returned from his coma." Jonathan folded his hands primly behind his back.

The nurse nodded. "Yes, your highness. Please go in and see him. I'll bring his medicine in a bit." She motioned with both hands toward Frederick's room.

Jonathan smiled cordially and brushed past her. He didn't show it—couldn't show it—but Frederick's state had worried him greatly. He and his brother had always been close. No one under-stood the burdens of the royal family like a blood brother. It was only in the most recent year or so that Frederick had decided to go wild. He used to be a sweet and sensible little brother.

A knock on the door was unnecessary. Jonathan stepped in and closed the door behind himself.

Frederick, hair a mess and eyes blurry, used his good arm to push himself up to a sitting position. "Oh, gracious. You've come to scold me, haven't you?" His voice sounded raspy, gruff from disuse.

"I see you've come back to yourself." Jonathan marched closer and took a seat in the chair next to Frederick's bed. "Someone who claims to be as virile as you... shouldn't you have woken sooner?"

"I wanted to take a good rest while I had the chance." Frederick's dry humor came out more serious-sounding than he meant.

Jonathan shouldn't pick on someone who had been in an accident such as Frederick's, but he couldn't help it. "We retrieved the security footage of your accident." Jonathan briefly debated whether to tell him their suspicions or not.

Frederick grunted in the affirmative. "It wasn't an accident. Someone did it on purpose."

"That's what we suspect."

"Stop suspecting, it's a fact. The driver accelerated into my lane, and as far as I could see he wore a mask and dark clothes. No doubt he wished to slip away into the night unnoticed. Have you found him? The nurses said it's been a week."

"You shouldn't speak of this so calmly." Jonathan didn't like the dull resolve in Frederick's demeanor. What ever happened to the lovable little brother he grew up with?

Frederick shrugged his good shoulder. "It's in the past. Hindsight is much clearer than foresight. I shouldn't have taken the motorbike. I should have listened to mother when she insisted I take more security personnel. All things I will be sure to remember in the future."

"We suspect the Anti-Monarchists." Jonathan felt it necessary to tell him that much.

Frederick's wry grin did little to ease Jonathan's troubled heart. "Undoubtedly. When you're king, I suspect you'll want to appoint me as Crown Prince. It's not an office to be taken lightly."

"You're the only one who can do it justice. I trust you."

"I don't. You shouldn't either." Frederick looked away from his brother. "You shouldn't involve me in palace affairs anymore. Not the important political kind."

"Every prince has his scandals." Jonathan reached out to rest a hand on Frederick's shoulder. "Even if they don't, someone makes them up. Your scandal doesn't make you any less a part of the family."

"Family, yes. I wouldn't give that up. Just don't expect me to be a part of the politics. I've had enough of them. Enough of all the unfairness." Frederick leaned his head back. "I'm tired."

"I'll allow you rest, then. Mother sends her love."

"I love her, too. Tell her she should come see me. I won't be here too long, you know."

"Yes, they say you're healing nicely. Father and mother will transfer you to the palace for the remainder of your recovery. Just as soon as the hospital clears you to leave."

Frederick finally smiled, if only a small, sad one. "Thank you, *Jean.*"

Jonathan grinned at the old nickname. Pronounced like a French 'John', he had always liked the familiarity it built between himself and those who used it. "When you're ready to discuss what really happened, I'll be here."

"I don't know what you mean."

Jonathan shrugged his shoulders. "You will. I'm glad you're awake. I look forward to spending the Heritage Festival time with you."

Frederick winced. "Don't overextend a wounded man. Will there be pretty ladies?"

"You're hopeless." Jonathan laughed. "I'm thinking of bringing my pretty lady overseas for it."

"You have a pretty woman? Ooh, this is a story I'd love to hear." A yawn escaped Frederick's lips. "Later, after I've rested some more. Come back and tell me of her."

"Not likely." Jonathan rolled his eyes. As if he would build Alissa up to Frederick, of all people. Jonathan loved his brother, but his brother loved one too many beautiful women. He refused to give him an inch when it came to Alissa.

Frederick settled back into his bed. "Have Gaspar bring a change of clothes and my personal belongings."

"I'll have Guillaume make the call. Sleep well."

Jonathan waited only for Frederick's nod of affirmation before he left. Frederick needed all the rest he could get right now. It would be a tedious road to recovery, but Jonathan had no doubt that Frederick would make a full recovery, one way or another. He only wished he understood the source of his brother's angst and anger.

೮೨೮೩

Alissa pulled her knees to her chest as she scrolled the article on her phone. The internet had its charms, especially when one's boyfriend was a public figure. Jonathan smiled back at her from the cover photo, but his eyes didn't sparkle like usual. That usual diplomatic smile.

The short public speech suggested that Jonathan's brother had gone home to complete his recovery. Alissa relaxed with that news. It was the news of the Anti-Monarchists behind the accident that made her frown.

Of course, Jonathan had mentioned the Anti-Monarchists before, but it never dawned on Alissa how much of a real problem they might become. If they had attempted to attack Jonathan's brother, wouldn't they come after him, as well? How selfish had she been to never care whether danger stood in Jonathan's path?

Maybe being a Crown Prince wasn't all it was cracked up to be.

Feeling guilty, Alissa found the video-chat app that she and Jonathan used. She didn't know if he would have time, but she felt the need to apologize for her own stupidity. Jonathan's destiny included so many people.

The call rang through. Rang some more. Eventually, Alissa gave up. He must be busy again. Understandable, but no less hurtful. The last week, they kept missing each other. Sometimes by mere seconds, but usually by far too long. Messages left didn't equal time spent together. Alissa found she missed Jonathan.

"Yo, sis!" Cody poked his head into the room. "I'm out for the afternoon, so don't do anything crazy."

Alissa put her phone down. "Where are you going?"

"Hanging with the guys. Oh, and would you grab the mail?"

"The mail?"

Cody grinned sheepishly. "I'm supposed to be grabbing it daily and I've missed it the last two days."

"So grab it on your way out." That seemed the most logical explanation. Their mother had delegated the chore to Cody, not Alissa.

"Nope, too late, I already asked you." Cody blew a dramatic kiss in Alissa's direction. "Love you, sis! See you later!" He disappeared down the hall. The front door opened and closed.

Alissa rolled her eyes. Cody had a way of getting out of his own chores. Almost every time. This is what she got for having a clumsy, tricky older brother. It's also what she got for letting him stick close by. He should have gone to his own place by now, yet he insisted on staying at their parents' house with Alissa. Sometimes, Cody could overreact.

Whatever. A walk would do her good. Adison had calmed down his security over the last few weeks. Alissa had freedom to roam around now. Thank God. With all these guys hovering like watch-dogs, Alissa needed room to breathe.

The outdoors greeted her with bright rays of sunshine and a cool breeze. Alissa loved her home. Even the weather here knew how to calm her.

Gravel crunched under her feet as Alissa started down the drive. The oak trees on either side greeted her with a rustle of their leaves. Alissa allowed her thoughts to roam back to her childhood, when she and Cody would race from one end of the lane to the other. When they would climb the trees to see who could go higher. Cody broke his leg on one of those trips.

At the end of the lane, Alissa flipped open the mailbox. True to Cody's words, two days' worth of mail stuffed the small space. Alissa finagled her hands onto either side of the stack and tugged. Envelopes and flyers spilled out. She barely managed to catch half.

"This boy, I swear..."

Alissa sighed and bent to pick up what she'd dropped. With everything secure, she started back up the lane.

Most mail was easy to sort through while walking. Coupons went to the bottom of the stack, magazines in the middle, and non-junk mail on top. Most of it consisted of bills and sales. Alissa only paused when she came to an envelope with her own name scrawled across it.

Who would send her mail here? Red flags shot up in Alissa's imagination. A quick glance revealed half the distance back to the house still stretched out before her. Suddenly, it felt too far. Too exposed.

Alissa stopped and stared down at the envelope. No return address. That couldn't mean anything good.

Trepidation spread, starting as butterflies in Alissa's stomach and accelerating through her heart and head. Alissa closed her eyes tight and took a deep breath.

"Adison!" She called up the lane. "*Adison!*"

"What happened?" The voice came from the trees beside her.

Alissa squealed and skittered aside. "Can you not sneak up on me like that? Where did you come from anyway?"

"I followed you." Adison's gaze fell on the mail in Alissa's hands. "What's wrong?"

Alissa held out the letter. "I'm getting weird vibes."

"You have good instincts." Adison motioned her forward. "Let's get back to the house before we open it."

Alissa nodded. She had every intention of doing what Adison said. He seemed competent and Jonathan trusted him. There wasn't any reason she shouldn't, as well.

Alissa didn't relish the thought of interacting with the police again, but she saw the necessity in it. Reporting this would create a trail of evidence. Besides, if she kept reporting things, they might find the culprit sooner. If this was even anything bad. Her fear could be an overreaction. Those ran in her family.

Adison seemed extra cautious as he escorted Alissa back into the house.

"Set the mail on the kitchen table."

Alissa didn't like being told what to do, but Adison was the expert here. She could recognize that. Alissa dropped the whole pile on the table and took a step back. The message at Violet's apartment had been a warning. What if this time, the envelope contained something more?

It may not be anything, you dimwit, Alissa chided herself.

The sound of shutters flipping closed echoed from the next room. Adison checked outside each window in the kitchen, as well, before he closed them off from the outside world.

"If you'll step aside, please." Adison, all business, waited patiently.

Alissa worried her lip through her teeth. "Where's the safest place for me to be?"

Adison searched the room and finally pointed to a corner. "That has the least visibility from outside."

Without a word, Alissa tucked herself away in the place Adison pointed out. Her fingers shook and her heart pounded, awaiting the final verdict. When did her life become a novel? When did it become normal to ask where she would be safest?

Adison tossed a glance over his shoulder, then reached for the envelope.

Alissa held her breath, expecting the worst.

Chapter 15

"You're ten minutes late for the Cause for Orphans charity event," Markum pointed out. He flicked through a few more screens, then held the tablet out to Jonathan. "And you'll need to approve the speech for tonight, as well as the opening speech for Heritage Festival."

Jonathan scanned the most pressing speech first. "Take out the part about Frederick's whereabouts. The people only need know he's safe and cared for at this juncture."

Markum retrieved the tablet and made a note. "The Heritage Festival speech?"

"I will read it after the Cause for Orphans event." Jonathan stepped out the doors into the sunlight. "Call and tell them we'll be fashionably late. Instead, assure them I have every intention of staying as long as I can today."

"Yes, sir." Markum jogged to the far side of the day limo and climbed in.

"Jonathan!"

Had Jonathan not learned at a young age to control his reactions, he might have shuddered at the voice. Even if he had told Estrella to return to Veldoria, he didn't expect to see her in the palace. Least of all today.

Jonathan turned with a pleasantly neutral expression on his face. "Estrella. What are you doing here?"

"We haven't seen each other since your return. I came to give my greetings." Estrella pursed her lips into an exaggerated pout. "I've missed you."

Of course. Jonathan knew Estrella too well to think she would give up on him just because he told her they had no chance at any romantic feelings. Once she knew what she thought she wanted, Estrella became relentless. She was too good a friend to alienate her. Beside that, Estrella's father was the Prime Minister and one of the King's most trusted friends.

"Your Highness..." Guillaume stepped forward. "We must be going."

"So soon?" Estrella asked.

"I'm afraid so. I have schedules to attend. We will speak later." Jonathan shot Guillaume a small nod of thanks, then slid into his own side of the car.

Ever since he returned to Veldoria, he had been running non-stop. His father's declining health meant Jonathan needed to take on more responsibilities, both public and private. Killer schedules became the consequence of Jonathan's vacation time.

The day limo rolled out of the palace gates and into traffic.

Jonathan breathed deeply for the first time all day. He pulled out his own phone while Markum made quick work of reassur-ances to the Cause for Orphans.

A missed video call from Alissa made Jonathan frown. He hated not being able to answer her calls. No matter how busy he became, he didn't want to neglect her. He had time while they drove. Jonathan returned the call.

It rang for far too long before a message told him Alissa wasn't available. It wasn't like her to not answer, so Jonathan tried again. He got much the same result.

Left to wonder why Alissa didn't answer, Jonathan went to the next best avenue. He dialed Adison's phone.

Adison answered immediately. "Your highness."

Jonathan smiled softly at the abrupt tone. Just like Adison. "I've tried to phone Alissa and she isn't answering. Are the two of you out?"

"No."

Maybe he shouldn't ask yes-or-no questions. Jonathan pondered how to phrase his curiosity. "Where are you?"

"The Cassidy residence."

"Then why isn't she answering her phone? Did the battery run out?"

"No, sir." Adison paused. An air of hesitance hung like smoke, clouding the atmosphere and worming its way into Jonathan's lungs.

Jonathan sat straighter in his seat. "Where is she?"

"She's indisposed right now." Adison hesitated again, then sighed. "I'm sorry to say, sir, that she's with a police officer right now."

"Police?" That couldn't mean anything good. In fact, Jonathan's mind went to the worst scenario. "What happened? Is she alright?"

"Lady Alissa is fine, just shaken," Adison assured.

Jonathan closed his eyes briefly. He shouldn't have dragged her into this. Never, ever. Yet, it was too late now. "What shook her? I need details."

"Lady Alissa received a letter again. They found her."

Three words shook Jonathan to his very core. *They found her.* If they wouldn't hesitate to injure a prince, what would keep them from attacking a mere citizen? They had few choices now. Even fewer ways to keep Alissa safe and sound.

Jonathan made the decision almost before he could ponder at all. "Bring her."

"Is this really the best idea?"

"I don't care what it takes. She's no longer safe there. Bring her." Jonathan refused to sit by and watch from half a world away. If staying away from Alissa didn't change anything, he would keep her right by his side. He intended to marry this woman. He wouldn't allow anyone to harass her.

A long pause on the other end of the line made Jonathan think that perhaps Adison had hung up. Finally, two glorious words put Jonathan's mind at ease. "Yes, sir."

"As soon as possible."

"Yes, sir."

Jonathan relaxed in his seat. Adison would keep his promise. Ever since the palace hired him, Adison had been nothing but loyal. Jonathan trusted Adison as implicitly as he trusted Guillaume.

"I'll send the jet. Make sure she's on it when it returns." Jonathan waited for one last affirmative answer before he ended the call.

The thought of Alissa coming to Veldoria eased Jonathan's mind. He could see her again. Could hold her hand and watch her smile. It would be worth it, no matter what happened going forward. As long as they were together, Jonathan knew they could overcome many obstacles.

Markum pushed his glasses up on his nose. "You're sending the jet for a woman?"

"Don't look at me like that." Jonathan wrinkled his nose. "It's within my rights."

"It may not be the best option. In the view of the Public Relations team. What if the press gets word of this?"

"Then we'll deal with that." Jonathan shrugged a shoulder. "I put her in danger, so I need to protect her."

Guillaume coughed, but it sounded more like a laugh to Jonathan.

Judging by Markum's expression, he heard the same. "Is there something more I need to know?"

Jonathan cleared his throat. "I've met her parents."

Markum pushed at his glasses again. "This is something you didn't think it wise to tell me about? I could have been making a strategy to deal with the rumors."

"They aren't rumors. I'm dating her." Jonathan left nothing up for discussion. Even Markum, his most trusted aide, wouldn't dissuade him from this path. He had every intention of seeing it to the end.

Markum huffed, but he didn't argue. By now, he knew better. Jonathan could bend about many things, but his personal life was one thing he stood firm about.

In a short while, the only woman who had ever truly caught his eye would be on Veldorian soil. Jonathan could hardly contain his excitement and nervousness. *Not long now.*

ಐಲ

Violet's squeal ricocheted around the private hangar. "The dude owns a jet *and* a Benz? Marry him."

"First of all he's not a 'dude'." Alissa rolled her eyes at her best friend's antics. "Secondly, please calm down."

Violet grabbed Alissa by the shoulders and shook her. "This is a dream, right? There isn't something I'm totally missing about this guy? Is he a millionaire? Billionaire? Does he own a small tourist country?"

Alissa winced. She should tell Violet everything. It would only make Violet angry to find out later. However, Alissa didn't quite know how to break the news to her best friend. How did one explain that their boyfriend did, indeed, own a country?

"About that..."

Adison pushed his way between the two girls. One hand rested against Alissa's elbow. He used his free hand to motion toward the Mercedes-Benz. "Let's talk after we're in the vehicle."

As much as she wanted to argue, Alissa didn't. Adison had been nothing but helpful. She should listen to his instructions. Especially here, where she didn't know anyone.

Adison held the door for both girls, like a true gentleman.

Violet slid down in the plush seat and splayed her hands over the leather. "It's so soft! I've never ridden in a Benz before, but I am loving it. Seriously, keep this guy around. I don't care what he does at this point." She sat up abruptly. "Unless he's a part of the mafia. Then, no. Never."

"He's not mafia," Alissa assured Violet.

Violet grinned. "Then we're good."

Alissa debated whether or not to tell Violet about the whole crown prince situation. On the one hand, Violet deserved to know. On the other, Violet seemed too happy. Alissa hated to burst her blissful bubble.

It couldn't hurt to let Violet have her fun for a little longer.

Alissa's brain was still on overdrive from trying to explain this whole situation to her parents. The picture, featuring Alissa's scratched-out face, had been bad enough. Explaining that her royal boyfriend had given orders to the security to take Alissa overseas... They hadn't taken it well. At first.

Eventually, Alissa's father saw the wisdom to the command. Alissa had left with his blessing. Not, however, before Violet heard the situation and insisted on tagging along.

Alissa didn't mind. With Violet by her side, Alissa felt like she could take on the world. Violet would back her up, regardless.

"How far until we get to... uh... Jonathan's house?" Alissa didn't exactly know where they were going. She figured Adison knew. He came from Veldoria, anyway.

Adison spared a glance from his seat in the front of the car. "It's fifteen minutes to Vitromont."

"Oh. Okay." Alissa didn't know what else to say.

She did her research. Vitromont referred to Vitromont Palace, a lovely place located at the center of Capitol City. After Jonathan mentioned it to her the first time, Alissa couldn't help but look it up online. Never in her wildest dreams did she imagine she would visit. Especially not as a guest. A tourist, maybe. A guest? Alissa didn't think that far ahead in this relationship.

"Vitromont?" Violet pursed her lips, thinking. "He doesn't live in this city?"

Alissa went rigid. This wasn't how she intended to tell Violet about Jonathan. She needed better timing.

Adison didn't waste time turning to answer. "Vitromont is his..." Adison blinked at the glare Alissa shot him. "Um... his estate."

"He has an estate?" Violet grinned wider. "I knew it. He must be rich. 'Lissa, you hit the jackpot. This is totally a Lizzie-Darcy situation."

"I'm not as stubborn as Lizzie." Alissa rolled her eyes. Violet, for all her faults, did have a love of classic literature. One of the reasons she and Alissa got along so swimmingly.

Violet clucked her tongue. "Look at you, still in denial. Sure. If you say so." She turned to watch out the window. "Oh my gosh! Look at the architecture! It's so gorgeous."

Alissa had to agree. As the car made its way through the Capitol City streets, one great piece of architecture after another soared by. Churches. Cathedrals. Old factories. A college. The entire aura of the city emanated ancient traditions and a bones-deep culture.

Friendliness pervaded anything else Alissa saw. People on the sidewalk stopped to chat with one another. Other drivers waved in greeting.

A thought struck Alissa, then. She wouldn't mind being a part of these people. The kindness she saw as they passed only made her want to know more.

Violet chattered away, but Alissa didn't pay her much mind. Most of what Violet had to say now had been said already.

The car passed a giant wrought-iron gate, set in stone.

Violet's head swiveled to look past the gate. "Is that a castle?"

"A palace, more accurately." Adison settled a communications device into his ear.

Alissa winced. She should tell Violet. Now. "That's Vitromont. Vitromont Palace."

"Cool."

"That's where we're headed." Alissa held her breath, waiting for Violet's reaction.

The car turned a corner and stopped at a solid metal gate. An armed guard stepped to the driver's side window.

Violet blinked, staring at her best friend like Alissa had grown a second head.

The driver rolled down the window and handed out his ID, along with Adison's.

The guard tossed a glance into the backseat. "Who are the ladies?"

"They're here at His Majesty's invitation. Guillaume will confirm." Adison wasted no time in answering. He never did.

The guard handed the identification back to the driver. "Just a moment."

"He's *actually* a royal?" Violet hissed in Alissa's general direction. "A real, live, honest-to-goodness royal?"

Alissa nodded. What else could she do? Violet would react how Violet wanted, regardless of anything Alissa said or did.

Violet grasped Alissa's shoulders in her hands. "Why didn't you tell me this sooner?"

"What?" Alissa didn't expect that kind of reaction. At all.

"You're going to be a princess!" Violet drew Alissa into a tight hug. "I'm so excited for you!"

"Um... thanks?" Alissa patted a hand against Violet's back.

Some days, even Alissa didn't know what to expect from her best friend. Violet's brain worked in mysterious ways. Alissa didn't claim to understand any of them.

"Wait, why didn't you tell me this earlier?" Violet pulled back to glare. "Isn't this something you should have told your best friend... I don't know... when you started dating the guy?"

"I didn't know how." Alissa shrugged. "Sorry."

The gates rolled open, allowing the vehicle entrance through a short tunnel. At the end of the tunnel, a courtyard lay open and sunshiny. A handful of other vehicles sat near the far end. On either side, arches allowed roads out of the courtyard and into... Alissa didn't know.

The driver stopped the vehicle near the far side of the courtyard. On second glance, Alissa could see the portico formed by the arches. It must lead into the palace.

Adison opened Alissa's door for her and stood at attention. Alissa had never seen him so stiff.

Violet didn't wait for anyone to open her door. Far too impatient, that woman. She burst into the courtyard with a smile and a laugh, arms thrown wide. "Oh my gosh, it's *beautiful!*"

Alissa giggled. "You're right." Even with the old, weather-worn stone that lined it, the courtyard felt homey and warm.

"It should be beautiful, what with the budget to keep it up and all," a new voice floated from the portico.

Adison and the driver both dipped a bow.

Alissa spun to look for the source.

The soft swish of a wheelchair on concrete filled the air. A thick-shouldered security guard pushed the wheelchair into the sun.

A houndstooth blanket covered the man's legs and lower torso, contrasting with his forest green V-neck sweater. He seemed young, for a wheelchair.

The man in the chair turned his head to address the guard behind him. "Gaspar. You don't have to hover."

Gaspar dipped a bow and took a few steps back.

Violet appeared at Alissa's side and linked arms. "Who's this guy? Looks like a playboy to me. Don't let the invalid status fool you. It's probably fake."

Alissa cleared her throat, trying not to laugh too hard at the look that the man tossed in Violet's direction.

After a brief hesitation, the man turned to Alissa. "You must be my brother's woman."

"Don't assume things. It could be me." Violet arched her brows.

The man huffed his own breathy chuckle. "My brother's woman wouldn't call me a playboy. And she would know my invalid status is because I still have a gimpy leg."

"Oh." Violet shrugged a shoulder. "That's fair."

Alissa gave him her best smile. "You must be Frederick, then."

"As accused." Frederick spread his hands through the air in a here-I-am gesture. "But don't believe everything that every wayward little girl tells you."

"Little girl?" Violet dropped Alissa's arm and took a step forward.

Frederick smirked.

Alissa caught Violet's arm and pulled her back. "Vi, calm down."

"Did you hear his tone? He might as well have called me an urchin!"

Frederick clucked his tongue. "Such language. I said no such thing. I'm sure, deep down, you're a lovely person."

Darn it. Violet's temper. Even a slight provocation like that could throw Violet into a tantrum.

Alissa stepped in front of Violet to keep her from outright attacking. "Where's Jonathan?"

"I'm sorry to be the bearer of bad news, but my brother is indisposed today. He asked that I see to his guests until he returns." Frederick motioned a hand back the way he came. "Shall we go in?"

"You really don't have to do that." Alissa tucked her hair nervously behind her ears.

Having Jonathan meet her family had been one thing. Spending the day with Jonathan's brother, with only Violet to keep the conversation going, was a completely different matter.

"I'm bored out of my skull. Besides, my brother would quite literally have my head if I let you go wandering alone." Frederick motioned Gaspar forward with a flick of his wrist. "I should show the two of you where you'll be staying, I suppose."

"Yes, let's do that." Alissa flashed Frederick a brilliant smile. Grasping Violet's arm in her hand, Alissa started down the indicated corridor, five steps behind Frederick and his guard.

Violet didn't struggle very hard, which meant she either cooled off fast or she decided to plot Frederick's demise. Neither option sounded pleasant to Alissa. The first meant Violet didn't care that she had been insulted. The second meant she cared too much.

Frederick and Gaspar led the way inside, down beautiful halls filled with ancient and modern treasures, alike. Alissa had no words. None to comment and even less to ask questions. Everything seemed too perfect inside these walls.

Gaspar pulled the wheelchair to a stop beside silver elevator doors.

Alissa glanced around them. "An elevator?"

"I can't take the stairs." Frederick motioned to his blanket-covered legs. "This is the only other entrance to the private residence floor."

"P-Private... residence? What?" Alissa didn't know whether to be flattered, shocked, or outraged.

Frederick smiled gently up at her. "Tourists visit the palace all the time. They are only allowed in specific areas. The private residences are where the family abides. Of course, we have many guest suites as well. You will be staying there."

Violet leaned around Alissa to glare suspiciously. "Just her? Are you ignoring me on purpose?"

"Naturally, you follow where Alissa goes. If she stays in the guest suites, you stay there as well. Am I wrong to assume this?" Frederick's smile didn't waver.

"No. You're not." Violet relaxed a little. "But remember, I have my eyes on you."

"You won't be the first woman to say that." Frederick shrugged a shoulder. "Do as you wish. I have no preference one way or another."

The elevator opened with a ding.

Gaspar rested a hand over the pocketed door to hold it open.

Frederick motioned to the girls. "Ladies first."

Violet shot Frederick a suspicious glance, but it was far from the glare she usually wielded. Alissa figured that Violet didn't quite know what to make of Frederick. Honestly, neither did Alissa. One second he seemed like a good-humored mansour. The next, he seemed quiet and sad.

Still, Alissa couldn't bring herself to dislike him. Frederick, at heart, seemed genuinely kind.

The elevator, once all had loaded, took them up to a floor marked simply by a button emblazoned with the royal crest. Gaspar used a key to confirm its destination.

Not a single person spoke. Not even when the elevator doors slid aside to reveal an open lobby. This one felt more residential. More like someone decorated it to live in, not to show off.

Gaspar wheeled Frederick out of the elevator and dipped a short bow.

Frederick dismissed him with a wave of his hand.

Alissa and Violet both turned to watch Gaspar stalk down a hall.

"Where is he going?" Alissa spoke first.

Frederick chuckled. "We're in the residences now. Gaspar won't be needed for protection."

"That depends on your definition of danger," Violet muttered.

Alissa pinched her best friend's arm. Violet had a way of over-exaggerating everything. This wasn't the time to speak everything on her mind.

"The guest wing is this way, if you don't mind." Frederick planted his hands on the wheels of his chair. For someone who recently learned how to navigate a wheelchair, Frederick didn't do a half-bad job. Apparently, steering took less effort than Alissa thought it would.

Alissa strode after Frederick, mesmerized by the beautiful interior of an equally beautiful home. This part of the palace didn't feel as grand, but it somehow held a weight. As if reality seeped into a fairytale and wound the two worlds together.

"When will Jonathan be back?" Alissa ventured.

Frederick kept rolling as he answered. "Jean will return this evening. Didn't you know? Today marks the start of Heritage Festival."

"Heritage Festival?" This time, Violet voiced Alissa's question.

"It's quite the ordeal in Veldoria. Did you not do your research? It's long and detailed, so I suppose you wouldn't have been able to commit all the proceedings to memory, but you should both know a bit about it."

Alissa didn't know how she missed hearing about a festival. Especially one as large as Frederick made this out to be. Her heart sank, weighed down by the heaviness of failure.

"Ah, here we are." Frederick stopped at a door and leaned forward to push it open. "The Cygne Suite. Jonathan was insistent that it be this suite you stay in."

The door swung inward to reveal the most beautiful entryway and parlor that Alissa had ever seen. Decorated in shades of white and ivory, elegance sparkled from the crystal chandelier all the way down to the marble floors. A pair of creme sofas sat facing each other in the middle of the parlor, a stone fireplace their backdrop.

"It's amazing." Alissa didn't know where to look first, or what to do.

Frederick wheeled out of the way. "You can enter. For the time being, it's yours."

"What about me?" Violet pouted.

Frederick shooed her inside, as well. "You'll stay here, of course. There are three bedrooms to choose from. I'm sure you'll find one of them satisfactory."

Alissa stepped foot into the suite and couldn't stop herself from smiling. Jonathan knew how to impress a girl. Alissa couldn't be sure why he chose this suite, but she loved it. It felt clean and bright. Both things she needed in her world right now.

Forgetting the two behind her, Alissa made her way to the first door she could find. It opened into a spacious bedroom, decorated in creme and black. Violet's luggage already sat at the end of the bed.

Alissa grinned, figuring Adison had done his job properly and then left. She moved on to the next door. This one opened into the most luxurious bathroom Alissa had ever seen. A rain-fall shower, a claw-footed tub, and a basin sink were just the highlights.

One more door sat on the other side of the bathroom. Alissa stepped inside without hesitation. This time, she found herself in the middle of a sea of red and gold. A four-poster bed covered in red silk. The windows, adorned with golden curtains. Alissa's luggage stood sentry at the foot of the bed.

Alissa couldn't help a happy squeal. Without a second thought, she raced for the bed and leaped into the center. She had never felt anything softer in her entire life.

A rap on the open doorframe drew Alissa's attention. She sat up with a grin.

Frederick glanced around the room. "I see you're pleased with your new quarters."

"This room is awesome." Alissa gave another bounce, like a child. She didn't care what Frederick thought of her.

"I'm glad." Frederick held up his phone from his lap. "My brother won't be back in time to see you, so I'll have to relay the message. There's a joust tonight. An opening ceremony of sorts, for Festival."

"A joust? Really?" Alissa turned to better face Frederick. "That sounds fun."

"It should. You're invited, of course. Someone will be around to fetch you and your friend when it's time to leave." Frederick motioned around the room. "Settle in well. I'll see you soon."

Alissa jumped to her feet. "Wait!"

Frederick stopped, his hands already resting on the wheels of his chair. "Yes?"

"Thank you. For making sure we got in safely and for being so nice."

"You shouldn't thank me."

"Why?"

Frederick shrugged a shoulder. "I'm not as nice as you want to think."

"Thank you anyway." Alissa didn't believe it for a moment, but she didn't argue with Frederick. If she knew anything about people, it was that they all felt pain in their own way. One day, Frederick would come to terms with whatever hurt his heart.

Without another word, Frederick turned and left the suite.

Alissa wished she could help him, but instinct told her he wouldn't accept her help if she tried. So, instead, she would do her best to be a friend.

"This place is amazing!" Violet burst into Alissa's room and flopped onto the bed beside her. "If I haven't said it yet today, I'll say it now. Please marry him so I can come stay here as often as I want. There's a super soft black mink blanket in my room and I want to make all of my clothes out of it and live inside them."

"How do you know it's mink?"

"It's labeled, dummy." Violet rolled over onto her stomach. "How about you? Do you like it here?"

Alissa nibbled at her lip and shook her head. "I love it. It feels right. I didn't think it would."

"Do you like Jonathan that much?" Violet rested her chin in her hands.

"I think I do." Alissa tapped a finger against Violet's head. "What about you? Frederick's attractive."

"Attractive, yes. But a bit of a jerk. I've read the articles. I'm putting up with him because he's your future brother-in-law. Doesn't mean I have to like him."

"Methinks you protest too much." Alissa raised her eyebrows. "I'm going to shower and change. We're invited to a joust."

"You mean one of those things where grown men with long hair and muscles try to pummel each other to death with a giant stick?" Violet sprang to her feet. "I'm in!"

Alissa laughed, freely and giddily. Even if she hadn't been able to see Jonathan yet, Veldoria had been more than welcoming so far. She couldn't say as much for the days ahead, but Alissa wanted to believe that Jonathan's most beloved subjects would continue to welcome her with open arms.

Chapter 16

Alissa didn't realize that jousting fields existed in the real life, modern era. Nor did she think that she would ever have to pass through security to get into one. The security at the gate hadn't asked many questions after they spotted Adison trailing Alissa and Violet. Even without a ticket, they let the two girls pass.

Now, Alissa and Violet stood within a galley, perusing various trophy cases and concession stands. Truth be told, Alissa didn't know where they were supposed to go. She could always ask Adison, but Alissa enjoyed exploring, too.

Frederick hadn't lied when he said Heritage Festival was a big deal around Veldoria. A television above one of the concession stands played a live news station. A flash of a number of different celebrations made it perfectly clear. Alissa had only seen such country-wide celebration when it came to things like Mardi Gras. Even that barely held a candle to this level of celebration.

The audience for the jousting match entered with one of two auras around them. Stuck-up and rich, or regular people who saved up to buy a ticket. The field and surrounding bleachers could hold a thousand spectators at most. Yet, the atmosphere spoke of an excitement that superseded all that.

Violet wrapped her arms around Alissa. "I'm running to the bathroom, be back in a minute. Don't let Adison out of your sight."

"Oh, yeah, because that's how that works." Alissa gave Violet a quick hug. "I'll be around here somewhere."

"No sitting down in the bleachers until I return." Violet skipped off toward a sign marked *restrooms*.

Alissa rolled her eyes. Such a drama queen, that one. Then again, Alissa's life would be dull without Violet. Alissa looked over her shoulder to make sure Adison still followed.

She ran smack-dab into another person.

"Oh, I'm sorry!" Alissa reached out to steady the woman in front of her. "I didn't mean to hit you."

"You wouldn't have if you were in the right section of the galley." The woman straightened her spine and shoved Alissa's hands away.

Alissa blinked, realization finally settling over her. She had met this woman before. Briefly. It hadn't been the most pleasant experience then, either. What was her name again? Right. Estrella.

Estrella tucked a strand of perfectly silky blonde hair behind one ear. "Commoners are seated in that direction." She pointed down the long hall. "Though I'm not even sure you count as common."

"If not common, what am I?" Alissa didn't like conflict, but she knew better than to allow herself to be insulted. She may not be as royal as Estrella, but that didn't make her any less of a person.

"Desperate?" Estrella shrugged her dainty shoulders. "I don't know how you weaseled your way in, but you shouldn't even be here. I suggest you leave before I call security."

"I'm afraid security would only escort her to her seat."

Alissa turned at the sound of Frederick's voice.

Frederick shot her a quick grin before he turned to Estrella. "If you're going to show your mean side, please be sure to determine what status the other person holds. In this situation, you are lower than Lady Alissa."

"*Lady* Alissa?" Estrella scoffed her displeasure. "She has no official title. Even you must know that, Frederick."

"I'll thank you to address me properly outside of palace walls. No matter how long you've known our family." Frederick looked up at Alissa. "I will escort you to your seat."

"I can't go without Violet." Alissa looked back down the length of the galley.

"Adison will wait for her and stay by her side. Gaspar will be more than enough to watch you and I, both." Frederick tilted his head back to address the guard at the back of his wheelchair. "Let's go."

"Are you going to ignore me now?" Estrella shrieked.

"Yes." Frederick signaled Gaspar forward with one hand.

Estrella stepped into Alissa's path. "I have things I need to discuss with her."

"Think twice about it." Frederick reached out for Estrella's wrist and tugged her out of the way. "If it's still a good idea, ask my brother for permission later. We should be getting to our seats, Alissa."

Alissa knew better than to refuse the escape that Frederick gave her. She hustled to his side. "Thank you."

Frederick gave a nod. "I think Jonathan might kill me if I let any harm come to you. Estrella seemed harmful."

"Still, thanks."

"No need to thank me. I've never expressly liked Estrella. She's been more of a pest than a friend."

Alissa didn't know why Frederick wouldn't receive thanks, but it really grated on her nerves. She had been raised to be polite. Standard manners dictated that she thank him for extricating her from an uncomfortable situation. Alissa couldn't figure out why Frederick wouldn't accept such simple things.

Gaspar and Frederick led Alissa through a well-secured gate and into the arena.

"This is the royal box." Frederick rose from the wheelchair, standing on one good foot. The blanket went back in the chair. Gaspar helped Frederick into a seat in the front row.

Alissa looked around at the small arena. As Frederick indicated, not just anyone could enter the box of seats. Short walls on either side prevented common folk from accessing it from the bleachers.

"My lady?" Gaspar motioned Alissa to a seat beside Frederick.

"Should I really sit there?" Alissa asked aloud.

Gaspar nodded.

Frederick motioned her closer. "I told you, Jean left very express instructions. Come have a seat and don't mind the stares. They all know I wouldn't toy with a woman of your caliber. You're not my type, sorry."

"You're not my style, either." Alissa settled into her seat and rubbed her sweaty palms down the fabric of her jeans. "I didn't think people would dress up this much for a joust."

"I'm in denim." Frederick stretched out one leg. "You're in fine company. Don't worry. Enjoy the games."

Alissa nodded, wanting to do as Frederick requested. His presence felt similar to Cody's, so it didn't bother Alissa. In fact, it put her somewhat at ease. Still, she would feel better with Violet beside her. At least she knew Violet would beat anyone that got out of line. Violet had a protective streak as high as the sky. Alissa glanced toward the gate.

"Your friend will sit at the back of the box with Adison." Frederick didn't look away from the tethered horses at the far end of the field.

Alissa turned her full attention to Frederick. "Then what am I doing up here?"

"Jonathan. Instructions." Frederick sighed and sent a glance heavenward. "I swear, the man wants to start a scandal with this," he muttered.

"Scandal?" Alissa cowered back in her seat. She couldn't be the cause of Jonathan's first scandal. What would she do if everyone hated her? She couldn't bear the pressure.

Frederick planted a finger in the middle of Alissa's back and pushed. "Straighten your spine, chin up. At least present a good front while you're here."

"I don't know what you think you're doing, buddy boy, but watch where you're touching." The loud voice carried from behind them.

Frederick pulled his finger away. "I see your friend has joined us."

"Yeah." Alissa fixed her posture. "She's like that." She wouldn't apologize for Violet. Violet did as Violet pleased. Alissa learned not to get in her way.

Frederick shrugged his shoulders. "With her personality, she'll probably enjoy jousting more than others." He leaned a fraction of an inch closer so his lowered voice could be heard. "It's violent."

Thinking back to how Violet had described jousting back at the palace, Alissa couldn't help but snicker. Frederick had pinned

Violet's personality within hours of meeting her. Alissa didn't think anyone could do that. Turned out, she had been wrong.

Frederick pointed down the field. "Today's last contenders are Sir Claude and Sir Alain. The horses are Fairydust and Beetle-juice. There will be two rounds before they ride, but they are the main attraction."

Alissa listened as Frederick explained the whole event, from beginning to end. She had always heard of jousts, but never experienced one in real life. It all sounded as exciting as she imagined.

The announcer stood atop the podium and bowed toward the Royal Box.

Frederick lifted a hand in greeting. Alissa had a sneaking suspicion it was also a signal to start the games.

The first two rounds were split by a short trick show. The horses seemed more than eager to run, happier still to obey their riders. They must be well-trained. Young citizens of Veldoria took turns running out to fetch broken lances, as happy as a child gathering candy from a parade.

Alissa watched in awe, not caring how much time had passed.

The announcer took his podium again, a too-cheerful smile plastered on his face. "In the tradition of Veldoria and in honor of its vast heritage, Sir Claude and Sir Alain will choose a lady to fight for. A moment, please, while they make their decision."

Both knights spurred their horses down the sides of the field.

Alissa watched in awe at the sheer power of the horses' strides. The stately way both men sat tall in the saddle. She would never be able to do so.

One of the men—Sir Alain, she thought—stopped his horse in front of the royal box. With one giant, gloved hand, he presented a rose and leaned down. "If your ladyship would be so willing to lend me your favor."

Alissa blinked. She didn't exactly know what that meant, but she never expected him to come to her, of all people.

Frederick nudged his good foot against Alissa's toe. "Everyone is waiting. Stand up and accept it, don't make the man wait."

As if in a dream, Alissa rose to her feet and gingerly accepted the rose from the knight's hand. She offered him a smile.

The crowd cheered.

Sir Alain dipped his head in a bow and turned his horse away.

Frederick produced a second rose from somewhere nearby and tapped it against Alissa's arm. "Take this one, as well. It won't do to hold only one, since it's the language for love."

Alissa sank into her chair and took Frederick's rose, as well. "I thought it was just a symbol of who they're jousting for."

"Yes, but a single rose means 'I love you.' Trust me, Jonathan would not appreciate you accepting love from another man." Frederick grinned and motioned toward the field. "Watch your knight. Cheer him on. He's supposed to be the best."

Alissa thought she also heard a "I hope this goes as planned," but she couldn't be sure.

The final joust began.

Sir Claude and Sir Alain lined up on either end of the field, their horses prancing to run. Someone checked armor and weapons for both men, then scuttled off the field.

The announcer settled in his chair to watch.

Someone raised a flag and swept it down in one smooth motion.

The horses took off toward one another, their riders at the ready with lances and determination. Sir Claude's lance glanced off Sir Alain's gardbrace.

Alissa twirled the roses in her fingers. Part of her felt responsible if Sir Alain didn't do well in this match. He had chosen to represent her, after all. She could feel the pressure rising in her chest.

"Come on," she muttered as the horses took up a stance to start again.

Lances lowered, the men lunged toward one another. This time, neither hit anything. Alissa figured it must be hard to aim when bouncing atop a steed.

"The third run will be the last," the MC declared.

The horses lined up, one snorting and the other side-stepping. Both knights braced their lances.

The horses took off, careening the men toward one another.

Sir Alain's lance struck Sir Claude's gardbrace.

Sir Claude tumbled off his horse and hit the dirt.

The crowd rose to their feet. First, in stunned silence. Then, as Sir Claude sat up and threw aside his helmet, in uproarious applause.

Frederick lifted his hands above his head and clapped loudly, considering he couldn't stand.

Alissa let out a breath and slumped back in her seat. At least no one had gotten hurt.

The announcer pulled the microphone closer. "Sir Alain has dismounted Sir Claude and thus, by default, wins this tournament." He, too, joined the applause.

Sir Alain raised his arms in victory. Even his horse seemed happy with the outcome. Together, man and horse started a victory lap around the field. Sir Alain stopped, once again, in front of the Royal Box.

"Would you like to join me, my lady?" Sir Alain extended a hand toward Alissa.

Alissa shot a look sideways to Frederick. "Is this customary?"

"To some extent, yes. He did joust on your behalf. Traditionally, and hypothetically, your favor gave him the strength to win." Frederick waved a hand. "Go on. Just a ride around the field."

"I can't ride a horse." Alissa didn't know what to do. On one hand, it would be rude to refuse. On the other, she had never been on a horse before. She would look awkward and clumsy. In front of everyone.

"I won't allow her ladyship to come to harm." Sir Alain reached his hand closer toward Alissa.

"That settles it, then." Frederick raised a finger and beckoned Gaspar. "Help Alissa onto the steed. It should be a memorable experience for her."

"Wait, what are you doing?" Alissa shot Frederick a panicked look, even as Gaspar helped her to step up onto the railing. "Frederick? Frederick!"

Frederick grinned and waved a hand in greeting.

Sir Alain helped situate Alissa side-saddle on the front of the saddle. Before Alissa could protest any more, the horse began to move.

Alissa squealed and clutched at the roses she had forgotten she held. If Frederick was still in the box when she returned, she would kill him herself. Nevermind his royal title. She didn't care at this point.

The horse slowed after a few paces. Alissa was surprised to see Gaspar had followed along at the side of the arena. With a grin that said he knew more than he let on, Gaspar lifted two more roses and placed them in Alissa's lap.

Confused and surprised, Alissa tucked them with the others. The horse took off again before she could question Gaspar.

The next time the horse stopped, it was in front of Adison, who also handed up two roses.

Alissa looked around in wonder. What was going on? Had someone planned this? Frederick had known about this, of course. He gave her one of the first two roses. What was at the end of this little charade?

The third time, Violet handed over a pair of roses and then shot Alissa a wink. Someone had pulled her into this, too?

When the horse reached the front of the arena, Sir Alain gingerly helped Alissa down onto the stage. The MC presented three roses from his podium. With no words, just a short bow.

Alissa looked back over her shoulder at Sir Alain. He didn't say anything, but he did incline his head in respect before he and the horse took their leave.

At this point, Alissa was well aware of the eyes on her. Who wouldn't be curious what was going on? No one in this place knew her, yet not one looked away. Alissa tried her best not to shrink into herself. Not here, not now. If she could get through this, she could get through anything.

A collective gasp preceded the crowd's murmuring.

Alissa rolled her lips together and turned around to see what they were all staring at.

Jonathan took the last step up onto the stage. His lips lit in a smile.

Alissa didn't miss the single rose that Jonathan twisted in his fingers. As if this whole thing made him nervous. A perfect bloom, scarlet red. One rose that would complete the count of twelve total.

Jonathan stopped in front of Alissa and held out the rose. "I am sorry. For not arriving sooner. For making you wait. Please accept these as a token of my heart."

"What were you going to do if Sir Alain didn't win?" Alissa couldn't help but tease him.

"Don't you know? I always have a backup plan." Jonathan twirled the rose again.

With such a sincere expression on his face, Alissa couldn't torture him any longer. She reached out and took the rose, placing it in the bouquet within her arms. "Forgiven."

In front of God and at least a few hundred people, Jonathan broke the stoic presence of a crown prince. He reached out to draw Alissa into his arms, wrapping her in a secure embrace she hadn't felt in almost a month.

Jonathan rested one hand against the back of Alissa's head. "I've missed you."

"I missed you, too." Alissa sank into his hold and closed her eyes, finally secure.

Undoubtedly, the entire audience uttered some form of shock, but Alissa didn't care. Right now, the tall and stately man cradling her close was all that mattered. They could deal with the aftereffects as they rolled in.

&C3

Jonathan knew, without a doubt, that this would find its way to the front page of tomorrow's tabloids. A prince that set aside his dignity for a woman? The press would have a field day with that alone.

The tabloids wouldn't count on the amount of disinterest that Jonathan had in what they said. Alissa stood before him, finally. He couldn't care what anyone thought about their relationship. He meant to make it crystal clear where the whole thing was heading.

It had been a while since Jonathan felt so nervous. Of course, he never stepped into the spotlight without a bit of anxiety, but this perched on a brand new level. What would his people think of Alissa? That thought rose high above the rest. He wanted his people to like her, because that would eliminate all objections to Jonathan's marrying her. Jonathan had confidence that his parents would love Alissa, and Frederick had already mentioned his approval.

Alissa tilted her head up. "Everyone is staring."

"It was meant to make a point."

If he wanted to introduce her, Jonathan knew a big splash would do the job better than a slow leak. Besides, if she became a public figure, the Anti-Monarchists would have a harder time using her to their advantage.

Jonathan released Alissa from his embrace and instead took her hand. "Let's go. We've done all we can here."

Without another word or a glance to the crowd, Jonathan led Alissa down the back stairs of the stage. He didn't miss how she waved excitedly to Guillaume as he fell in line. Not proper etiquette, but Jonathan could understand the joy of seeing someone she knew in a foreign land.

One of the security guards opened the back door of Jonathan's day limo.

Jonathan helped Alissa inside, then slid in beside her. Finally, a moment where they could speak. Phone calls and video chats weren't the same as face-to-face communication. Jonathan turned to Alissa as soon as the security guard shut the door.

Alissa grinned back at him. "That was quite the show. Did you pull Frederick in from the beginning?"

"Of course. What are little brothers for?" Jonathan leaned back in his seat. He couldn't take his eyes from Alissa, even when he knew he was staring. "I can't believe you actually came."

"Adison is pretty convincing when he wants to be. Besides, Violet wanted to visit. Once she gets it in her head, she doesn't let it go." Alissa laughed. The sound widened Jonathan's smile. It really had been too long.

"Shall we have dinner together?" Jonathan didn't mention that he had already prepared a reservation. Alissa didn't need to know. He intended to treat her like a royalty. Soon enough, she would be his queen.

Alissa nodded enthusiastically. "I have something to tell you. Oh, and thank you for the flowers. They're beautiful."

"We'll be sure to have one of the palace staff put them in a vase in your room." Jonathan leaned toward the front seat. "Pierre-Leon's, if you don't mind."

"That sounds fancy."

Jonathan reached out to take Alissa's hand again. "It's about time I treated you to something fancy. I promised you a month and I've barely spared you any time at all."

"You're busy running a kingdom."

"That's no excuse." Jonathan lifted Alissa's hand to press a kiss to her knuckles. "A man should always make time for his love."

Jonathan knew the risk, bringing up the word *love* at a time such as this, but he couldn't help it. He had made known his sentiments at the beginning, with Alissa's father. Love had always been the final outcome for Jonathan. Being absent from Alissa had only made it clearer that he viewed her in that light. Things were going too fast, but Jonathan had no control over it.

Alissa looked down at their twined hands and let out a short breath. "If you keep saying things like that, I might melt."

"Are you sure that isn't my intention?"

Alissa laughed. "Now I see the resemblance between brothers."

Jonathan, despite Alissa's happiness, couldn't help but frown at her insinuation. "Frederick flirted?"

"Not with me. With Violet." Alissa shrugged her shoulders. "I'm not even sure you could call it flirting. More of a verbal sparring match. You know how Violet is."

"Verbal jousting? Interesting. That isn't normally how he flirts." Then again, Frederick could have changed his flirting style over the course of the past year. "I'll be sure to post someone to watch him. I apologize on his behalf."

"No need. Violet can handle herself."

Jonathan had no doubt that Violet could handle herself. However, handling Frederick? Even the most experienced family member had a hard time controlling Frederick. When the man set his mind to something, he didn't take no for an answer. Jonathan made a mental note to have a chat with Frederick at a later date.

The short caravan of cars pulled to a stop before an exquisite stone entrance. Jonathan knew the restaurant well. The Royal

Family frequented their premises for meetings and dinners. Pierre-Leon's also had an excellent room for a small, intimate date.

Guillaume pulled open the door and dipped a bow. "Adison is also on his way."

Jonathan nodded. Good. Since he had assigned Adison to Alissa's protective detail, he expected nothing less. Adison probably left Violet under Gaspar's care. It might not turn out well in the end, but for now Jonathan trusted Gaspar to watch over Frederick and Violet, both.

Guillaume escorted Jonathan and Alissa inside, through a series of doors and finally to the receptionist's counter.

The receptionist bowed to Jonathan. "Your private room is ready, Your Highness. If you'll come this way."

Jonathan didn't utter a word. No one expected the Crown Prince to address them personally. In comparison of stations, Jonathan sat too high above the rest for them to expect anything of the sort. Besides, it would be rude to address the girl without knowing her name.

The receptionist led Jonathan and Alissa to the back of the restaurant.

Guillaume entered the room first, checking all the corners and windows before he returned. He bent at the waist. "It's clear, Your Highness."

Jonathan patted a hand against Guillaume's shoulder. Guillaume took his job so seriously, sometimes it made Jonathan feel bad. Nevertheless, he wouldn't trade Guillaume for anyone else.

"Shall we?" Jonathan offered a hand to Alissa.

She had been accepting of the security protocols, a fact for which Jonathan was grateful. Not everyone would stand quietly while these kinds of things went on around them. Truly one of a kind, his Alissa.

Alissa grinned at him and took his hand. "I feel under-dressed."

Jonathan looked around at the crystal chandeliers and satin seat cushions. "Nonsense. What you're wearing doesn't matter. It's just the two of us. Let's enjoy the time."

Alissa nodded, but she still pulled her lip through her teeth.

Jonathan gently tugged her into the private room and shut the door behind her. "There. Now no one knows if you're under-dressed or not."

"Next time, a little warning?" Alissa didn't seem upset, but she didn't seem as elated as Jonathan had hoped.

He pulled her chair out for her. "Next time, I will be sure to give you the proper dress code. Forgive my rudeness."

Alissa's shoulders sank with her sigh. "I'm sorry. I waited a really long time to see you. I shouldn't start off by nagging."

"I probably deserved it." Jonathan motioned to the chair. "Have a seat. Let's catch up."

Alissa sank into the seat and placed her napkin on her lap.

Jonathan smiled to himself as he pushed her chair back toward the table. At least Alissa wasn't an unreasonable woman. In fact, each word that left her mouth made him fall a little farther into her charm. There would never be any going back on Jonathan's part. As far as he was concerned, he found the one woman beside whom he could spend his lifetime.

Jonathan took his own seat across from Alissa. This way, face to face, he could at least watch over her. Jonathan liked that idea. He missed being able to spend time in Alissa's presence.

Alissa opened a menu and choked.

Not the reaction that Jonathan expected. He flipped open his own menu. The answer came to him immediately. Alissa had seen the prices. An ordinary, American girl wouldn't imagine spending so much on a single dish. He should have thought that through, but Jonathan had only thought of impressing her. With his schedule, they had so little time to spend together.

"Don't bother about the money." Jonathan tried his best to sound encouraging. "What should we have for an appetizer, hm? How one begins a course is very important. It sets the mood for the rest of the meal."

"What mood are you trying to set?" Alissa lifted her eyes over the top of the menu.

This time, Jonathan choked. Did she have to phrase it like that? She knew better, but as always, Alissa liked to taunt him. She had been this way since their first meeting. Jonathan would admit that her attitude had drawn him to her. A little.

"I think the roasted artichokes will set a good atmosphere." Jonathan, trained diplomat, avoided Alissa's question altogether.

He didn't miss the mischievous smile that tugged at the corners of her lips. Behind her innocent facade lurked something of a devil.

A waitress slipped into the room with a cart. Silently, she settled two glasses of water onto the table.

Jonathan ordered their appetizer without any hesitation. Alissa didn't seem to mind, so he decided to do what he wanted. The main purpose of this dinner was to talk. The food came as a bonus.

"Our special tonight is filet mignon, I've heard it's delicious." The waitress pointed it out on Alissa's menu.

Jonathan waited for Alissa's response, a small nod. "We'll take that for our entree, then."

"It will be just a few moments." The waitress accepted both of their menus and backed her way out the door. It shut with a solid click.

Alissa took a sip of her water. She set her napkin aside. "I'll go to the restroom really quick." She stood to her feet and headed for the door.

BANG!

Glasses shattered on the table.

Alissa hit the floor. Jonathan dove the opposite way.

Smoke rose and swirled around the ceiling.

"Alissa? Are you alright?" Jonathan rested an arm over his nose and mouth, trying to block the tear-inducing haze.

Crash!

Windows shattered. Once-perfect panes scattered over the floor in tiny pebbles.

Combat boots hit the floor, crunching the shards beneath.

Jonathan recognized the weapon pointed at him right away. Not a standard palace-issued weapon, but a military-grade rifle. Illegally obtained, for sure. Next, Jonathan saw the intent in the dark eyes peeking out of the ski mask at the other end of the barrel.

Jonathan rolled to the side, quickly finding shelter behind his knocked-over chair.

A bullet lodged itself into the floor nearby.

A piercing female scream shook Jonathan to his very core.

"Alissa." He moved to stand, but another bullet buried itself by his hand. Jonathan curled into a ball and searched the foggy room for his girl.

In a corner by the door, Alissa cowered. The second attacker had long ago stepped away from the window and now seemed to be enjoying the game of hunter and prey. Even when he clearly knew Alissa had nowhere to go, he stalked toward her, one step at a time. A thick blade worked between his fingers, twirling in a psychotic hypnosis.

More boots from the windows. A smattering of male voices.

Jonathan reached for a fallen dinner knife and clutched it in his hand. He wouldn't go down without a fight.

One by one, black-garbed figures took stances around Jonathan.

Jonathan braced himself, ready to launch at the first attacker. He tossed another look in Alissa's direction.

Alissa's attacker raised his arm to plunge the knife down at her.

"No!" Jonathan dove in her direction.

A firm hand snagged his shoulder and pulled him back.

The knife descended in slow motion, its intent all too clear.

A thick, tall body wrapped itself around Alissa from the side. His shoulder took the brunt of the stab.

Adison looked up at the attacker with sheer fury blazing in his eyes. The next stab, Adison blocked with his arm.

"Grab him, let's go." One of the voices finally took charge of the situation.

Hands grabbed at Jonathan as he struggled to escape their grasp. He had to get to Alissa. Though Adison was trying, fighting, he didn't have a weapon. Hand-to-hand combat only worked if Adison and the man he fought were evenly matched.

Adison blocked the knife as best he could, moving closer and closer to the attacker. In the process, he pushed the attacker farther and farther from Alissa.

The attacker dodged a blow from Adison and buried the knife deep in Adison's abdomen.

Jonathan shook out of the hold of the men dragging him. Long enough to toss the knife in his hand and watch it skid closer and closer to Adison's foot.

The attacker landed another blow to Adison's side. Adison went down, but Jonathan saw him artfully snatch the dinner knife as he fell. He slashed at the attacker's ankle first.

After that, Jonathan lost sight.

A shot rang out in the room. One of the men manhandling Jonathan went down in a pool of his own blood. The others panicked as more shots rang out.

Jonathan managed to turn enough to see Guillaume climb through one of the windows, followed by the rest of the Royal Guard. He assumed they hadn't been able to get through the door, or they would have come sooner.

"Finally," he muttered.

Jonathan threw an elbow behind him, making contact with his attacker's nose in the process. As if he wouldn't know how to protect himself. He had gone through the military, as was required of all princes. Even if it didn't last long, Jonathan learned more than his fair share of combat skills.

"Adison!"

Jonathan spun at the sound of Alissa's panic.

Guards swarmed the room, tackling each and every insurgent. One of them found the source of the smoke and covered it.

"Sire, you have to come with us." Guillaume wrapped a hand around Jonathan's arm.

Jonathan shrugged him off. "Alissa."

"Will be brought as well. We must get the both of you away from here." Guillaume grabbed Jonathan's arm again and steered him toward the tall window.

Jonathan did as he was told, stepping out into the cool evening air. He didn't like it, but he understood Guillaume's job. Jonathan shot another look over his shoulder in search of Alissa.

All he saw was Alissa curled over Adison's form, shoulders shaking with sobs.

Jonathan refused to believe what had happened. Adison wouldn't die. He swore his life to the crown, but Adison wouldn't give up his life so easily.

Ambulance sirens sounded in the distance. They would get here in time. Adison would be fine.

"Make Alissa leave," Jonathan ordered.

Guillaume opened the car door and ushered Jonathan inside. "I will see to it personally." He tapped a hand on top of the car. "Take His Highness to the palace. Now."

Jonathan didn't like leaving Alissa behind, but he understood the urgency. This hadn't been an accident. It had been a direct attack. Something like that needed to be addressed. He had no doubt there would be a meeting as soon as he arrived home. Jonathan only wished that he could see to Alissa's safety, himself.

Chapter 17

Alissa couldn't stop the tears from falling. It should have been a nice dinner with her boyfriend. Why did it always end up like this? She brought bad luck to everyone around her. She might as well break up with him now, but her heart had gotten too involved. She couldn't walk away. No matter how much bad luck she brought.

Guillaume had promised to give her updates on Adison's condition. The only way he managed to pull her away from the restaurant. Now, Alissa sat still and silent in the back of a diplomatic vehicle, Guillaume beside her. Apparently, Guillaume made a promise to Jonathan about her safety. Otherwise, why would he have stayed behind?

Alissa didn't know what to think. She couldn't close her eyes without seeing that stupid knife. She couldn't open her eyes without seeing Adison's blood on her hands. Her fault, that Adison ended up like that. She didn't deserve his loyalty.

"We've arrived." Guillaume's voice bore a tone meant to soothe.

Alissa swallowed, but managed to look up and out the window. This time, they hadn't stopped in the open courtyard. Instead, rows of overhead lights brightened a granite garage.

Guillaume climbed out of the car and came around to open Alissa's door. "Please."

Alissa nodded. She wanted to hold it together, but she could barely contian the tears that pressed at her eyes. How did anyone expect her to push forward as though nothing happened?

Inch by dutiful inch, Alissa stood from the car on wobbly legs.

Guillaume shut the door behind her. "This way." He motioned toward a well-lit opening in the wall.

Alissa swallowed her emotions and marched toward the light. She couldn't focus on the bad. Not here, not now. Even if it had been ten times more terrifying than any stalker's letter, she couldn't think on it. If she did, she might allow fear to paralyze her. No one could afford that.

Once through the doorway, Alissa identified the hall as a tunnel. White lights lit every inch of it, all the way to the glass-and-metal door at the far end.

Guillaume typed a passcode and slid his security badge through a scanner. The door opened with a hiss of air. "If you please." Guillaume motioned Alissa inside.

Alissa took the offer gratefully. She didn't care where they were headed, nor what would happen when they got there. Right now, her limbs felt too heavy to do anything.

One corridor led to another. Alissa didn't pay attention to which way they went. She noticed when they passed a door labeled "Security Headquarters", but past that she didn't care.

Guillaume led her into an elevator much like the one she had used with Frederick earlier. Had it only been hours ago that she arrived in the palace? It felt like years.

Alissa didn't recognize the hall that appeared on the other side of the elevator doors. It seemed similar to the residences' lobby, but somehow very, very different. Could they let her go to her own room now? Or, at the very least, leave her with Jonathan? She felt safe with him.

No such luck. Guillaume escorted her down a red-adorned hall. At the end, he knocked twice on the door before he pushed it open.

"After you."

Alissa sighed, but it did little to lift the weight on her shoulders. She didn't have the strength or inclination to argue with Guillaume, so she stepped over the threshold.

Across the room, a formal, gold-flecked couch held an equally golden woman. Though her blonde hair had dulled with age, she held herself with dignity and poise. Perfectly manicured fingers folded loosely in her lap, the woman kept a pleasantly neutral expression. Behind her stood one man and one woman, at constant attention.

Guillaume stepped into the parlor behind Alissa. "This is Alissa Cassidy. As Your Majesty requested." He dipped a bow. "If it please Your Majesty, I will return to his highness, the Crown Prince."

Alissa shot a startled gaze over her shoulder. Guillaume meant to leave her? With this woman? Why would he do such a thing?

"Of course you should return to your duty. Thank you, Guillaume." The woman's voice came out soft, yet at the same time authoritative. Like the ringing of classical bells.

Alissa didn't know how to ask Guillaume to stay. She didn't want to be alone, but she dreaded how he might answer her even more. So, instead of speaking, she watched Guillaume step out and close the door.

"Have a seat."

Alissa turned back around, only to find the woman motioning to a chair nearby. As much as she wanted to believe she had a choice, Alissa didn't think she had the power to make a decision in anything at the moment. She sank into the chair and clasped her hands tightly in her lap. Maybe then, they wouldn't shake so much.

"I suspect you do not know my identity."

Alissa shook her head. Talking seemed too difficult. Besides, she wouldn't know what to say.

The woman smiled softly. "I am Jonathan's mother, Mireille Isabella of the House of Manon."

"The queen?"

Of course, the queen, you dolt. Jonathan's mother would obviously be the queen, since his father was the king. Alissa didn't know why she had to ask such idiotic questions. She should know better.

The Queen lowered her head in a single nod. "Yes. The queen. However, you may call me Mireille."

Alissa didn't like the sound of that. It sounded far too informal. "That's okay. Using your first name doesn't seem like a good idea, either."

"Then, perhaps..." The Queen raised her gaze, studying Alissa with some form of interest. "Mother?"

Alissa blinked. What was with this family? Just because Jonathan showed interest and intention with her, did that mean she had become part of the family now? It didn't seem likely, but The Queen's eyes held no ill intent.

"If that's what you want."

"Perhaps now isn't the time to speak on such trivial things. You've endured quite the ordeal."

Alissa dropped her eyes to her hands. The blood had almost dried now. In the creases of her hands, it left red stains. On her fingers it smeared in a grotesque reminder of what had happened.

The Queen followed Alissa's gaze. "Oh, child..." A soft sigh fell from her lips. "Nicole, fetch a change of clothes and draw a bath."

The woman behind The Queen bowed her head and hastened to do as told.

"No, it's okay, you don't have to do that. I just need... I need to wash my hands." Alissa stood from the chair.

The Queen rose, as well. "You haven't looked at yourself. You are covered in filth. The bath will relax you."

"I'd rather wash my hands first." Alissa could feel her walls crumbling, her resolve weakening. She would rather be anywhere other than the queen's presence. "May I go back to my room now?"

"It's safer here, at the moment." The Queen looked toward a door at the short end of the parlor. "You may use my bathroom, instead. Lucian, please show her—"

"I'll find it myself. It's no problem." Alissa shot for the door, unable to stand it any longer. She couldn't take the pity or the coddling. She could deal with this on her own. It wasn't so bad, now that she had moved past the initial trauma.

The door led to a bedroom to which Alissa barely paid attention. She found the bathroom easily enough. A massive display of elegance, with a round jet tub in one corner and a waterfall shower in another.

Alissa shot straight for the sink and cranked the hot water to full blast. If she could scrub away the blood, she could be at ease. She knew it.

The water scalded her fingers, but Alissa paid it no mind. Using her nails, she scrubbed and scratched at the blood stuck to her skin.

Images replayed in her head like a bad horror film. Knives. Dark eyes. Glass shattering and bullets splintering the floor. One reassurance whispered in her ear, even as a knife punctured Adison's flesh.

"You're okay."

The first tear escaped Alissa's eye. Her breath caught in her throat, then broke through again.

What did she ever do to deserve the loyalty of a royal guard?

The answer came in a rush that Alissa hadn't prepared for: they were friends.

On top of that, she could have lost Jonathan, too. In one moment, her whole world could have crumbled and left her all alone. She could have been responsible for the death of a future king. Of a nation.

A sob shook Alissa's shoulders. Then another. She crumpled to the floor in a heap of regret and rusty water. She had almost lost everything, including her life. She had watched as a man bled out on the floor.

Alissa didn't know if she would ever be okay again.

"Alissa!" The Queen's surprised voice didn't pull Alissa from her sorrow.

A pair of thin, but strong arms wrapped around Alissa. A delicate hand cradled Alissa's head against The Queen's own shoulder.

"Nicole, the bath. Lucian, contact Jonathan's security and brief them on Alissa's location and the situation." The Queen spewed orders like it came naturally to her.

Meanwhile, Alissa simply wept.

⅋ℹ℺

Jonathan shifted in the seat beside his father. He understood the need to handle these matters as training for his future reign, but he didn't have to like it. Keeping a calm head came with more cons than pros. How did they expect Jonathan to think rationally when someone had tried to murder the love of his life?

"Do we have an update on Adison's condition?" The King jotted down a short list of topics to discuss as he asked the question.

One of the royal advisors leaned forward to better see the king and crown prince. "He arrived unconscious at the hospital. They took him immediately to surgery, but we've yet to hear how it's going."

"Be sure to house him in the Royal Ward," The King looked up from his notes. "He served beyond his duty today. Prepare a medal for when he recovers."

Jonathan understood his father's optimism. They didn't know if Adison would pull through or not, but all of them wanted to believe he would get better. Best to remain positive.

The King set down his pen and straightened in his chair. "I want a complete briefing of the incident."

One of the advisors cleared his throat. "We haven't finished our investigation yet—"

"Now." The King's tone brooked no room for argument.

The Minister of Defense rose from his seat. "As it has been stated, the investigation is ongoing. However, I will present Your Majesty with the facts that are available."

Jonathan mimicked his father's body language and leaned in to better hear. Whatever the case, Jonathan had questions. Loads of them.

"The Crown Prince and Alissa Cassidy arrived at Pierre-Leon's, a five-star dinner restaurant, at five-twenty-seven in the evening. They were escorted to a secured, private room." The Minister of Defense glanced up from his notes, cleared his throat, and looked back down. "At five-forty-three, a waitress entered with a cart containing a pitcher of water. At five-forty-six, the waitress exited the chamber. At five-forty-seven, an incendiary device disguised on the cart's lower level detonated. Six members of an insurgent militia found a weak spot in our security near the south windows. They took advantage of that to enter the room. One cornered Alissa Cassidy while five threatened and surrounded His Royal Highness the Crown Prince. Two shots were fired in the direction of his person. Insurgent One pulled a knife on Ms. Cassidy with intent to do bodily harm. Adison Cebon, arriving on scene at a later date than His Highness' security, assessed the situation and arrived through one of the broken windows. He was in time to protect Ms. Cassidy, but not without incurring several critical wounds. Mr. Cebon incapacitated Ms. Cassidy's attacker. His Highness' detail entered at five-forty-nine and detained the rest of the insurgents. His Highness was brought directly to the palace. These are the known facts of the situation."

With a heavy breath, the Minister of Defense took his seat.

No matter how the facts were stated, the whole scenario irked Jonathan and shook him to the core. He had seen the murderous intent. They had meant to kill Alissa while he watched. He couldn't stand the thought of any of them getting away with it.

"Are they in custody?" The King asked.

Another Minister bent his head. "Five are being detained in the palace. The last went to the hospital for his injuries. We have men watching him."

"I want to see the detainees." Jonathan refused to sit back and listen any longer. They pulled guns on a royal. They tried to murder the future Crown Princess. He was done playing their game of rules and regulations. The best idea would be to face them head-on.

The King shifted in his seat and suppressed a cough. "That isn't a wise decision."

"If it was the Anti-Monarchists again, they know how we think. They know what we'll do, which laws we will state." Jonathan faced his father properly. "I want to unbalance their schemes. Allow me to see the detainees."

"First, let's set a strategy for the next few hours." The King turned to the PR Manager. "We should issue a statement on behalf of the palace. Don't commit to anything, with the exception of our bringing charges against the intruders."

"Yes, Your Majesty." The PR Manager bowed along with his words.

Jonathan breathed deeply in an attempt to control his anger. "Allow me to see the detainees, father. I'm not asking to inter-rogate them, myself."

"Guillaume will take you and you will have exactly five minutes to say what you feel you must." The King reached for his royal seal. "Except for the parade, The Royal Family will not be partici-pating in Heritage Festival events outside of the palace proper." The seal thudded against the king's notes from the meeting. According to tradition, they would now be taken to the royal archives and stored in the King's Records.

A monarchy had nothing if it didn't have a history. A story. From the beginning of Veldoria's independence, each king cautiously stored his diaries and edicts. They held as much impor- tance as the monarchy, itself. Without them, no one would know how each king truly ruled. In the future, logging what happened each day would be one of Jonathan's most important responsibil- ities.

Today, Jonathan's most important responsibility was to Alissa. First, he would meet the men who blindsided them. Then, he would check on Alissa.

The King rose.

Jonathan followed suit.

"Go now." The King lifted wise, aging eyes to his son. "I under- stand your emotions. It's a low blow, to toy with the Crown Prince's woman. Don't think I will be lenient, either. I have merely learned to control my emotions. You should do the same."

Jonathan dipped his head in a semi-bow. "Yes, Your Majesty."

The King patted a hand against Jonathan's shoulder. An affec- tionate gesture, in its own way. Jonathan knew that it meant many things, but most of all it meant that he shouldn't blame himself. That was one of the problems, being a royal. Everyone else blamed the monarchy even when the monarchy already blamed themselves. One never won, regardless of the situation.

Jonathan waited until his father exited the room, then lent a bow to the Ministers and made his own exit.

Guillaume fell into step next to him. "Which detainee would you like to see? You only have five minutes and there are five of them."

"The one who shot at me." Jonathan didn't hesitate for a second.

He already knew which would allow a more effective meeting. The one who pulled a knife on Alissa had the most to fear. Since that man sat in a hospital Jonathan had no intention of visiting, the man who had the second-most to fear would do.

"Yes, sir. This way." Guillaume turned toward the detainment rooms.

In a few hours, the men would be handed over to Veldorian police, but the Palace insisted on their own investigation, as well. For the first time in his life, Jonathan was grateful for that regulation. It afforded him a few moments to discover the plan behind the incident.

Guillaume stopped beside a door on the right. "Would you rather observe him from the secured room?"

"No." Jonathan appreciated the thought, security-wise, but he had no intention of backing down now. They declared war, in their own way. He planned to bring them a fight they would never forget. "It's enough if you come in with me."

"Yes, sir." Guillaume sighed, but he opened the door and stepped inside.

Jonathan lifted his chin and put on his best haughty face. No need to let the man see how much the attack affected him. Jonathan's dress shoes clicked against the tile floor as he crossed the threshold.

The man at the table didn't flinch. He merely lifted his eyes, then lowered them again.

Jonathan could have said something sarcastic, but he chose to keep his silence and his dignity. He braced his hands against the chair on his side of the table.

The man plucked at one handcuff. "I see they're sending in the big-shots."

"You should address His Highness appropriately," Guillaume snapped.

"Why?" The man sniffed. "I don't see any real leader in this room. Just a spoiled brat who got bested in a fight."

"It wasn't a fair fight to begin with." Jonathan flexed his fingers against the chair. He didn't have much time, but he wouldn't speak unless he calculated his words.

"If we asked for a fair fight, your side wouldn't allow it." The man rolled his eyes. "It's time the people see you for who you are."

"Then I should return the favor. Let the people see you for who you really are, as well." Jonathan tossed a glance toward Guillaume's corner. "What's his name?"

"It's recorded as Stephan Harper."

The man blinked, then looked away with a chuckle. "Of course it's recorded as that. Stephan Harper is my name."

Guillaume straightened his jacket sleeve. "In actuality, his identity is Maxwell Leopold. A naturalized Veldorian, but not born or raised here. He didn't arrive in the country until he was thirteen."

"And he dared to fire at an unarmed man." Jonathan clucked his tongue. "Shameful, isn't it? Someone who wasn't even born in Veldoria trying to eliminate the monarchy? It could be considered terrorism."

"Hey! I'm not a terrorist, just a realist. Trying to do my best to secure my country's future." Maxwell sneered.

Jonathan leaned forward, leveling his gaze at Maxwell in a way he hoped portrayed all his disdain. "No. You're a terrorist. Pulling a knife on an unarmed woman. Backing her into a corner and attacking when she didn't do anything wrong. There's nothing that better defines a terrorist."

"That's your fault, not mine. Besides, I didn't pull the knife." Maxwell jerked at the handcuffs holding him to the table. "This is real terrorism. If you wanted to keep her so safe, you should have left her alone. She's part of the monarchy now. You all have to go."

"By killing us?"

"Deposing you is ideal. Abolishing the monarchy? Even better. But we're prepared to do what we have to do. It's a revolution, *your highness.* Brace yourself."

"The monarchy is well established. I would worry about yourself, Maxwell." Jonathan gave his best diplomatic smile. "I've heard prison isn't very accommodating for murderers like yourself." Jonathan turned for the door. "Guillaume, make sure he's put in a very special cell in prison."

"Yes, sir."

"Hey! You can't do this to me! I didn't do anything!"

Jonathan spared one last look in Maxwell's direction. "Your people assaulted the wrong woman."

It didn't matter how many expletives the man shouted. The investigators would get out of him whatever he had been fed to say. Jonathan walked away knowing that he had done all he could.

Guillaume locked the door behind them and waved to one of the other security personnel to keep watch.

Jonathan waited for Guillaume to catch up before he asked the next pertinent question. "Where is Alissa right now?"

"Well... that is..." Guillaume cleared his throat. "It seems she isn't taking the situation well. It was reported that she collapsed in hysteria."

"What?" Jonathan spun to face Guillaume. "When? Where?"

"She is in your mother's quarters." Guillaume shook his head grimly. "She doesn't seem to be holding up so well."

"Where is Violet?" In Alissa's time of need, her friend should be with her.

"News hasn't spread to her yet. Gaspar returned Frederick and Violet to the palace. It seems they're taking tea in the library."

At least Frederick hadn't dared try to take Violet to his personal residence. That would have caused quite the stir in the palace. Jonathan could be thankful that Frederick seemed to still have some sense.

"Don't alarm her yet. Allow me to check the situation first. Has Frederick been advised?"

"He hasn't been told. The Queen only asked for you to know." Guillaume motioned down the hall. "Shall we?"

Jonathan nodded. He hated keeping it from Violet, but he had half an inkling that the woman would only end up punching him if anyone told her. Not that Jonathan did anything wrong. Violet had a nasty temper. He didn't want to be on the wrong side of it.

Guillaume escorted Jonathan as far as the door to the queen's parlor. There, he stopped beside the queen's personal guard, Lucian.

Jonathan rapped twice on the door, then let himself in.

The room seemed too quiet. Even if his mother had a soft personality, the constant bustling of maids and butlers always created some noise in her wing. Strange, the complete silence that permeated the atmosphere.

"Mother?" Jonathan called out, knowing she would hear him.

The Queen appeared from the direction of her bedroom, shutting the door behind herself. She pressed a finger to her lips. "Quietly, Jean."

"Where is Alissa? Is she alright?" Jonathan craned his neck in an attempt to see through the minuscule crack in the bedroom door.

The Queen smiled wryly. "She just fell asleep."

"May I see her?" Jonathan didn't want to have to ask, but he and Alissa were nothing official yet. His mother, higher in rank, had the final say over Alissa's visitors.

The Queen reached out to rest a hand against Jonathan's cheek. "For a moment. She has been through quite an extraordinary circumstance today. I know you'll take responsibility for her, but... Do be careful, Jean."

"I'm attempting to be careful. Things aren't going my way."

"Life rarely does." The Queen stepped aside. "Nicole will stay in the room with you. For propriety's sake."

Jonathan expected nothing less from his mother. The Queen treated protocol and honesty with great solemnity. Of course she would situate her lady's maid in the room when a man and woman were alone together. That way, rumors wouldn't dare rear their ugly heads. Jonathan didn't mind. In fact, he appreciated her forethought.

Jonathan tiptoed his way into his mother's bedroom. Only then did he breathe a sigh of relief.

Alissa lay curled under the covers, her hair damp and spread everywhere. His mother must have lent her the shirt, since it didn't quite fit. Still, with the rich silk coverlet pulled up over her, Alissa reminded him of Sleeping Beauty.

She must have been shocked at the restaurant, so Jonathan couldn't blame her for her sudden tiredness. All he could do was pull up a chair beside her and watch over her, hoping sleep would restore her.

Chapter 18

A room full of green wallpaper hung foggy in Alissa's vision as she woke. A single stream of sunshine glared against a mirror on the far wall. Alissa groaned and rolled from her side onto her back.

A large, warm hand tightened around Alissa's fingers. "Thank God."

Jonathan? Alissa didn't remember him being there when she fell asleep. Did his mom call him or did he come on his own? A thousand questions exploded through her head. No going back to sleep now that her brain decided to be awake.

Jonathan reached out and smoothed Alissa's hair away from her face. "Do you feel better this morning?"

Right. Her mental breakdown. Alissa almost forgot about crying on the queen's shoulder. Not her most shining moment.

Alissa sat up abruptly. "What about Adison?"

How could she sleep when Adison went to the hospital? He got hurt saving her. She should have taken the responsibility to stay up until she heard how he was doing. The least she could do for the man who saved her life.

Jonathan released Alissa's hand when she tugged it away. "He pulled through the surgery well. They say he's stable and, with some physical therapy, should be back to normal sooner rather than later."

Alissa closed her eyes and breathed deeply. At least he made it. She would have felt so much worse if Adison died because of her.

"This isn't his first time being so injured." Jonathan's tone brought Alissa's attention around. "You wouldn't have any way of knowing it, but Adison came from the Black Forces. This is nothing but a scratch by their definitions."

"What's the Black Forces?" Alissa couldn't stop the question. She should have expected stupid inquisitions like that with her overactive-but-sleep-addled brain.

"Military elites." Jonathan shrugged a shoulder. "Similar to your Special Forces. If that's any help."

Alissa nodded. Of course, the example helped. It didn't make Adison's injuries any less serious, but it made Alissa feel better about his state of mind. He would recover well, since he trained for this sort of situation. At least, that's what she hoped.

Jonathan offered a wry smile. "I couldn't keep the news of your collapse from your friend any longer last evening. We managed to hold her off for this long, but she should arrive any moment." He checked a watch on his wrist. "Will she hate me forever if I'm beside you when she arrives?"

Despite the situation, Alissa couldn't help but laugh. "Maybe not forever, but you might get hit."

"How hard does she punch?" Jonathan's expression dropped, his cheeks paled. As if getting punched by Violet truly scared him.

Alissa folded her legs and pulled the blanket up around her waist. "Hard enough that I wasn't worried about leaving her alone with your Casanova brother."

"Frederick knows better than to bite the hand that feeds him, anyway." Jonathan glanced toward the door, clearly nervous. "I should vanish before she arrives."

"Were you here all night?" Alissa finally managed to clear her brain enough to think through the situation.

"No. I wanted to stay by your side, but my mother kicked me out to deal with Violet. I just arrived a few moments ago."

"Oh, that's right. This is your mom's room." Alissa mentally kicked herself.

What kind of guest trudged in covered in blood and then stole the queen's bed for the night? Did everyone think her presumptuous now? They must think she wanted to stake a claim to a royal position, but Alissa had no intentions of taking anything from anyone.

"Stop fretting." Jonathan pressed a palm to the top of Alissa's head. "I have duties to attend, but I will see you later. Mother swears she has plans for you and Violet, both. Don't let her push you around."

"Pretty sure I don't have a choice about that." Alissa didn't know if she should look forward to spending the day with The Queen. Should she dread it?

"I'm relieved to see you're better." Jonathan rose to his feet. "If anything at all bothers you, call me immediately."

"I can take care of myself." Alissa rolled her eyes.

Jonathan smirked. "And yet we keep ending up in these situations. Be sure to call."

Well, she couldn't argue with that. Besides, Alissa took any and all excuses to talk with Jonathan. On the phone or in person. "I'll call."

"Good." Jonathan paused as if he wanted to say something else. His gaze never left Alissa, nor did it waver in its intensity. Alissa didn't know what went through his head, but his eyes darkened, then lightened, like a thousand emotions were trapped inside.

Someone cleared their throat from the other side of the room.

Alissa startled.

Jonathan averted his gaze.

A woman in a black skirt and suit jacket stepped forward from the corner. She dipped a bow. "It's better if you go now, Your Highness."

"Yes, well." Jonathan cleared his throat.

Alissa didn't know how to read the situation. All she knew is the woman in the corner seemed to know something that Alissa didn't. What had she spotted that Alissa missed? Alissa wracked her brain for an explanation. She came up empty.

Jonathan hesitated once more, then stepped away from the bed. "The royal physician will send a tonic. Drink it all."

"Gosh, let it go, Jonathan." Alissa scooped a hand back through her hair. "I'm fine."

"You are not. Don't try to convince me otherwise." Jonathan stopped at the door to nod his head at the lady in the corner.

Once again, she bowed.

Alissa didn't know what kind of silent understanding they had, but if telepathy were a real thing, they could very well be the poster children.

Jonathan shut the door on his way out.

Alissa rested her hands in her lap. "So, remind me who you are again?"

"I am Nicole. Her Majesty's lady's maid." Nicole dipped a bow in Alissa's direction.

Alissa wracked her brain and finally came up with the answer. The woman who had been standing behind the queen the evening before. The uptight one. The title of Lady's Maid fit her too well. Like a role in a historical drama. Down to the spotless black pumps on Nicole's feet, she screamed posture and modesty.

"I can call you Nicole, right?"

"Of course." Nicole kept her eyes downcast, the perfect servant. She must have had this job for years.

Alissa couldn't think of anything else to ask in order to keep the conversation rolling. Should she apologize for the night before? Probably. But she couldn't quite find the words to do so.

"It literally took you long enough!" Violet's loud, boisterous accusation hailed from beyond the bedroom door.

Alissa let out a deep breath. This could be a long conversation. On top of the questions that Alissa knew Violet would have, Alissa had questions of her own.

Nicole stepped to the door and dipped a curtsy. "I will fetch your breakfast."

"Thank you." Alissa smiled, but got nothing in return. Not even a flinch. She probably shouldn't have expected much, anyway.

Nicole opened the door and stepped aside when Violet came sailing through.

A black-clothed man, probably from someone's security detail, peeked in after Violet, then disappeared again.

Nicole shut the door behind herself.

Violet raced to the bed and flopped down next to Alissa. Her arms snaked their way around Alissa's shoulders and pulled her tight to Violet's chest. "I swear, everyone who works here are either imbeciles or turtles."

"Turtles?" Alissa tipped her head back awkwardly to try to get a look at Violet's face.

Violet smushed Alissa's head back into her shoulder. "Yes, turtles. You have no idea how slow they move around here. I should have been with you yesterday. What happened? Are you okay? I heard about Adison. He was a good guy."

"He's not dead, dummy." Alissa wrapped her arms around Violet in a return embrace.

"He's not?" Violet finally let Alissa go. Thank heavens.

Alissa shook her head. "Clearly you only got part of the story. He's fine, after surgery."

"Well, that's a relief." Violet tapped a finger against Alissa's knee. "What about you? You doing okay? I heard there was a killer and an emotional breakdown."

"Other than almost getting stabbed, I'm fine. I just... had a moment." Alissa hated how weak the whole situation made her feel. Couldn't she hold herself together at all?

Violet rolled her eyes. "You got overwhelmed, get over yourself. I wouldn't be fine after that, either. I'd be better than you, but not *fine*."

"Gee, thanks for the vote of confidence."

"Hey, I speak the truth and only the truth." Violet shot Alissa a wink.

Great. Now that they had that out of the way, Alissa had some things to clear up with her best friend. Starting with... "What were you doing while all that was happening?"

"Me? Oh. Um... nothing much." Violet scooped her hair behind her head and secured it with a hairband that she kept on her wrist. Then, she cleared her throat. Tucked a strand of loose hair behind her ear.

Alissa folded her arms. Interesting. Violet told her everything, always, so why did she lie about something that simple? "I mean...

you had to be doing something. You're not the kind to sit around and do nothing."

"I am when there's a snooty bodyguard watching my every move." Violet laid her head in Alissa's lap. "Comfort me. He was awful."

"Sounds to me like you're trying to change the subject." Alissa flicked her fingers against Violet's forehead. Leave it to Violet to try to hide things by seeking reassurance. Even with that temper of hers, Violet had a cute side. Or so she wanted people to believe.

Violet shook her head. "I'm not changing the subject."

"Yeah, you are."

"Am not."

"Then tell me what you did while I was gone."

Violet wrinkled her nose. "I got stuck with Frederick. For tea in the library. It was *so boring!*"

Something told Alissa it didn't bore Violet half as much as she wanted Alissa to think. However, Alissa liked to take her friends at their word. She would live by that principle today.

Alissa leaned back on her hands. "Boring enough that you didn't realize I hadn't come back yet? Didn't they tell Frederick what happened?"

"That's the other thing!" Violet sat bolt upright, then turned so she could look at Alissa properly. "Apparently they told him before they told me. How bogus is that? Sure, he's a prince, but I'm your best friend!"

"I don't think they take things like that into consideration at a place like this."

Alissa could barely contain her amused smile. She hadn't seen Violet in such rare form since... she didn't know when. It took little to upset Violet, but a lot to make her rant like this. Alissa had missed the constant rambling of her lifelong friend.

Violet rolled her eyes. "I don't care if they take that into consideration. You're not a princess yet, so your guardian should be told what's going on first and foremost."

"My guardian is...?"

"Me! Of course I'm your guardian. You wouldn't have survived childhood without my guardianship."

Alissa did recall several times when Violet had been especially helpful. As an introvert child, Alissa had been the target for ridicule. Violet, being the extrovert, didn't stand for a single misplaced word regarding her friend. Alissa didn't even remember when Violet decided they were friends, she only remembered no one dared cross Violet. It had been a lifesaver on multiple occasions.

Alissa reached out to gather Violet into a hug. "Thank you."

"Okay, we're hugging now. That's cool." Violet wrapped her arms around Alissa. "Why are you thanking me?"

"For everything."

Alissa had no doubt that Violet would have made some sort of snarky comment, but she didn't have the time. The door opened, allowing entrance to both Nicole and Jonathan's mother.

Violet shot to her feet and dipped a much-too-dramatic curtsy.

Alissa rolled her eyes. Leave it to Violet to overreact. Since when did Violet react in a normal manner, anyway?

The Queen inclined her head with a soft smile. "Good morning, ladies. Alissa, I am relieved to see you much improved. I hope you feel able to rise to our schedule today."

"We have a schedule?" Violet spoke first. Apparently, her curiosity got the better of her. Or, perhaps, she didn't care what she said. The latter seemed more accurate.

The Queen's smile widened. "The two of you can't attend a ball without a proper gown."

"There's a ball? When? We're invited? What do we have to do?" Violet fairly vibrated with ecstatic energy.

Alissa couldn't help the butterflies that fluttered in the pit of her stomach. A ball? Her? She had never done anything like that before. What if she messed up? Still... she shouldn't disappoint anyone.

"You are my son's guests. Of course, you're invited." The Queen nodded once in Nicole's direction. "Please eat first. We'll join the designers after you've properly gotten ready."

Alissa didn't know whether to thank her or beg for it all to stop. What did she step into when she agreed to date Jonathan? Could she handle everything it entailed?

ॐ☾

"You failed to get rid of her!"

The voice on the other end of the phone wasn't one The Boss wanted to hear, but it the outburst had been inevitable. He never should have made a deal in the first place. He never had, in the past.

"If I had done it your way, do you think I would have gotten out unscathed? You're not as smart as you think you are." The Boss plucked a cigar from the box nearby.

"If we had done things my way, it wouldn't be a problem for me now!"

Oh, good. He had infuriated her. It always made these sessions so much more interesting. The Boss sighed heavily. "It isn't my job to take care of your romantic interests. If you can't seduce him before he's a king, how do you expect to influence him when he *is* a king?"

"What is that supposed to mean?"

"I'm beginning to doubt your ability to be of any help to me." An understatement. If he had the choice to do so, The Boss might do away with the woman once and for all. She was a loose end he couldn't afford with his status. It wouldn't be his first time to make someone quietly disappear.

The woman scoffed. "See if anyone else cleans up your mess next time you're on foreign soil. If you didn't have my connections, what were you going to do about the photographs and videos?"

"You aren't my only connection."

"Oh? Then why was I your first phone call? You know politics well. It's a game of push and pull. Give and take. You've taken, but you haven't given much."

The Boss pulled the phone away from his face to swear. Dang it, if the woman didn't have a point. He needed her if something like that happened again. He could only ask so many favors from so many people. Anyone else would have reported him to the authorities. She only helped because he promised to help her in return. A woman who wanted to be queen would do anything for her ambition.

Which is how The Boss found himself sitting here, several thousand feet in the air.

"I'm coming to take care of the situation myself. I have a connection I think can help improve our chances. Dramatically."

See if he ever did anything for a woman ever again. This went too far. He shouldn't be here, but he had no choice. Not if he didn't want his name in the tabloids tomorrow morning.

The woman paused as if she needed to correct her composure. "Meet me at the same place as last time. We should discuss this. I would hate to have to hand those videos over."

"You said you destroyed them." The Boss felt every last drop of blood drain from his face. She promised to destroy them.

"You think I wouldn't keep insurance? A man like you isn't trustworthy."

The Boss could almost hear the smirk on her lips. If she didn't have so much dirt on him, he would take his time and enjoy wiping that smirk off of her elegant little face. "I'll see you when I land."

The Boss shoved the phone back into its pocket. If he spoke to her for too much longer, he might lose control of his anger. Last time that happened, it didn't end prettily. The Boss leaned his head back and took a cleansing breath. Everything would work out. Just in time for the next race. He couldn't lose. Not after all he went through to get to his position. He wouldn't back down now.

Chapter 19

Heritage Festival didn't feel the same without events out among the people. Jonathan didn't care for seclusion, especially when he should be endearing himself to everyone's hearts. His father intended to cede the throne to Jonathan in a few months. Jonathan had many things to learn about running a country.

Jonathan wanted to be a king with power, not a puppet for the governmental body. To have power, he needed the people's love. Their trust. He needed them to look up to him for direction and answers. Shying away from Heritage Festival wouldn't win him any favors.

Jonathan tapped his pen once on the desk, then twirled it between his fingers. He had two chances to win hearts this week. Once at the Royal Ball, when the titled citizens would attend. Second, at the festival's Closing Ceremony Parade. Smiles often won more favor than words.

"Are you listening, Your Highness?" Markum's voice broke through Jonathan's solitude.

Jonathan lifted his gaze. "Something about a meeting with the Prime Minister. A lunch date?"

Markum shoved his glasses up on his nose. "I would appreciate it if Your Highness would apply his attention to his daily schedule."

"Do I have time to spend with Alissa today?" Jonathan set his pen down. Thinking didn't seem to be getting him anywhere. He might as well ask what he wanted to know.

"I think that will be a bit difficult."

Jonathan froze. For a moment, his heart stopped beating. When it started again, when he could remember that Alissa would be safe inside palace walls, Jonathan lifted his head. "Why?"

"The Royal Ball is tomorrow. Her Majesty has Alissa in fittings and spa sessions all day." Markum turned his attention back to the tablet in his hands.

"What about breakfast?" Jonathan didn't want to pout, but he couldn't help it. His mother had monopolized Alissa's time the day before, as well. Didn't she understand that Jonathan was attempting to romance Alissa? How could he do that if he never saw her?

Markum shook his head. "Her Majesty is introducing Alissa to her new guard. I'm afraid breakfast isn't an option, either."

"Dinner?"

"Your father requested a private dinner for the two of you."

Jonathan wrinkled his nose. Sometimes, being a prince had its cons. Today, those cons far outweighed the pros.

"Can I cancel the lunch appointment with the Prime Minister?" Not that he wanted to cancel, but Jonathan didn't like it when his schedule didn't allow him time to see Alissa. He needed to be sure she felt alright. Especially after what happened.

"Your Highness, it's best if you wait until tomorrow. I will instruct Lucian to update Guillaume with all progress." Markum slid the tablet beneath his arm. "If there are no other objections, I will bring your morning reading."

Jonathan dismissed Markum with a wave of his hand. *Morning reading* didn't often mean enjoyment. Newspaper articles about the royal family. Internet propaganda about ridiculous rumors. Reports, requests, and requisitions. If he could get through this part of his work, Jonathan could move on with more pleasant activities.

Just because he bore the title of Crown Prince, it didn't mean that Jonathan always enjoyed his job.

Thankfully, morning flew by with little trouble. Jonathan signed and approved so many files he couldn't remember them all.

Markum escorted Jonathan to the car that would take him to lunch. Even though Markum could have stayed at the palace, he chose to come along. Jonathan knew the reason. Markum didn't trust him to keep the appointment.

"It's the Prime Minister. I shouldn't get on his bad side." Jonathan settled into his seat.

Markum opened his tablet and scrolled through it. "That doesn't mean you wouldn't. Anything is possible when you're pining after a woman."

"I'm not that fickle."

"You're not that trustworthy, either."

Jonathan rolled his eyes. "If you're going to be that way, at least allow a stop at a florist's."

"I already scheduled time in for that. No more than twenty minutes. Make your selection wisely."

"I'm well-versed in things of that kind. You've met Mother."

Markum chuckled. "Your mother raised you well. The woman you marry is lucky, indeed."

"You meant to say that Alissa is lucky, indeed." Jonathan had no intention of marrying anyone else. He had made his decision and he didn't stray from already-decided courses.

Markum didn't answer. It hadn't been a question.

The aide sat in silence while the vehicle maneuvered Capitol City streets. They stopped before a white stone building. A green-rimmed chalkboard on the sidewalk announced that the florist on the corner was open for business.

Jonathan stepped from the car and buttoned his suit jacket. Twenty minutes to make a decision. He should only need ten, depending on what he found inside the florist's shop. He stepped inside.

"Welcome!" A short, petite woman called from the back, her hands buried deep in a bouquet. She pulled them out to wipe them on her apron. "Please feel free to look around, or if there's anything I can help you with..." Her eyes went wide at the sight of Jonathan and the guard behind him.

In a rush, she shoved loose hair from her face and scuttled out from behind the counter. "Your Highness." She dipped a bow. "Forgive my rudeness. What may I help you with?"

Jonathan scanned his keen gaze over the fragrant little shop. "I would like some flowers delivered."

"Yes, of course. Do you have any idea what kind?"

Jonathan smiled. "Perhaps you could make a few recommendations."

Nine minutes and one very flustered florist later, Jonathan returned to his vehicle.

Markum looked up, then glanced at his watch. "That was fast."

"The woman who owns the store had excellent suggestions. I'm pleased with your choice. We will order from here in the future."

The car rolled forward, this time on its way to lunch. Jonathan leaned his head back and took the next few minutes to recenter himself. He couldn't lose his focus in a meeting with the Prime Minister. Politics were tricky waters to navigate.

With strict punctuality, Jonathan's vehicle parked in front of the restaurant. Just in time for Jonathan to see the Prime Minister head inside. Followed by Estrella.

Jonathan shot Markum a glare. "Who invited her?"

Markum held up his hands in surrender. "It wasn't on the schedule, I swear. I didn't know she would be attending, either."

Of course. Jonathan stepped out of the vehicle and squared his shoulders. Today's meal might present more of a battle than a relief. There were so few tactics that would get through to Estrella. Jonathan had thought that the event at the joust would silence her. Perhaps he underestimated her persistence.

Markum and Guillaume fell into line behind Jonathan. They stopped inside the front door. Since the lunch meeting had invited only Jonathan, they would wait at a respectable distance until he had finished. Protocol demanded it.

Jonathan wished he could do away with protocol and force both of them to join the uncomfortable discussion sure to take place. His fingers itched to twitch against his slacks. Jonathan didn't allow them the pleasure.

The Prime Minister stood from his seat as Jonathan approached. "Your Highness."

"Sir." Jonathan shook the Prime Minister's hand firmly. "A pleasure, as always." Or so he hoped.

"Please, sit." The Prime Minister motioned to the empty chairs on Jonathan's side of the table.

Jonathan took a breath and settled into one of those chairs. He would war if he had to, but he hoped Estrella would remain docile. "To what do I owe the honor of this luncheon?"

"It's been a long while since we met as acquaintances, not professionals." The Prime Minister motioned a hand to Jonathan's menu. "Today is my treat. Please, order what you would like."

Jonathan felt a truckload of other intentions behind the request. Politics, most likely. Yet... The Prime Minister brought his daughter. Jonathan tapped a finger against his leg beneath the table. Watching. Waiting. Hesitating.

In an amazing feat of patience, they made it to dessert before anything went wrong. Just about the same time as the waiter placed a small dish of creme brulee in front of Jonathan.

The Prime Minister cleared his throat. "A few months ago, your parents and I had talked about getting together to discuss your engagement."

There it was. The real reason for calling him out. Jonathan cracked his spoon against the hard sugar topping a little too forcefully. "Did you?"

"Yes. We thought the spring would be a nice time for the two of you to get married, but we needed to discuss the details."

"That was a few months ago." Jonathan tried his best to keep his face neutral and his tone calm.

Estrella reached out to wrap her hands around her father's arm. "I told you, daddy. Jonathan has someone now."

Jonathan arched a brow. Estrella didn't back out of these kinds of conversations. She wanted something. Definitely. He had to put a stop to this before it got out of hand.

"It's been planned for quite some time now," The Prime Minister patted a hand over his daughter's.

Jonathan set his spoon down and lifted his gaze. "Apologies, sir, but I will not be marrying your daughter. I have someone I am rapidly growing fond of, and I intend to remain faithful to that love."

Estrella's look of shock told Jonathan he had chosen the right words. Left no room for her argument. Now, she would back down. He hated to hurt her, but if it was the only way to make his intentions clear, he would.

"Is that so?" The Prime Minister didn't look happy, but Jonathan couldn't decipher the emotion on his face. Betrayal? Anger? Shock?

"I intend to introduce her formally at the ball tomorrow evening." Jonathan rose from his chair. "Seeing as I've ruined the mood, I will take my leave first."

Without another word or regret, Jonathan turned and walked away.

Chapter 20

Alissa wished she had more time to spend with Jonathan, but alas, she couldn't say no to The Queen. Who could? Because of that, Alissa found herself in The Queen's parlor for the second day in a row.

Today, instead of tailors and seamstresses, there sat a half-finished gown on one side of the room. A man clad in a black suit and a security earpiece occupied the other side.

A cup of tea had gone cold on the table in front of Alissa. She didn't mind cold tea. She did, however, mind the tension of the unknown. How did one bring up the subject when The Queen hadn't brought it up herself?

In the end, curiosity got the better of Alissa. She wrung her hands in her lap. "If I may ask... um... who is he?" Timidly, Alissa pointed a finger in the general direction of the new security personnel.

The Queen glanced his way. A small, tinkling laugh rolled off her tongue. "My apologies. I should introduce you." With a single wave of her hand, The Queen beckoned the man forward. "Alissa, this is Joffrey. Your new personal guard. After what happened with Adison, we are remiss to leave you unprotected. Joffrey will guard you in Adison's absence."

Joffrey bent at the waist. The motion did nothing to upset his close-cropped hair, but his unbuttoned suit jacket moved plenty. "I pledge my life as yours, Lady Alissa."

"Oh. Um... okay." Alissa nibbled at her lip. What did she do in this situation? "I'm not... really a lady. You know that, right? I don't have a title. I'm a commoner, you can talk like we're friends."

"Apologies, my lady." Joffrey bowed again.

Okay, so that wasn't going to work. *Friends* didn't seem like a word in Joffrey's vocabulary. Alissa reached for her tea and took a sip. Neither the temperature nor taste registered with her. Alissa was too busy thinking of ways to make Joffrey see things her way.

The Queen settled her teacup in its saucer. "The Royal Parade has been rescheduled for tomorrow afternoon, before the ball. I think it would be lovely if you would accompany Jonathan."

Alissa swallowed to avoid spitting her tea in The Queen's face. The liquid stuck halfway down. "What?" Alissa squeaked.

The Queen laughed softly. "Did you not understand that Jonathan has every intention of making you his queen? Oh, dear, perhaps he hasn't been clear enough."

Even though Alissa heard the facetiousness in The Queen's voice, she couldn't quite process it. What kind of woman let a relationship progress this fast? Alissa wanted to scold herself. To tell her own head that it had gone crazy. She couldn't. Everything about the relationship felt too right.

"Please don't look so shell-shocked." The Queen rested her hands primly in her lap. "All you need to do is sit beside him, smile, and wave. We will release the official information about your relationship to the press."

"The press?" For a moment, Alissa felt small and insignificant. Why didn't she think all of this through before she let herself fall for a prince?

The Queen nodded. "The parade is televised. They will want to understand why there is a woman beside the Crown Prince. Then, tomorrow evening at the ball, we will formally introduce you to the noblemen and ministers."

"What about Violet?" Alissa grasped at the first and last straw that came to mind.

"We will ensure that she is comfortable and cared for during the time we are out. She may, of course, attend the ball."

Alissa nodded slowly. So... no way out of this one. She could either break up with Jonathan now and never see him again, or she could let the world know that she intended to be by his side forever. In the end, the choice ultimately fell to Alissa. Even if she felt that she couldn't handle the pressure, Alissa knew holding the country's expectations on her shoulders would be easier than running away. If she ran away, she may never forgive herself.

"Okay. I'll do it."

The Queen didn't bother to try to hide her smile this time. "I will make the preparations and alert Jonathan."

"Do I have to ride in the carriage the whole time? What if I get stressed out or start to panic? Can I walk?" Alissa didn't want to admit to the level of sheer fear that plagued her thoughts.

The Queen reached out and tucked Alissa's hand inside her own. "Dear girl. Future daughter. Don't worry. If something of the kind does happen, Joffrey will walk alongside you for a moment while you breathe. I'm sure our people will be lenient toward you. They know you haven't grown up in such a life."

"When can I see Jonathan?" Seeing Jonathan always calmed her down and made her feel better. Especially after the attack at the restaurant. Alissa wished he didn't have to attend to royal duties so often. It would be better if she knew where he was at, at all times.

"Jonathan has a full schedule today. You have a full schedule, as well."

"I do?"

"You can phone him after lunch." The Queen stood. "For now, we should move on to your fitting."

Alissa rose to her feet.

Joffrey took a step forward.

Great. He's going to be one of those people. Alissa shot him the sweetest smile she could muster. "Can you please not act so intense? It freaks me out."

"I've been told not to venture more than three meters from your person. It's for your safety."

"Three... what?" Alissa pushed a strand of hair behind her ear. "I'm sorry, but is it possible for you to use the American metric system to translate what you just said?"

"Apologies, my lady." Joffrey bent his head in a bow.

Alissa clenched her fists instead of pulling her hair out in frustration. "Fine. Whatever. Regardless, just... just stay about five more steps away and don't make jerky movements."

"I will do my best." Another bow.

Alissa blew out a breath. She could do this. She could handle this. She could make it through the next twenty-four hours. If anyone could withstand this, she could. *Dear Lord, help me.*

A knock sounded on the door, seconds before a female employee stepped inside. She lifted the vase of flowers in her arms. "I was told that Lady Alissa had come to your quarters, Your Majesty. His Royal Highness had these delivered."

Alissa couldn't help but smile. How did Jonathan have such good timing, even when he couldn't be by her side? She didn't understand how he knew she would be feeling so down today.

The Queen motioned to the table. "Set them here. I think, perhaps, Alissa would like to view them more closely."

The woman set the vase on the table and retreated with a bow. The bouquet didn't carry much of a scent, but the blossoming pink flowers were pleasant to look at.

Alissa snatched the attached card and opened the dainty creme envelope. Jonathan's familiar scrawled handwriting greeted Alissa.

The language of flowers is diverse, but I thought I must send you these as a message. Do you know what azaleas mean? The florist has included their meaning in the vase. I promise to see you later. Until then, Your Prince.

Alissa couldn't help but grin. It wouldn't be like Jonathan to tell her outright what his flowers meant. Besides, it seemed more fun to search for the meaning.

Alissa grabbed hold of the vase and turned it, hoping to find a card or a sign. Instead, she found script-like lettering spiraled on the vase, itself. *Take care of yourself for me.*

Azaleas would never look the same to Alissa ever again.

Chapter 21

Jonathan stopped outside his father's offices. A deep breath stilled his heart and mind. He didn't expect to feel so free and refreshed after he had made things clear to Estrella. Now that he had cut that leash, he could move forward freely. Even though Estrella had been a close friend for so many years, Jonathan couldn't continue to lead her on.

With a now-clear conscience, he stepped into his father's office.

The King wrapped his hands over a walking stick and rose to his feet. "Welcome."

"Have you waited long?" Jonathan glanced at his watch. According to the schedule Markum had given him, he arrived only seven minutes late.

The King chuckled. "There aren't many people who can make me wait at all. It was no bother." He lifted a hand to motion to the chair nearest his desk. "Sit down. We have many things to discuss."

Jonathan took his seat with seasoned grace. "Many? And here I thought you wanted only to eat a meal with me."

"I will admit to that ulterior motive." The King settled into his chair and set the walking stick to the side. "The schedule for Heritage Festival activities has been rearranged. We added a family member, at your mother's behest."

A new family member? Jonathan reached out to lift his glass of water from the table. He could easily deduce the new addition, but even if he wanted to shout for joy, he would retain his decorum before his father.

"I see. What schedules have been rearranged?" Best to act like his feet still sat solidly on the ground, even when Jonathan felt he could fly.

The King grinned, a boyish action that belied his age. "The parade has moved up. Tomorrow morning is the date. It should grant enough time to prepare for the ball in the afternoon."

"It's unprecedented for the parade to change its time."

"The attacks from Anti-Monarchists are unprecedented, as well. It's best this way." The King shifted in his chair, as if his hip suddenly hurt him. "Alissa will ride in your carriage. Your mother has already provided the necessary information to the media. We can formally introduce her during the ball."

A spot in the Royal Parade and a formal introduction, all in one day? To Jonathan, it seemed too much to handle. Especially for a simple girl like Alissa.

"Has she agreed to all this? I don't want her to feel we are rushing things. I would rather do nothing than have her run away from me."

"She has agreed." The King paused as the doors opened.

Kitchen staffs wheeled in a cart full of The King's favorite dishes.

Jonathan wrinkled his brow. This meal felt different than others he had spent with his father. His father seemed... more serious than usual. Much more solemn than Jonathan remembered.

The kitchen staffs bowed to both the King and the Crown Prince before they exited.

Jonathan stared at the salad before him. "Father. What's really wrong?"

"We should eat first." The King reached for his knife and fork.

"No." Jonathan tore his eyes from the salad to stare directly at his father. "I will not eat until I know what has happened."

"Nothing has happened that we did not prepare for." The King motioned to the food. "Eat."

"I said no." Jonathan turned in his seat. It wasn't like his father to delay a conversation like this. The King faced everything head-on. "Tell me. Why did you insist we meet this evening?"

The King set down his utensils with a sigh. "I had hoped we could enjoy a nice meal before I broke the news."

"What news?" Jonathan clenched his fingers against his knees. What kind of terrible ordeal must his father have gone through to be so hesitant to speak? Did the Anti-Monarchists strike again, in a more personal manner? A million worst-case scenarios flitted through Jonathan's overactive imagination.

None prepared him for the words that fell from his father's lips.

"The doctors have given me, at most, six months to live." The King averted his gaze. The first time he had done so since before his reign. "I want to make another announcement at the ball. That I will abdicate the throne to you. Effective immediately."

"Six months?" Jonathan rolled his lips together, trying to determine what went wrong. His father had always been in good health. "Why?"

"Even a king can develop a tumor, I'm afraid." The King finally brought his eyes back around to his firstborn son. "It cannot be operated on. It is your time, my son."

"A tumor..." Jonathan tried his best to process the information as quickly as it had been given to him.

He wouldn't let his father give up his reign like this. His father had always been a good king. He couldn't back down now. It would change how the people saw him. Besides, Jonathan was hardly ready to be a king. How would he manage without his father's assistance?

"How about this, then?" Jonathan grasped at straws that would help both parties. "I will accept a regency. While I am your regent, I will learn from you how to be a good and wise king. Please, father, do not abdicate. Remain by my side. I will rule in your stead, but please do not leave."

Jonathan knew he should have phrased the whole request in a more positive light, but right now he didn't feel like a crown prince. Right now, as portrayed in his desperate plea, Jonathan was just a little boy who didn't want to lose his father.

The King leaned forward in his seat, his eyes softening toward his child. "I know that becoming a king is the hardest and saddest moment in a man's life. I, too, had to endure the grief as if it were a joy. I will not leave you without a mentor. A regency is a good idea."

"Thank you, father. You won't regret this decision." Jonathan tried to pull a solid breath, but it didn't come easy.

The King smiled softly. "However, you must promise me one thing."

"Anything. Say it."

"Prepare yourself well. My leaving is inevitable, so guard your heart from bitterness and anger. Let me leave in peace. Let your rule begin with happiness."

Jonathan knew why his father made the request. Even though Jonathan had been little when his father assumed the throne, he knew the stories. His father had loved the former king very much. It changed Jonathan's father when the old king suddenly died. Jonathan's father hadn't had time to prepare his heart. Jonathan would have a small period to accomplish what his father never had.

"I won't let you down," Jonathan promised.

The King motioned to the food. "Then, eat. We have much to prepare before tomorrow. An announcement such as this doesn't come easily."

Jonathan's heart ached in his chest, but he knew all his life that a moment like this would come. Becoming a king brought the heaviest burden and the foggiest sadness. A king might be loved by his country, by hundreds of thousands of people, but his role brought only loneliness. In the station of a king, someone always had to pass away for another to assume his rightful role.

&OCG

The Boss folded his arms across his chest, then unfolded one to check his watch. She should have been there a quarter hour ago. All his training told him not to wait at all. He ignored it for the sake of blackmail. Why did he think he could trust her in the first place? As conniving as she turned out to be, he should have shot her to begin with. No loose ends.

But... she held the heart and hand of two of the most powerful men in Veldoria. If she had left any evidence to them, they wouldn't hesitate to expose a foreigner. Countrymen sided with countrymen. Until the right incentive appeared.

Stiletto heels clicked against rough concrete. The sound echoed around the metal beams in the ceiling.

The Boss huffed a sigh and lifted his glass to have a swallow. Alcohol might make him gentler to the crazy woman.

Estrella slipped her skinny form onto a stool beside him. "You said you were good at your job."

"You said you didn't want it to be obvious." The Boss downed the end of his drink. "You should trust my judgment."

"Your judgment didn't do anything but push her into Jonathan's arms. How could I trust that?"

The Boss snorted. Women were all alike. A one-track mind, without any sense of the big picture. She could only think about her one-sided love. There were plenty of other balls in the air. Pieces of a grander puzzle that had nothing to do with Estrella's unhealthy obsession. Estrella thought she wanted that girl out of the picture. The Boss held a much larger grudge against the girl.

"Your plan hasn't worked either, which is why I'm here now." The Boss grabbed a liquor bottle from the back of the counter. "Want a drink?"

"I think I'd better not. I've seen what you're capable of." Estrella shot him a bitter smile. "Has your plan changed? Is it now time accomplish what should have been accomplished weeks ago?"

"He must have rejected you pretty hard." The Boss poured another drink. It went down smoothly. "Don't worry, I want the girl out of the way just as much as you do. I can't have her telling everyone my secrets."

"You said you had connections. I doubt they're as good as mine. I've received an offer that you should accept." Estrella folded one long leg over the other. "These people are very persuasive and they know how to handle things without too much of a mess. You'll barely even have to get your hands dirty."

"What's their offer?" The Boss didn't like bringing in outsiders if he didn't have to, but if he could put the full blame on Estrella and her kind, he would take the deal.

"They don't want anything but the girl. You extract her, they'll take her off your hands."

The Boss knew a too-good-to-be-true deal when he heard it. He doubted he would walk out of the exchange alive. "A hundred thousand US dollars to purchase the girl and you make the exchange instead of me."

Estrella stood and hiked her bag up onto her shoulder. "I'll present the offer to them and call you. Don't expect too much. And don't do anything rash."

The Boss chuckled as Estrella stalked away. He had never done anything rash in his life. Estrella, on the other hand, seemed the walking definition of the word. Her irrational behavior would fix his problems without any fuss. All he had to do was sit back and watch.

Chapter 22

"Wake up, wake up! It's your big day..." Violet pounced on Alissa with far too much enthusiasm for the early hour. When Alissa barely stirred, Violet poked a finger against her cheek. "There are people waiting at the door and they've been standing there for ages. Get up and deal with them so I can go back to sleep."

"I wanna sleep, too." Alissa pouted at her best friend in an attempt to get an extension for her slumber.

Violet sighed heavily. "Okay, you've forced my hand. I didn't want to do this, but you leave me no choice."

Violet's weight lifted from the bed. Her footsteps faded into the parlor.

Alissa cuddled down under the covers and closed her eyes. Just five more minutes. She'd had a rough couple of days.

"Violet says you refuse to awaken."

Alissa's eyes shot open. She yanked the blankets up to her chin as she sat up. "Jonathan!" Her voice squeaked. Alissa took a moment to clear her throat. "What are you doing here?"

Jonathan tucked his fingers into his jean's pockets. "You're already running thirty minutes behind schedule. The Royal Family is very prompt about these things."

"I didn't mean to make people late." Alissa nibbled at her lip, trying to decide if Jonathan was angry or just informing her of the situation.

Jonathan chuckled to himself. "Stop pouting and get up. You're far too adorable when you pout." He cleared his throat.. "I should go get ready, myself. I will see you at the parade."

Alissa opened her mouth to say something, but Jonathan had already high-tailed it out the door. She only briefly heard him mumble some sort of instructions.

A half-dozen women invaded Alissa's room, all with their arms full.

Alissa's brain couldn't process the amount of items they carried, let alone the identity of each. Why did they need so much to prepare her for a parade? Alissa had walked in exactly one parade in her life, and it had been one of those t-shirt, shorts, and tennis shoes deals. People didn't care what you wore as long as you gave them candy.

Then again, a *royal* parade must have its differences from an American celebratory parade.

One of the women stepped to the end of the bed and bent her head. "If you wouldn't mind climbing out of the bed, we have much to do."

"Much?" Alissa ran her hands back through her unruly morning hair. "Is it that bad?"

The ladies' maid pressed her fingertips to her lips to stifle a laugh. "It is... typical. We have very specific instructions, as this will be your first televised appearance. If you please." She motioned to a vanity at the side of the room, where a host of beauty products had suddenly appeared.

Alissa gulped. "How long is this going to take?"

"It will move along faster if her ladyship will cooperate." The ladies' maid gave her best smile.

Alissa believed she meant it. She didn't seem hostile and Jonathan had sent them in, himself. With a trepidatious heart, Alissa crawled out from under the covers and tiptoed toward the vanity.

Before she even sat down, a flurry of hands and whispers surrounded her. As if she might get offended if they talked too loudly. Alissa gripped her hands in her lap, closed her eyes, and let the ladies' maids do their jobs.

Brushes and irons pulled through Alissa's hair in rapid-fire succession. Someone worked quickly to apply makeup to Alissa's face. Somewhere along the line, one of the ladies' maids got a hold of Alissa's fingernails and toenails. They, admittedly, needed a new coat of polish.

Alissa didn't know how long they worked on her appearance before the swarm finally dispersed. They left one lone ladies' maid at Alissa's side.

"If you'll follow me, your wardrobe has been prepared." The ladies' maid motioned Alissa to get up.

A quick glance in the mirror convinced Alissa that these women were all miracle workers. The Alissa in the mirror looked like a far better version of the real-life Alissa. When did her eyes get so big and bright?

"Lady Alissa?" The ladies' maid kept a smile, but tense urgency reflected from the rest of her face.

Alissa smiled back and rose from the chair. If she had learned one thing since coming to Veldoria, it was that the palace operated on a strict time schedule. Heaven help her if she held up an entire parade because she had refused to wake up.

The ladies' maid motioned delicately to a dress and shoes displayed on Alissa's bed. "This is your wardrobe for today's event. Would you like my assistance to put it on?"

"Just with the zipper, if that's okay." Alissa hesitated to reach out and touch the dress. It looked... expensive. "You really didn't need to go through all this trouble for me."

"It's imperative that you look lovely perched next to His Royal Highness. This is the least we could do." The ladies' maid motioned again to the dress. "If you would."

Though Alissa and the maid moved hastily, they moved carefully. Alissa would bet money that the maid had the same motive for caution as she did. Neither wanted to wrinkle or ruin the dress. Why, out of all the colors in the world, did they have to choose a dress with a white base?

Still, Alissa didn't like to argue. She wore the dress. The shoes, she didn't have any qualms with. Alissa had always had an affinity for shoes. The ones chosen for her looked divine. Gold and strappy, with an emblem from a brand that Alissa and every other shoe lover knew by heart. Alissa didn't listen to her hesitation when it came to those heels.

The ladies' maid motioned Alissa toward the door next.

Alissa didn't expect the round of applause that greeted her in the sitting area.

Violet, the leader of that antic, skipped to Alissa's side. "Oh my gosh, you're so pretty! Of course, I already knew that, but now everyone else will, too. I'm so happy for you!"

Alissa laughed heartily. "You should come to the parade, too."

"And miss out on my blissfully silent morning and these yoga pants?" Violet shook her head. "No, thank you. I'll see you when you get back. There's a ball to attend this evening, you know."

"You don't let me forget." Alissa patted a hand against Violet's head. "Be a good girl while I'm gone."

"Good luck with that." Violet shrugged her shoulders. "I'll try, but..."

"Whatever. I'll make someone keep an eye on you."

Violet saluted her best friend. "Ma'am, yes ma'am."

Alissa laughed at Violet's grin. "Just don't burn down the place while we're away."

"Miss?" The ladies' maid from earlier, who seemed to be in charge, took a step forward. She held up a small jewelry box. "Her Majesty had these specially delivered for you to wear today. She thought them quite appropriate, given His Royal Highness' gift to you yesterday."

Confused, Alissa accepted the little burgundy box. The lid stuck slightly, then flipped open. Alissa smiled softly at the contents.

A pair of earrings, made of one delicate golden chain each. At the tip of each earring hung a single, porcelain azalea blossom.

"I should wear them?" Alissa confirmed. She wanted to wear them, regardless, but today she stepped into the world of royalty. She should abide by their rules.

The ladies' maids all gave a bow.

Alissa took that as a yes and slid the earrings on. The Queen had impeccable taste. Alissa handed the empty jewelry box off to Violet and squared her shoulders. She didn't know if she was ready for any of this, but Alissa was willing to try.

Chapter 23

Jonathan didn't understand the nervous energy fluttering inside his stomach. He had done this parade dozens of times in his life. If he smiled and waved, all would be well. There was no reason to have such anxiety. Security would be tight. The press would be everywhere. Jonathan pressed a hand to his beating heart. There was no need to feel this anxious.

"Is your lady friend on her way?" Markum checked his watch, then the schedule on the tablet. "The parade begins in five minutes. Isn't she pushing the time a little too closely?"

Jonathan sighed and shot Markum a glare. "She's new at this. Do not make her feel inferior. I like you as an aide, but she's more important."

Markum wrinkled his nose. "I should stick closer to your side."

"Please refrain from doing so." Jonathan raised a finger to hail the head of security.

Guillaume stalked over and bent a traditional bow. "Sir."

"Assure Markum that the schedule will continue as planned and for the love of everything holy, get him out of my sight." Jonathan pressed a palm to his head, this time.

"What? Your Highness!" Markum's eyes went wide with shock. "Whyever for?"

"I need to remain calm and if Markum stays, I don't know if I can keep my composure." Jonathan waved a hand to dismiss them.

Guillaume snagged the back of Markum's collar. "I'll see to it that he doesn't bother Your Highness any longer." Jonathan didn't miss Guillaume's amused grin as he dragged Markum away.

One of the ladies' maids that Jonathan had assigned to Alissa came skittering out from the portico. "Your Royal Highness." She curtsied, gulping in a breath to calm her rapid-fire breathing. "She is on her way. Apologies for our tardiness."

"It is no large matter. Return to your duties, then."

The girl smiled and darted off the way she had come.

She had barely cleared the portico entrance when Jonathan heard the rush of heels and rustle of feet headed his way.

"I'm sorry! I'm late!" Alissa's voice floated on a slight breeze.

Jonathan opened his mouth to say something, but once he saw her, nothing could be said. The same breeze that carried her voice brushed an errant piece of hair from Alissa's face. The white dress selected for her first outing faded to red at its hem. Paired with gold shoes, it made her appear positively regal. Exactly how Jonathan had seen her all along.

Alissa came to a stuttering stop beside Jonathan. "Sorry. I'll listen better next time."

"You made it with two minutes to spare." Jonathan smiled and offered his hand. "Shall we?"

Alissa smiled and tucked her fingers into Jonathan's. "You look nice. I like the... sash and stuff."

"Thank you. I worked hard to earn the 'stuff', but the sash comes with my title." Jonathan pressed a kiss to her fingers before he started toward their open carriage.

Alissa's reactions never ceased to amuse him. She thought about things so simply. On such an ordinary level. The palace could use that kind of refreshment. The residents therein had become too jaded to the world around them.

"The horses are gorgeous." Alissa stared at the black steeds as they passed.

Jonathan gave her hand a squeeze. "The finest in the palace. If we have time, perhaps we can reward them with a sugar cube later."

"Feeding horses sugar cubes is an actual thing?" Alissa smiled up at Jonathan. "I thought they made that up for movies. I've never had to research horses."

"It is, indeed. Watch your step." Jonathan switched out the hand holding Alissa's so that he could use both hands to balance her. With little difficulty, she took the two steps up into the carriage.

"Thirty seconds," came a familiar voice behind Jonathan.

Jonathan tossed a precursory glance to Guillaume. "Yes, thank you. I'm getting in now. Assure Markum that all is going according to plan."

Guillaume would, of course, keep watch on Jonathan's side of the carriage, while Alissa's bodyguard would stay on the other side. Jonathan gave thanks to Heaven for that. Until they caught whoever wanted her dead, Jonathan had no intention of ever leaving her unguarded again. He couldn't bear if something happened to her because of him.

He couldn't bear if something happened to her at all.

The palace gates opened to the sound of thunderous applause and cheers from the subjects.

Jonathan straightened his spine and fixed his expression. He shot a glance sideways to Alissa.

Alissa rested her hands in her lap, one thumb nail picking at the other. Her heel tapped against the carriage floor in a sporadic, tentative rhythm.

Despite all his years of training, despite every caution he ever heard, Jonathan couldn't watch her anxiety. If someone had been beside him during his first parade, perhaps he wouldn't have suffered such nervousness. Alissa didn't need a trial by fire. She had him.

Jonathan reached over. With a little finagling, he managed to unclasp her hands and take one inside his palm. "Relax. Smile. I'm here."

"They said I can get down and walk if I feel too nervous." Alissa heaved a breath.

"You may, but at least try to begin." Jonathan gave her fingers a squeeze. "I won't let anything happen. You're safe."

"I'm not worried about that." Alissa nibbled at her ruby-tinted lower lip. "I'm worried they'll all hate me."

"Impossible." Jonathan could have said more, but the carriage gave a soft lurch as it started forward.

Alissa's attention ventured elsewhere, outward, as they crossed from Royal Property into the cordoned-off parade route.

Subjects lined the streets, a mass so thick that Jonathan couldn't see the light through them. Humanity pressed close together to view the figureheads of a monarchy.

Jonathan lifted his free hand to give his first wave. He could only pray that Alissa would remain calm. If she could get past this, she could get past anything else they threw her way. To win the hearts of the people was to win the heart of the nation. Once the nation loved her, Alissa could thrive in the palace.

Lord above, make her thrive.

Chapter 24

Alissa hadn't prepared herself for the sheer amount of people lining the streets. Not to mention a half-dozen television cameras trailing along beside them. She didn't even count the cameras around the other carriages.

She would wager that the King's and Queen's carriage garnered the most attention. Frederick sat alone in a carriage behind them. Beyond that, everything seemed like fanfare and costume. Palace guards, mounted police, a few titled noblemen. The Prime Minister brought up the rear.

All these things, Alissa knew from the short briefing The Queen had given her the day before. Let it never be said that Alissa couldn't memorize her teacher's words.

Jonathan hadn't let go of her hand since they left the palace gates behind. Alissa couldn't thank him enough for that particular comforting gesture. Still, with all these eyes on her, it became hard to keep a smile on her face. Especially when she couldn't tell what any of them thought about her.

After a while, Alissa ventured a look past the cameras and television crews. The onlookers all carried different expressions on their faces. Surprise. Shock. Elation. Anger.

Alissa took a breath to steady her shaking nerves.

Jonathan turned and leaned close to her ear. "Do you need a small break? We can stop and allow you to walk off-camera for a moment."

Alissa thought it over, but she needn't have. If she focused on the cameras for much longer, she wouldn't be able to keep up her smile. She gave a short nod of affirmation.

Jonathan rested his free hand on the side of the carriage and tapped his palm twice.

Guillaume jogged to the driver and spoke only a few words.

The horses whinnied softly as they pulled to a stop.

Jonathan gingerly helped Alissa to her feet and toward the step on her side of the carriage.

Joffrey immediately stepped forward and offered his hand to help her down.

"Take good care of her."

Alissa glanced over her shoulder when she heard Jonathan's comment. He sounded concerned and, though his face bore a smile, his eyes held only somber insistence.

Joffrey dipped his head toward the prince. As soon as Alissa was steady on the street, he released her hand.

"This way, my lady." Joffrey motioned toward a small space between the press and the barriers holding back the public.

Alissa tossed Jonathan a smile. "I won't be long. Just enough to breathe."

"Hurry back." Jonathan chuckled and gave Alissa a small wink. "I'm not a very patient man."

"Trust me, I know." Alissa raised her hand in a half-wave. It wasn't really a goodbye, more like a see-you-later, so she didn't find anything else necessary.

The carriage started rolling again.

Alissa stepped into the safe space behind the cameras and took a deep breath.

Joffrey fell in line behind her.

"Mama, is that the new princess?"

Alissa's step faltered. She turned to see the most precious, cherub-cheeked child staring straight at her. Alissa couldn't help but smile, even though moments before she hadn't wanted to do so.

The child's mother quickly shushed the little girl.

Alissa stepped closer and bent to the girl's level. "What's your name?"

The little girl pulled back. Her thumb and forefinger lifted to rest on her pouty lips.

Alissa looked up to the little girl's mother. "What's her name?"

"Angelique." The answer was accompanied by a small curtsy, as if the woman didn't know what to do with herself.

"It's a beautiful name." Alissa turned her attention back to Angelique. "It's a pleasure to meet you, Angelique."

Angelique's fingers pulled away from her lips, a fraction of an inch. "You talk funny."

"I'm from America. I can't help it." Alissa laughed softly. "I think Prince Jonathan talks funny, too, because he speaks differently than I do."

"Your hands look soft." Angelique pressed up against the barrier. "Can I touch them?"

Alissa looked down at her own hands. Thanks to this morning's manicure, they did look lovely. She couldn't blame the little girl for wanting to know more. With a smile, Alissa held out her hand to the child.

Angelique reached small, pudgy fingers through a slat in the barrier.

Alissa held her little hand as long as she dared before she gently pulled back. "You should come visit the palace sometime, Angelique. Would you like that?"

Angelique nodded. "Then I can be a princess, too."

"Perhaps." Alissa wished she had something to give the little girl, but alas, she came empty-handed. "I'll be sure to bring a present for you next time."

"That's very kind of you, my lady." Angelique's mother dipped another awkward curtsy. To Angelique, she rested a hand on her head. "Say your goodbyes now. Her ladyship needs to move on."

Angelique lifted both hands to wave.

Alissa held her hand out to the girl's mother. "You have a beautiful daughter."

"Thank you, my lady." The mother briefly shook Alissa's hand.

Alissa didn't mean to start anything. In fact, the whole exchange had been innocent. However, Alissa didn't have the heart to refuse the other outstretched hands. These were Jonathan's people. Alissa wanted to love them as much as Jonathan loved them.

One by one, Alissa shook hands and gave greetings. The carriages rolled past at a faster pace, but for the moment she didn't care. For the first time, Alissa felt a true connection with the Veldorian people. Even if it was just shaking hands, Alissa could feel their sincerity.

Until one hand didn't let go.

Alissa pulled up short and gave a gentle tug. Still, the hand didn't release hers. Alissa looked up to the owner of the hand and attempted a smile. "I should move on now. Please let go."

The man said nothing. He simply tightened his grip. His eyes made no sense, dark and brooding and devoid of merriment. With a single tug, the man pulled Alissa flat against the barrier.

Alissa raised her other hand to pry their fingers apart.

The man released her hand, but in the same moment caught both her wrists in his palms.

"Joffrey." Alissa looked behind her, hoping that Joffrey hadn't broken his promise and strayed too far.

The man pulled at Alissa's wrists, using Alissa's body to scrape the barrier a few inches across the concrete.

"Joffrey!" Alissa cried, louder this time.

Joffrey appeared down the road and jogged in Alissa's direction.

Alissa tried to breathe easier. Why wouldn't this man let her go? What did he plan to do here? The press stood feet away from them, yet no one seemed to pay attention. Did they not hear her over the roar of the crowd? Maybe taking a break had been a bad idea.

Joffrey slid to a stop beside Alissa and rested one hand against her back.

Alissa turned to look at him, eyes wide in desperation.

Without a word, Joffrey hefted Alissa up and over to the other side of the barrier.

"Joffrey? Joffrey!" Alissa twisted her head wildly, trying to make sense of what happened. All her fuzzy mind could compute was Joffrey's back as he walked away.

The man from the crowd yanked at Alissa's wrists, giving her no option but to follow him.

Hands pressed in on all sides as he dragged her through the masses. Bodies crushed together and ran into each other. Alissa stumbled behind the man, unable to do anything else. Voices rose around her, but nobody saw. They were all too focused on the parade.

"Let go of me!" Alissa didn't think it would work, but she hoped it would garner a reaction. At least then she could figure out what he wanted.

He didn't react. Not at all. He remained the same stoic, silent threat all the way past the crowd.

A black car sat waiting along a side-street. The man opened the back door and shoved Alissa inside. The door slammed before she could regain her footing to try to escape. The locks clicked.

"So this is where we meet again."

Alissa froze, afraid to look. Yet, her curiosity got the better of her. She swiveled her head to the man on the seat beside her. Someone stately. Someone with an aura of power. Someone who seemed vaguely familiar.

"Who are you?" she asked.

The man chuckled and drew a long inhale of the cigar in his fingers. "Let's go."

Chapter 25

Jonathan maintained his smile and wave with one hand, while the other drummed nervously against his leg. Hadn't it been far too long? Alissa said she would take a short break and come back. How long had it been? Why didn't he wear a watch this morning?

He should focus on his people, but after everything Alissa had been through lately, Jonathan couldn't stop worrying about her.

He spared a glance to Guillaume. He could always ask the man to check in with Alissa's new guard. That seemed like the best idea. Jonathan dropped his hand over the side of the carriage and gave three taps.

Guillaume sauntered closer, his eyes still wandering the crowds and cameras. "Yes, sire?"

"Make sure Alissa feels well. She fell behind a little while ago." Jonathan did his best to maintain his composure.

Guillaume's lips shifted as if he wanted to laugh. "Yes, sir. Give me a few moments and I will report back to you."

Jonathan didn't bother with any thank-yous. The press didn't need to suspect anything about his request. The people needed him to continue smiling and waving.

The carriages approached a T in the road. The parade wavered for a second before the first carriage veered left and picked up its pace.

Tension coiled in the pit of Jonathan's stomach. It took every ounce of strength to remain smiling and not alert the press or the people. In the original plan, the parade veered right. Left meant one thing and one thing only. The emergency route.

Jonathan curled his fingers against the side of the carriage. He didn't like the connotations of this route. He didn't like the foreboding that pervaded his head and heart.

Guillaume wouldn't look his direction, too absorbed in perusing the surrounding area.

Jonathan continued to wave, even when he didn't feel like doing anything but panicking. In times like this, the people needed a strong king, not a blubbering little boy. Jonathan hated that part of the job. Remaining calm in difficult situations.

The parade trailed its way down the street and into the courtyard of one of the city's finest hotels. Jonathan knew the location well. It had been in the briefing. One of the safe locations in case of calamity.

"This way, sire." Guillaume motioned toward the back entrance where they had stopped.

Though Jonathan wanted to ask a million questions, he held his tongue and followed Guillaume's directive. Security multiplied once inside, swarming around Jonathan like bees to a hive. Dread wormed its way into Jonathan's heart. He knew what he had to ask, but he hated even the thought of the answer Guillaume would give.

Security escorted Jonathan to a suite on the top floor. Four guards stepped into the room with Jonathan, while two waited in the hall. Guillaume wasn't among them.

Jonathan stopped to stare down one of the guards. "What's going on?"

The man dipped a bow. "Guillaume will come explain as soon as he finishes briefing His Majesty."

Jonathan didn't like the answer, but he couldn't do anything about it. He could wait. That's what he told himself, but his head didn't take the hint.

Jonathan liked to claim intelligence. Unfortunately, that intelligence meant he could deduce many things. If Alissa were with the parade, she would be in this room with him. Which meant something happened to her. Come to think of it, Jonathan hadn't seen Joffrey either.

The lock on the door beeped. The latch clicked as it opened.

Jonathan shot across the room to greet Guillaume at the door. "What's happened? Where's Alissa?"

Guillaume held up a hand to stop Jonathan before he could continue. With a single crook of his finger, he ushered Frederick into the room, as well.

"What is going on?" Jonathan asked again.

"I thought it would be easier to tell both of you together." Guillaume stepped into the living area. "Please have a seat."

"No, please tell us now." Jonathan didn't think he could sit down if he tried, at this point. He spent his energy trying to keep the people calm. How did Guillaume expect him to remain composed now, in private?

Frederick sighed and settled onto a chair. "You're making him panic, Guillaume. What in the world happened?"

"Your Highnesses, it is my deepest regret to inform you that we seem to have... misplaced Lady Alissa." Guillaume winced as if he knew the backlash that would come next.

"Misplaced?" Jonathan didn't want to think on the inferences declared by that word. "Contact her personal guard. Surely she wandered off on her own. Violet. Violet will know where Alissa is. Frederick, phone Violet."

Frederick sighed at his brother. "I don't have her number."

"You spent an entire day with the woman, how do you not have her number?" The strange revelation momentarily distracted Jonathan from the situation at hand.

Frederick shrugged. "She is oddly dense when it comes to taking hints and rather resilient when it comes to standing her ground."

"Then call the palace and have someone put her on the phone."

"Wouldn't it be best if we keep her from panicking for now?" Frederick looked to Guillaume. "Surely someone at the palace would know if Alissa went back there. Who was her personal guard today?"

"His name is Joffrey Eisel. We cannot contact him, either. A thorough search has begun from the place they were last seen." Guillaume cleared his throat. "His Majesty has instructed we continue with today's scheduled events as though nothing has happened."

"How do you expect me to do so?" Jonathan raked a hand through his perfectly gelled hair. "I cannot continue on knowing that something has happened to Alissa—*again*—and I failed to protect her."

"It is your duty as future king to abide by the traditions and rules," Frederick reminded him.

"You want me to sit back while no one does anything about this? While we throw a party and pretend everything is fine?" Jonathan hated the idea of smiling while Alissa might be scared and alone.

Frederick shook his head. "I never said as much. You have to abide by traditions and rules, but I have leeway. I have a few contacts and I will enlist the help of Alissa's trusted friend. She and I will wrack our brains for her whereabouts while you attend the ball. Leave fashionably early and come find us. I'm positive security will be more than happy to assist me."

"You just said it's better not to upset Violet."

Guillaume raised a hand. "If I may? Alissa's friend is very loyal to her. Though she is emotional, Violet will use every ounce of her power to locate Alissa. If you cannot help with the search yourself, she and His Highness are the next best option. Until we hear more, until there is a call to confirm, we will assume Alissa's life is in imminent danger."

Both princes paused at the way Guillaume had phrased it.

Jonathan scoffed a humorless laugh. "You believe she's been taken as a pawn."

"Of course he does. Why else would he wait for a call to confirm her life isn't in danger?" Frederick rose from his chair. "Guillaume, is there something you aren't telling us?"

Guillaume cleared his throat again. "Nothing has been confirmed, but... it is too coincidental and with everything that's happened..."

"Speak plainly." Jonathan took a step closer. "Explain."

"I shouldn't say anything." Guillaume closed his lips tightly.

Frederick slung an arm over Guillaume's shoulders. "I think it's best if you tell us everything so we can plan accordingly."

Guillaume inhaled through his nose. "I think it might be the Anti-Monarchists."

"No proof?" Frederick absently picked at apiece of fuzz on Guillaume's jacket.

Guillaume shook his head. "Just a hunch."

Jonathan gritted his teeth together. First they tried to kill her and now they took her for... what? Ransom? It didn't make sense.

Why change their plan? Why take her in such a public area? To prove that they were more powerful than the monarchy?

"Alright." Jonathan conceded, knowing what he must do. "Enlist Violet's help, but do not let her out of your sight. Restrain her physically if needed."

"We will work the maps in the security office, don't worry." Frederick released Guillaume's shoulders. "We will find her, Jean. There is no other option."

"Don't call her family until we are sure. Frederick, you will have to ensure Violet doesn't say anything to them until we're ready for them to know."

Frederick gave a two-fingered salute. "Leave it to me. Accept the regency. Don't let them ruin this most auspicious occasion." He turned for the door. "Guillaume, I'll be leaving with Gaspar. Send some extra men if you feel so inclined."

Before Guillaume could answer, Frederick sailed out the door and disappeared. Jonathan wished he had half of Frederick's pervasive confidence. Frederick had only volunteered to help with the search because he knew it would make Jonathan feel better. There was no need for Frederick and Violet to help security do its job. Still, Jonathan was thankful for their help. He only hoped neither injured the other in the process.

"May I speak frankly with Your Royal Highness?" Guillaume asked.

Jonathan nodded. He couldn't do much else right now. The fact that Alissa had disappeared sapped all strength he had mustered.

"I know that it is difficult to live with this knowledge, but I give you my word that we will find her. One way or another. For now... Your Highness, please attempt to hide these facts. For the peace of the country. Until we need their help, it's better that the people don't know about this."

"I know better than to say anything." Jonathan pressed a palm to his forehead. "When will we return to Vitromont?"

"As soon as we are given the all-clear."

"I'll lie down for a few moments." It was a clear lie, but Jonathan had no other excuse to leave the room.

He shut himself in the bedroom and sank to the edge of the bed. Negative thoughts rolled through his head like crashing waves. What if they had killed her already? What if Alissa lost her life because of him? Would he be able to live with the guilt?

A silent plea echoed over and over in his head, the only thing he could think. *Please be safe.*

Chapter 26

Alissa didn't dare speak a word, and the man from the car didn't offer any information either. She could die of curiosity. Alissa winced. That may not have been the best analogy. With the way things had been going today, she might actually die.

Not a pleasant thought. She should try to focus on the current situation.

The car pulled to a stop, but no one moved.

Alissa glanced out the window, unsure where they had parked. Steel pillars and concrete walls rose around them, like an abandoned warehouse she had seen on a movie. Apparently, these people had no originality.

"If you let me go now, you'll probably get away with this." Alissa hated the cheesy line, but it worked in most adventure novels. On the off chance that those novels had been telling the truth, Alissa figured she would give it a shot.

The man laughed aloud. "I wonder how you evaded my men at all, with that level of intelligence."

"I wonder why your men were after me at all. I don't know you or owe you." Alissa couldn't bring up the courage to look at him again. If she did, she might freeze in fear.

"Of course you know me." Strong, stubby fingers wrapped around Alissa's chin and forced her face around to look at him. "Take a good, long look."

Alissa inhaled sharply. His fingers dug into her skin and pressed too tight against her jaw-bones. What would Violet do in this situation? Alissa wracked her brain to think of what snarky remark her best friend would make.

In the end, Alissa locked eyes with the man beside her and arched her brows. "I have no idea who you are."

Alissa couldn't tell if the flash in his eyes bore anger or surprise. Either way, she didn't care much. It made him loosen his grip on her jaw.

"You don't know me? Impossible." The man tore his fingers away from Alissa in order to pick up his cigar. "You're an American, aren't you?"

"So are you. It's your accent." Alissa wished she could make her words stop, but she needed to know what got her into this situation in order to get back out of it.

The man snorted another laugh. "Maybe you're not as dumb as you look, but you're not smart, either. I may work for America, but I'm loyal to whoever pays the most."

A telling monologue. Alissa pressed her lips together while she thought. What would set him off? What would draw more information from his lips?

"Ask what you want. We have a few minutes left." The man took a drag of his cigar. Again.

She might puke if she ever smelled cigar fumes again. Alissa shut her eyes and took a breath. "Why am I here?"

"You heard what you shouldn't."

"Am I going to die?"

"That's not up to me."

"Who is it up to?" Alissa wished she could say she had as much courage as her questions denoted. In reality, she wished she could crawl under a rock and disappear.

The soft purr of an engine echoed against the concrete surrounding them.

"Time for questions is over." The man waved a hand toward the front seat. "Let's get her out of my car. If that woman is here, the others won't be far behind."

The large man in the front seat didn't bother to answer. He simply opened the door and stepped out.

"What woman? What others?" Alissa shied away from the door beside her as it opened. "Tell me what's going on."

The man outside the door wrapped a hand around Alissa's arm.

Alissa yanked out of his grasp. "I won't leave this car until you tell me what's going on!"

The man with the cigar laughed and waved a dismissive hand.

Try as she might to fight it, the man outside her door was much larger and stronger than Alissa. Though she attempted to flail her arms and squirm away, in the end he managed to haul her out of the vehicle.

Alissa's shoes scuffed against the ground as she struggled to remain upright. The click and slam of other car doors opening and closing mingled with the scratching of her desperate attempt at balance.

The man holding her didn't spare time or consideration on Alissa. He yanked her across the hard, rough ground. When she dropped her weight in an attempt to stop their progress, he wrapped his arms around her waist and hoisted her into the air. Try as she might, Alissa couldn't worm her way out of that.

"Being high and mighty didn't serve you so well, after all."

Alissa stopped squirming at the sound of *that woman's* voice. It couldn't be. Jonathan's childhood friend wouldn't betray him like this, no matter how bad she seemed. Even if she hadn't trusted Estrella, Alissa never thought she would stoop this low. She had no need to act like a hooligan.

Alissa took a short, shallow breath before she looked up. Hair that had come loose during her struggle blocked some of her view, but Alissa saw enough.

Estrella sneered, those icy eyes glittering with malice.

"What are you doing here?" Alissa choked on the words.

She already knew. Her life must be in Estrella's hands. Estrella would surely kill Alissa to get what she wanted.

Estrella snorted a humorless laugh. "What am I doing here? Oh, how silly of you. Don't you know who I am?"

Alissa clamped her lips shut. The more she said, the quicker her death. She had to stall for time. Jonathan would find her. She believed in him. In everything they had silently promised to each other. He wouldn't leave her like this. *Let him find me quickly.*

"When I pose a question, you answer." Estrella took a step forward. Her hand flew back as if she would hit Alissa square in the face.

Alissa lifted her chin defiantly. Before she could think to construct a decent comeback, a third and fourth vehicle roared their way onto the warehouse floor.

Every eye turned to look.

Far too many men exited each vehicle, all dressed in dark colors and armed with enormous automatic rifles. They definitely hadn't bought those weapons legally.

Alissa screamed as the man holding her waist tossed her toward the oncoming militia. Her feet hit the pavement before any of them caught her. Her ankle twisted on the way to the ground.

If she looked at it abstractly, Alissa could say the militarized men helped her up. Truthfully, they hauled her to her feet and held her still.

"Complete the deal so we can all get out of this place. There are other things on my schedule." Estrella folded her arms, but she looked angry that she hadn't been able to complete her physical slap.

Alissa tried not to smile in the middle of this dire situation, but if she was going to die anyway, she might as well find a little joy in the small things. At least Estrella wasn't satisfied, either. Alissa had never been vindictive before. She didn't wish anything bad on Estrella. However, seeing Estrella dissatisfied gave Alissa a small measure of morbid relief. At least Alissa wasn't the only one having a bad day.

Dress shoes clicked on the cement. The man from the car emerged from the shadows into the light. "You brought the money?"

One of the men from the vans stepped forward with a duffel bag and tossed it at the henchman's feet.

The man who had held onto Alissa stooped to open it, then gave a nod to the Cigar Man.

Cigar Man smirked. "Complete the transaction."

"She's all yours." The brute rose to his feet and slung the duffel bag over his shoulder.

Estrella turned to go.

The men from the van descended on her.

Without a word, both sets of kidnappers dragged their respective charges toward their own vehicles.

"Wait! Stop!" Estrella scratched at her abductors like an angry cat. "What are you doing? We made a deal!"

"Deals change," Cigar Man threw over his shoulder. "I can't have loose ends."

"I'll kill you!" Estrella kicked at one of the men holding her. "Charles! Charles!"

Estrella's driver—Alissa assumed he was the Charles that Estrella called for—reached for something under his arm.

A shot rang out.

Charles dropped to the ground, his fingers just shy of a gun handle.

Alissa screamed and tried to drop into the fetal position. The men on either side of her kept her upright.

For a brief moment, the entire warehouse went silent. Only the echo of another gunshot broke the stillness.

A river of red flowed from behind the far side of Estrella's car, dispelling any hope Alissa held for Charles' well-being. The thought of what she had witnessed made Alissa nauseous. If they would kill so easily, how would she survive?

"A shame." Cigar Man clucked his tongue.

"Monster!" Estrella spat at him. "I'll be sure to drag you down, one way or another."

"I wish you good luck." The man checked his watch. "Unfortunately, I won't be here to see it. I have a pressing engagement. I can't be late. Take care, gentlemen!"

Alissa barely felt the men on either side of her start to tug and drag again. Her heart hurt for Charles and his family. For everyone who suffered because of this whole plan. She even hurt for Estrella, dragged to the vehicle behind. And, for the first time,

Alissa doubted if the man with the cigar had really been behind it all.

She watched that man crawl into his vehicle. She watched the car drive away. Until someone slid the van door closed and tucked a black hood over Alissa's head.

She didn't know why they bothered. If she learned one thing from books, it came down to this. They had shown her their faces, so she would die. One way or another.

Chapter 27

Jonathan tugged at the bottom of his tuxedo jacket. In a few moments, he would accept a regency from his father. In front of hundreds of Veldorian elites and a few foreign allies. Yet, he couldn't stop thinking about Alissa. Where had she gone? What had happened?

Frederick and Violet hadn't contacted him yet. Jonathan had heard a rumor or two about Violet's dramatic outburst at the news. Frederick seemed to have found a way to calm her down. Jonathan didn't want to know how he did it. It couldn't have been easy. Violet didn't seem the type to let anything go once she had a hold on it.

Surely Guillaume would have contacted him if he knew anything about it, as well. Jonathan took a steadying breath. He couldn't let his fingers shake any more. Even if he was falling apart inside, he had to think about his people. The country needed him. He couldn't fail them. Alissa wouldn't want it.

The ebb and flow of stringed instruments washed over Jonathan like a restorative spring. Yet, as soon as it calmed him, Jonathan found another reason to be anxious. He refused to rest easy until this whole situation got sorted out.

"Jonathan?" The King rose from his seat. "It's time."

Of course. First things first. Jonathan straightened his shoulders. He would not look downcast in front of the world. No matter the turmoil in his head, he would hold his composure together.

The strings came to a lilting halt. A guardsman struck the ground with a staff, twice. The sound echoed around the grand ballroom, drawing everyone's attention.

"His Majesty, The King and His Royal Highness, Crown Prince Jonathan Henry Christophe of the house of Manon."

The doors swung open.

Jonathan pasted a blank expression on his face and marched into the hall. Step for step, always in line with his father. Chin high, as a royal should hold himself. Shoulders back to symbolize the pride of the nation. He couldn't afford to think past the basic lessons he learned as a child. If he thought, he might melt down again. Jonathan realized he couldn't show weakness. It didn't make hiding his panic any easier.

Up three steps. Across the stage to the podium.

Jonathan stopped next to the stand and turned to face the audience with military precision. Various reporters and a few scattered cameras greeted Jonathan and The King with bright lights.

The King braced his hands on either side of the podium. At first glance, it was a relaxed posture, but Jonathan knew better. He saw the tight grip his father kept. As if to center himself.

"My loyal subjects and dear friends," The King began, "I will make my statements brief, as I have no desire to steal the spotlight from this grand Heritage Festival tradition. I wish only to bring more reasons for our rejoicing this evening." The King looked sideways to Jonathan.

Jonathan gave a half-nod, reassuring his father that all would be well. That they stood on the same side.

The King lifted his lips in a smile. "Due to personal health issues, I have realized it is no longer within my power to reign as the sovereign this country deserves. Since I cannot offer my all any longer, I have presented my opinion to the Ministers of the Crown. I will step down from my position. Henceforth, my eldest son, the Crown Prince, will step into my place and rule as Prince-Regent until such a time as the throne is rightfully his to possess. I hope you all give him your support."

Applause erupted sporadically throughout the room. Some appeared surprised, others elated.

The King took a step back from the podium and dipped a half-bow.

Jonathan followed suit, bending at a forty-five degree angle. He counted to three before he straightened. Now the higher-ranking man on the stage, Jonathan lifted a hand to signal the music to start up again. It felt awkward, at least until everyone turned back to their dancing and socializing.

The King patted a hand against Jonathan's shoulder. "You did well. Go accept their congratulations."

"Yes, sir." Jonathan didn't want to spend his evening with a fake smile on his face, but he had little choice. In a few hours, he could slip out. Until then, he had to endure. It was his least favorite part of the job that came with his title.

The King went to his queen's side.

Jonathan swallowed in an attempt to silently fight the ache in his heart. No matter what happened, he had to be there for the people. Frederick and Violet would find something. If anyone in the palace needed to find something as badly as Jonathan, it was those two. They were the most invested in this.

With a sigh, Jonathan stepped down from the stage and ventured into the crowd.

The Prime Minister met him first. Strangely, Estrella didn't tag along at her father's side. She must have found something better to do.

Jonathan attempted a smile. "It's a pleasure to see you at such an event."

"I can't say no to a royal invitation, can I?" The Prime Minister extended a hand. "Congratulations on your regency. I look forward to working alongside you for the remainder of my term."

"Thank you." Jonathan shook the man's hand. He didn't seem as upset as he had at lunch the other day. All for the better. "I look forward to working with you, too."

"As for your situation with my daughter..." The Prime Minister shook his head. "It's a personal matter. I refuse to mix business and privacy. It's between the two of you and I shouldn't have interfered. My apologies."

"You didn't know the conversations she and I had with each other." Jonathan let his hand fall back to his side. "My sincerest apologies for misleading you or your daughter. It will not happen again in the future. I will be clear with all my intentions."

The Prime Minister laughed softly. "I will hold you to that, your highness. I've kept you too long. Please, join the festivities." He stepped out of Jonathan's path.

Jonathan spared one last smile before he stalked into the thick of the crowd. One after another, a whole host of Veldorian elites offered their congratulations. A few of the women suggested a dance or a drink. Jonathan politely refused them all. He had no intention of dancing when Alissa might be dying.

"Congratulations, your highness!" An over-exuberant man with an American accent approached Jonathan from the side. "On behalf of the United States of America, let me offer all the best to you."

Jonathan turned slightly, enough to size the man up. He was fairly tall, a bit out of shape, and smelled of a substance Jonathan couldn't quite place. "May I ask who you are to be offering congratulations on behalf of an entire country? I know the President, and you are not him."

"No, of course I'm not." The man held out a thick hand. "Senator Ron Lenley, at your service."

In the name of manners, Jonathan shook Ron's hand. Briefly. "I don't remember your name on the list of attendees."

"Well, I happened to be in the country. The palace extended an unofficial invitation when I arrived. Either way, thank you for letting me in." He laughed, but it felt hollow and shallow. "I hope Veldoria will continue to have excellent relations with us in the future."

"I see no reason to have any bad relations. Our two countries are allies, after all."

"Your Highness." Guillaume jogged to Jonathan's side and leaned close to the prince's ear. "It's about Joffrey."

"If you'll excuse me." Jonathan nodded at Ron and the man behind him. He didn't have time to spare for them. If he was going to waste time for any American tonight, it would be Alissa.

Guillaume led the way out a side door and down a hall.

"What's going on?" Jonathan asked as the doors closed behind them.

"Joffrey returned." Guillaume spat the words like venom. He probably felt responsible for the young guard's behavior, whatever it had been.

Jonathan didn't want to think that the palace's own employee had any part to play in Alissa's disappearance, but he couldn't afford assumptions. They would investigate every possible conclusion, even the one that made the least sense.

"Where is he?"

"This way." Guillaume slid his identification card through a keypad and pushed open the secure door.

Jonathan stormed down the hall. Fluorescent lightbulbs flickered in the ceiling above him. Jonathan rarely came to this part of the palace. He had been here too often lately.

Frederick waited outside the last door on the left. He pushed off the wall when he saw his brother approaching.

"Where's Joffrey?" Jonathan bit out through gritted teeth. The longer he thought about the man's failed assignment, the angrier he became.

Frederick tipped his head toward the door. "Have a look."

Jonathan shoved the door open and let out a breath.

Joffrey lay on a cot, an IV attached to one arm. His face bore bruises and swelling, along with a gash along his hairline. Consciousness didn't seem to be in Joffrey's near future.

"Where did you leave Violet?" Jonathan shot the question in Frederick's general direction.

"She's in the Hub watching camera footage." Frederick folded his arms across his chest. "He came back by himself, but..."

"I don't have a good feeling, either." Jonathan looked at his brother for the first time since the door opened. "Let me speak with Guillaume. Go make sure Violet doesn't do anything irrational."

"You mean other than hitting and kicking me upon learning the news of Alissa's abduction?" Frederick ran his fingers back through his dark hair. "I have people in place to make sure she stays in line."

"I don't doubt that. She isn't a one-woman show, however. Go help. At least she won't be alone."

Frederick nodded and shot one last glare in Joffrey's general direction.

Jonathan waited until he heard Frederick's bootsteps fade in the distance. He turned to Guillaume. "Tell me what's wrong with this picture."

Guillaume perused the sleeping man from head to to and then made eye contact with Jonathan. "His hands."

"His hands," Jonathan confirmed. "Call me the moment he wakes up. He and I need to have a nice, long chat. Find me evidence."

"It will be my pleasure." Guillaume snarled.

Jonathan stormed out of the room, fully expecting Guillaume to take care of locking up their new suspect. If Joffrey had done anything to assist Alissa's disappearance, Jonathan would personally ensure he was prosecuted to the full extent of the law. One didn't simply mess with royalty—with a nation—and expect to get away with it. Joffrey, of all people, must know that.

.

Chapter 28

Alissa abandoned any plans of escape after the dark-clothed men got her into the van. There were too many of them and she didn't know enough skills. Besides, now Estrella was a problem, too. Why did they want that idiot?

"Sorry," Alissa apologized to no one in particular. She meant it for Estrella, for calling her an idiot. Alissa had always thought of herself as a nice person, so it pained her to think such terrible thoughts about someone. Aside from not liking Alissa, Estrella hadn't done much wrong.

Okay, so she had something to do with the kidnapping, too, but it's not like she did the illegal part.

Alissa sighed. She couldn't lie to herself. It didn't work. Estrella gave her the creeps in more ways than one.

No one had bothered to take the hood off once they pulled Alissa out of the van. All Alissa knew was that they put her in some kind of chair and that this room had way too many drafts. Her toes tingled with cold. Her ankle throbbed where she had twisted it. Alissa wanted nothing more than to go home.

Somewhere nearby, a door opened and slammed shut again. Shoes clicked across the floor.

Someone yanked the hood from Alissa's head.

Alissa blinked at the sudden bright light. They could have at least warned her. She looked up, expecting to see one of the men. Instead, she met Estrella's eyes.

Her questions must have shown on her face, because Estrella chuckled. "I see our little kitten is confused."

"Why are you walking around all free and I'm like... this?" Alissa wiggled her arms, trying to loosen the bindings on her wrists. She only succeeded in pushing the zip-ties farther into her skin.

"You don't think I would be stupid enough to trust that senator, do you?" Estrella laughed outright. "I always have another plan. He's been trying to double-cross me from day one. I'm not a fool."

"So the whole kidnapping was just...?"

"A plan?" Estrella shrugged and tossed the hood onto a nearby table. "Something like that. They were my connections to start with. We're on good terms. They need my help for something, is all. It's the least I can do."

"Then what about the other guy?" Had she called him a senator? Maybe that's why he looked familiar. Even if Alissa didn't watch current news, Violet did. Alissa probably saw him on the television screen.

Estrella brushed off a chair by the wall and pulled it toward the center of the room. "I have my ways to take care of him. Don't worry, he won't get away with it."

"And your other friends?" Alissa glanced toward the door.

Estrella settled into the chair she dragged over and folded one long leg over the other. "They don't want anything much. Just an end to the monarchy."

That wasn't much? What kind of crazy person had Alissa run into? Even with her limited knowledge of kingdoms, monarchies, and hierarchies, Alissa knew it wouldn't be easy to topple a nation.

"What does that mean?"

"Wasn't I clear enough?" Estrella inspected her nails. "They need my father to pass a motion, so here I am."

"If he passes it, isn't it over then? Why do they want me here?"

"Oh, dear, you are naive. If you haven't figured it out yet, I think it's best if you don't strain yourself."

Alissa glared at Estrella. Did Estrella call her stupid? It felt like Estrella dissed her in some way. As if Estrella had ever done anything else. If Violet were here, she would have some snappy response to the insult. Alissa's overloaded brain wouldn't focus long enough to come up with anything.

Estrella glanced up. "You shouldn't be here more than a few days."

"And after that?"

She shrugged. "I don't know the rest of the plan. I supply the connections, not the strategy."

"For someone who insists that she loves Jonathan, you're doing a lot of things to hurt him."

"Are you saying that because you think you'll die?" Estrella laughed again. "Look at it from my perspective. If the monarchy ends, I don't lose anything. My family is independently wealthy, my father will hold the country together while we restructure, and Jonathan will only have me left to lean on."

"You're delusional." Alissa stared at the beautiful blonde, honestly scared for her own safety.

Estrella shrugged. "Aren't we all fools in love?"

What kind of person ruined another's life just to get together with them? That wasn't love, that was obsession. Estrella had a case of mental illness that Alissa didn't dare to diagnose. One wrong move and Estrella might well and truly snap. It would be best to change the subject.

"I get why you don't like me, but why drag a senator into this?"

"He approached me." Estrella stood to her feet. "I think that's all you need to know. You should prepare for the worst. These fellows aren't known for releasing prisoners."

"I'm not a prisoner. Just a hostage."

"You should already consider yourself lucky. They don't keep this kind of hostage very often. You've already lived longer than you should." Estrella strutted toward the door. "I'll see if I can convince them to bring you something to eat. Don't expect much from me."

Alissa rolled her eyes. She had never expected anything from Estrella. Least of all kindness.

As the door slammed and the deadbolt clicked, all Alissa could do was pray for help. One way or another, she would get out of this. If she had to die to save the things Jonathan loved most, so be it. Alissa wouldn't lie. She feared death. But, more than that, Alissa feared how Jonathan would react to losing everything.

⛤

Morning came bright and clear, much to Jonathan's chagrin. It felt more fitting for clouds to gather and rain to fall. With each passing hour, their chances of finding Alissa alive—or at all—diminished.

Jonathan glanced around the room. His bow-tie still lay where he tossed it the evening before. Security personnel flitted around the room, making phone calls and checking videos.

Sometime during the early morning hours, Violet had fallen asleep at one of the computer desks.

Frederick still sat in a chair at the conference table, his feet propped on the tabletop. He had slept for a while in the wee hours of the morning. Now, he scrolled through a laptop computer, searching for God-knew-what. Jonathan didn't dare ask. Frederick cultivated connections that Jonathan couldn't fathom.

Jonathan rubbed a hand over his eyes. He had duties today, but he couldn't quite bring himself to leave the Hub. Though he could trust Guillaume to do his best, Jonathan wanted to have his own hand in the whole situation. Keeping an eye on it from a distance didn't suit him.

Besides, this morning he would have to send for Alissa's family. He couldn't hide this from them any longer. If something happened to Alissa, they deserved to hear the news firsthand. Even if Jonathan hated to be the bearer of bad news, he had no choice.

Violet barely lifted her head from her arms. "Is it morning?"

"You should sleep a little longer," Frederick shot over his shoulder in her general direction.

Jonathan stood to his feet. As exhausted as he was, the rest of them must be even more tired. For Violet to sleep when her best friend had disappeared, she must have fully worn herself out.

"I'm up now. No use going back to sleep." Violet ran a hand back through her hair and pushed away from the desk. Her chair swiveled as it rolled toward Frederick's side. "How's the search going?"

"As well as can be expected. Whoever masterminded this knew what they were doing." Frederick sighed.

Violet leaned her elbows on her knees and rested her chin in her hands. "Or you're just an idiot."

"Not likely." Frederick rolled his eyes.

"What can I do to help?"

Frederick shook his head. "I don't have anything for you to do."

"I do." Jonathan made eye contact with Violet. "I have something for you to do. A small favor, if you will oblige me."

"Spill it, what's up?" Violet shot to her feet, as if Jonathan might ask her to run an errand.

Frederick lifted his eyes in a silent question, but he quickly went back to his computer.

Jonathan folded his hands behind his back. He hated to ask for this favor, but he had no one else who could accomplish the task. "I need you to make a telephone call for me."

"To whom?" Violet shoved her messy hair out of her face again.

"Alissa's family." Jonathan cleared his throat. "I will be sending a private charter to collect them. It should arrive this evening. I would like it if you refrain from saying anything about what has happened. I would rather tell them face-to-face."

"Good luck keeping her mouth shut," Frederick muttered.

Violet swatted a hand against his head. "You can stay out of this, *Freddie.* I can keep a secret, don't worry your spoiled little head."

"Apologize when I'm right."

"Not gonna happen." Violet marched to Jonathan's side of the room. "You want me to call right now?"

"I know it will be early for them, but we should bring them to Veldoria as soon as possible."

Jonathan left it at that. He didn't want to beg and plead, but he would if he had to. He felt a keen sense of responsibility for Alissa's abduction, it was only right that he bring her parents to Veldoria. Better to be near when they found Alissa, rather than half a world away.

Frederick dropped his feet from the table to the floor. "If she calls at this hour, won't they know it's an emergency?"

Jonathan had to admit, he hadn't thought that far ahead. He only thought so far as to decide that Alissa's family should be nearby.

Violet dug her phone out of her pocket. "It's fine, I'll call Cody instead."

"Cody is the brother?" Frederick's eyes never left the computer screen, his question indifferent.

Violet nodded. "He's dense, so he won't question it."

Cody hadn't seemed that way to Jonathan, but he could be wrong. Aside from a few interactions at Alissa's home, he and Cody had never spent time together. Violet would know better. Jonathan trusted her to take care of the matter.

Besides, Violet had dialed Cody's number before Jonathan had time to protest. To Jonathan's relief, she put it on speakerphone.

Cody answered on the fourth ring. "To what do I owe this displeasure?"

"We have a proposition and I didn't want to scare your mom and dad at this hour." Violet settled her phone on the table.

"So you called to scare me, instead?"

"Pretty much." Violet rolled her lips together, the first sign of nervousness she had displayed. "The pretty rich boys want to fly you guys over here."

"Boys? Plural?" Cody cleared his throat. "There's more than one of them?"

"Yeah, there's a brother. That's not the point." Violet blew out a breath. "Apparently they're sending a jet."

"Something's wrong, isn't it?"

"Why would you ask that?"

"Because you're the one calling, not Alissa. It's not like you, Queen Bee."

Violet rolled her eyes. "I..." She looked to Jonathan for help.

Jonathan shrugged his shoulders. He didn't have a clue how to distract Alissa's brother. If he pushed the matter, they would have to tell him. Not ideal, but sometimes situations called for difficult decisions.

Frederick set his computer down and leaned toward the phone. His gaze lifted, dark mischief aimed straight at Violet. "So, you think I'm pretty?"

"Is that the brother? Is this on speaker?"

Violet took another breath. "Yeah. Your problem?"

"Ugh. Fine. What time is the jet coming? We'll be there."

Violet looked to Jonathan again.

This time, Jonathan pressed his palms to the table and leaned forward. "I will have her text you the time and place. Please don't be late."

"Yeah, whatever. You better be taking care of my sister. And Violet..." Cody paused. "Stop behaving like yourself. Grow up, already."

"Says the baby. See you when I see you. I'm hanging up." Violet stabbed the *end call* button. She lifted her gaze to Frederick, who had turned away as soon as he instigated discord. "Thanks. I ran out of ways to avoid the question."

Frederick shrugged. "It was the most immediate solution to the problem. We didn't have time to explain. You shouldn't think that you need to answer the question I posed."

"I wasn't going to answer it anyway." Violet shoved her phone back into her pocket. "Anything else?"

Jonathan shook his head. "I need to get to work. Call me if you find anything."

"We have it well in hand. I'm waiting on a response from my source." Frederick stood to his feet and stretched. "At least trust me. I already told Gaspar not to let the little vixen out of his sight. She isn't going to get away with any irrational behavior."

Jonathan smiled sadly at his brother. Frederick was more than capable of this, but Jonathan still felt bad going to work with everything unresolved. Still, he had no choice. A country didn't cease to function because one woman disappeared. Today, Jonathan wanted nothing more than the space to breathe, but a king's job was merciless, devoid of any breathing room.

"Thank you for doing this, Frederick. Violet, as well." Jonathan snatched his bow-tie and jacket from the chair nearest him.

Before either could say anything else, Jonathan left the room. He refused to get sappy today. If he let any emotion take over, he would lose his composure. He had to hold it together, no matter how bad the situation. Alissa wouldn't want him to spiral into oblivion.

A quick stop by his residence gave Jonathan time to shower, change, and steady his shaking nerves. Today, he would take over his father's work. Decisions on royal appearances and events. Signatures on bills passed by Parliament. Matters of state that required a diplomatic hand. Jonathan didn't have the energy for any of it, but for the people's sake he wouldn't ruin his first day as Prince-Regent.

"Frederick will find her," Jonathan reminded himself. He didn't trust anyone in the world as much as he trusted Frederick. Every- thing would work out.

Jonathan dragged his feet on the way to his new office. Why did everything have to happen right as he stepped into his destined role? Why did everything go wrong?

Even though they had furnished his office richly, luxuriously, Jonathan couldn't appreciate it. He sank into the plush chair behind a mahogany desk and closed his eyes.

"Sire."

Jonathan bolted upright. His eyes flew open.

Markum dipped his head in a bow and closed the office door behind himself. "There is much work to be done today. However..." his sentence trailed off.

Jonathan knit his brow. What could possibly make Markum so speechless? A quick perusal of Markum's dress and stance didn't present anything amiss. "Spit it out. What's wrong?"

"I think Your Highness should see this." Markum strode to the desk and set his tablet atop it. "It seems urgent."

Jonathan picked up the offered tablet to see a paused video. "What is this?"

"Please watch it."

With a nod, Jonathan tapped the middle of the screen and gave the video his full attention.

Four men stood on each side. One side, with their backs to the camera. The other side, fully exposed. Between them sat a crate.

Someone from the visible side pried the crate open with a crowbar. The contents were perfectly in sight of the camera. Piles and piles of weapons in all shapes and sizes.

Jonathan paused the video, irate. "Do we know where this took place?"

"We're working on it. He seems to be the one selling. They give him money for the goods later in the video. Considering the weapons are identical to those used in the attack against you and Alissa, we think the buyers are with the Anti-Monarchists." Markum reached out and tapped the face of one of the men. "We're also looking into his identity."

Jonathan looked closer. A growl pooled in his throat and worked its way out his lips. "No need. Bring me Guillaume."

Markum bowed and headed for the door.

Jonathan glared at the video. Of course something else had gone wrong today. Since it might have something to do with the attack at the restaurant, it only fueled the fire of Jonathan's wrath.

Jonathan pressed a hand to his heart. It burned and ached all at the same time. He wanted to cry out in frustration, but he didn't dare. He had too many questions to ask and too many explanations to hear.

Guillaume didn't knock on the door, he entered unannounced. "Yes, your highness?"

Jonathan shoved the tablet toward the far side of the desk. "Why did the palace invite this man to the ball?"

"Who is he?" Guillaume ventured closer and lifted the tablet to look at the picture.

"He claims to be a Senator." Jonathan leaned back in his chair. If he stood, he might explode.

Guillaume looked up from the tablet. "He is. You met him during your visit to the United States. He attended the charity function where you spoke."

"Are you sure?" Jonathan didn't remember meeting him, but then again he had been preoccupied with the safety of a bright-but-queasy woman at the time.

Guillaume tossed the tablet back onto the desk. "I'm sure."

"Is he still in the country?" Jonathan set his jaw. He thought he would be able to do his job while in the middle of turmoil, but he had lied to himself. He had to intervene in the situation.

Guillaume shrugged a shoulder. "Probably."

"Bar him from leaving the country. Find him and bring him to the palace. Inform the police, as well, as they will be taking him into custody when we're through with him." Jonathan stood to his feet, his mind made up. "Markum!"

Markum opened the door and stepped over the threshold.

"Call an emergency press conference. I will write my own statement." Jonathan checked his watch. "Let's schedule it for an hour from now."

Both Markum and Guillaume had been with Jonathan since his teen years. They knew his temper. They knew when to leave him alone and when to push him. This time, neither spoke a word. They simply bowed and left to fulfill their respective duties.

Chapter 29

Alissa tapped her feet in an attempt to get feeling back into her toes. She didn't know how long she had been holed up in this room, but at some point she nodded off. Between the anxiety over the parade and the stress of this abduction, Alissa figured she must have been exhausted. Otherwise, she would never have fallen asleep. She didn't trust anyone around here enough to leave herself in their care.

Only one window let in any light. Because of that, strange shadows shifted along the streaks of sun. Dust and mold danced in the air, mocking Alissa with their freedom.

Too bad she couldn't see the full 360-degree view of the room. There might be something behind her that could be of some help. Even Alissa knew she needed a plan to get out of this place. Just in case Jonathan didn't come. The worst-case scenario.

In order to do anything, she first had to get rid of the stupid zip-ties on her wrists. Alissa jerked her wrists as far apart as they would go. Pain shot to the ends of her fingers and up her arms. A cry fell from her lips.

Alissa squeezed her eyes shut and waited for the feeling to subside. Something warm and liquid trailed its way down her fingers and drip, drip, dripped to the floor.

Alissa stopped struggling against the zip-ties. She wouldn't be able to break them like this. Especially not with raw and bleeding wrists. She would have to wait for them to cut her free.

She would get her chance. As long as she waited patiently.

Which turned out to be harder than Alissa anticipated.

Each second ticked by with the weight of hours. Feet shuffled outside the door. Voices rose and fell in whispered dialogues. No one spoke loud enough for Alissa to hear. Not for a long time. Until one shrill voice broke the silence.

"Do you want her to die before you reach your objective?" Strange, that Estrella would be the one to defend Alissa.

A man's voice answered, no less angry. "You're an idiot. Why didn't you tell me about this law before?"

"I don't write the laws. I simply alert others to their presence. If you want to succeed, she has to live."

"Feed her yourself."

"She won't eat food that I give her. I'm more likely to poison her."

"I wish I had thought to poison you."

"Pity that it's too late."

"Never say never."

The door crashed open against the wall.

Alissa flinched.

The man that marched in held himself like a general. Straight spine, chin up, anger and death in his gaze. He crossed the room in a few long strides. With a bang, the tray he carried crashed onto the table next to Alissa.

"The lady is insisting we keep you nourished. I can't argue with her logic, but I'm not a fan of her idea, so do not try anything foolish."

Alissa glared at his boots instead of his face. "If Lady Estrella sent it, I don't want it."

"She said you would say that. We shall see if hunger wins over hatred."

"Who are you, anyway?"

"No one to be trifled with." The man pulled a long knife from a sheath on his thigh. He shook it in front of Alissa's face. "No funny business."

Alissa kept her lips clamped firmly shut.

The man huffed a laugh and circled around to the back of the chair.

With utmost relief, Alissa felt the zip-ties loosen and then fall away. She didn't waste time thinking about injuries or consequences.

Alissa shot to her feet and raced for the open door.

The man reached out and tugged at her arm, pulling her momentum in the opposite direction.

Alissa lost her balance. Her already twisted ankle gave out. She hit the ground. Hard.

For a long moment, Alissa found she couldn't draw a breath. She gasped helplessly for the next intake of oxygen.

The man stood over her and tucked his knife away. "I told you not to try anything."

Alissa finally managed to take a short, wheezing breath.

The man reached down and hauled her to her feet. "You can sit here and eat or I can tie you to the bed for a nap. That's only because I'm considerate."

Alissa gasped another breath, wincing at the pain radiating through her body. "I... I'll eat." She barely managed the words, but she needed nourishment to remain strong.

"Fine." The man dragged the chair to the table and dropped Alissa onto its seat. "Then eat."

Alissa didn't like people watching her while she did things, but she didn't have a choice. She lost her chance at escape the minute she failed her first attempt. They wouldn't let her out of their sight now. Even Alissa knew that. They had never been stupid.

ಬೂಣ

Jonathan straightened his tie clip. Today, he didn't have time for nerves or anxiety. Today, he would solve things.

The press had done a spectacular job responding to the call for an urgent conference. A good thing, since Jonathan intended for the entire nation to see this interview. He needed to get the word out, one way or another.

Markum stood in the corner behind Jonathan. He seemed displeased, but at this juncture Jonathan didn't care. Markum would do as Jonathan instructed. A faithful aide, Markum never failed to remain loyal to the prince he served, no matter what Jonathan asked of him..

The minute hand on a nearby clock ticked as it moved.

Jonathan looked back at Markum. "It's time."

"Are you certain about this?" Markum pushed his glasses up his nose.

Jonathan nodded. "I'm certain."

Markum sighed, but said no more about it. With a sure march, he sailed through the door and behind the podium. Camera flashes popped and clicked. Fingernails clacked over keyboards. Video cameras rose to cameramen's shoulders.

Markum leveled his gaze somewhere in the middle of the room. "His Royal Highness, the Crown Prince, will be reading from a prepared statement. We will not be accepting any questions." With a respectful bow, Markum took a step back.

Jonathan marched to the podium that Markum had vacated. He had been the center of attention at a thousand press conferences, but never one like this. Tension hung so thickly in the air that he could taste it. Everything rode on the next few moments.

Jonathan set a black folder on the podium and flipped it open. His prepared statement. It was now or never. "Yesterday morning, in the midst of our nation's most joyous celebration, a terrible tragedy befell the royal family. Due to circumstances not yet known to the Royal Investigative Taskforce, Alissa Cassidy disappeared and has not yet been found. As future ruler of this country, I deeply regret that something like this has happened on Veldorian soil. As Alissa Cassidy's protector and future husband, I am devastated."

Jonathan paused to regain his composure. A future king did not cry in front of his subjects. He refused to show that amount of weakness and vulnerability to his enemies, whoever they may be.

"The palace will consider any request made by her captors, should they contact us. In the meantime, I ask that my loyal and kind subjects understand the gravity of this situation." Jonathan lifted his chin, removing his gaze from his statement and instead revealing it to the people. "If any of the people saw or heard something suspicious during the parade, I would urge you to contact the palace, as well. I am asking this favor of you, please. As it is my duty to help you, please assist me in finding her." A lump welled up in Jonathan's throat. A ticking time bomb of emotion. "That is all."

The folder clapped loudly as Jonathan shut it. His shoes clicked against the floor on his way out.

For the first time in their lives, the media didn't shower him with questions and demands. The room behind him remained eerily silent, an echo of their sovereign's breaking heart.

Markum followed Jonathan back through the halls, toward the Royal Administrative Offices. Neither said a word. Neither dared to utter what they were thinking.

"Jean!" Frederick's voice echoed down the corridor.

Jonathan stopped in his tracks. Frederick should be in the security offices, working. What brought him to the administrative offices? Jonathan spun to face him. "What's wrong?"

"The Prime Minister is on the phone. Something is going on. He sounds panicked." Frederick came to a stop beside Jonathan. "I think you should speak to him."

"What line is he on?" Jonathan took a step toward his office doors.

Frederick held out a cell phone. "He phoned me directly."

A frightening turn of events. Even though the Prime Minster was an old family friend, he never phoned Frederick or Jonathan directly. He always used the palace lines. For him to break his own protocol meant he must truly be desperate.

Jonathan snatched the phone from Frederick's grasp. "Prime Minister."

"My sincerest apologies, Jonathan. This is something that can be said only over a secure line such as this."

"Has something happened?" Jonathan wracked his brain for information that might tip him off to anything amiss. Last time he saw the Prime Minister, everything seemed fine.

"I'm going to help pass the anti-monarchy bill."

Jonathan blinked, stunned. "Sir?"

"It has nothing to do with you or your family, but everything to do with mine."

"I'm afraid I don't understand." Jonathan tried to wrap his brain around it. He really tried. The Prime Minister had never been hostile, so why now?

"The Anti-Monarchist faction has Estrella. If I pass this bill, they assure me that she will be returned unharmed." A pause. "I know you may not like her right now, but she's the only family I have left."

"Estrella went missing?" Jonathan would have thought the Prime Minister would have told him such important news.

"We found her car and her driver, Charles, this morning. He had been shot, and a note left on his body. Estrella would be returned in exchange for passing the bill."

Jonathan had always known that the Anti-Monarchists didn't mind killing first and asking questions later. He never expected them to be so blatant about it.

First Alissa. Now Estrella. What did the Anti-Monarchists think they were doing? What plan required both women? Clearly they meant to use them as pawns, since Jonathan had received neither a ransom note nor a body.

That's when it finally hit him. A very old law and a very constant tradition. For the first time since her disappearance, Jonathan held a bit of hope in his heart that Alissa would survive this.

"Pass the bill. Get Estrella back."

Frederick took a step forward, his mouth open to protest.

Jonathan held up a hand to stop him. "Prime Minister, do as they've said. We will handle everything else on our end."

"I am sorry, your highness."

"I know. I do not hold this against you. Proceed. Quickly." Jonathan didn't wait for any more of an answer. He merely ended the call and handed the cellphone back to Frederick.

Frederick trailed Jonathan toward his office. "What are you thinking? Why would you allow him to pass a bill such as that? We'll be out of a home and the country in chaos!"

"No, we won't." Jonathan left his office doors open so Frederick could follow him inside.

Frederick kept step at Jonathan's side. "What do you mean?"

"The bill doesn't go into effect because it passes in parliament." Jonathan dropped into his plush desk chair. "The ruling sovereign has to sign it. *I* have to sign it, for it to be effective."

Frederick huffed a wry laugh. "The reason they took Alissa."

"They have to make me sign it, so they will use her as a bargaining chip. We will use that to our advantage. Do not tell Violet just yet. Let's wait until the situation seems clearer." Jonathan breathed a deep breath. At last. A glimmer of light at the end of the tunnel. "Where is Guillaume?"

"He went to apprehend your senator friend."

Oh, yes. Jonathan had forgotten about that scoundrel. "He isn't my friend. Put Joffrey in an interview room, as well. I have questions."

"So do I." Frederick snarled. "But we'll need physical evidence. There isn't enough."

Jonathan met his brother's wrathful gaze with one of his own. They had trusted Joffrey, and he had let them both down. There would be no compassion or mercy if Joffrey had anything to do with Alissa's abduction. Because, if he had, Joffrey had betrayed them in the most personal of ways.

Chapter 30

The annoying clicks and dings of cellphones and security grated on The Boss's ears. Airports were such a nuisance. Thankfully, he would get out of the hustle and bustle soon enough. With all his loose ends tied up neatly, he could relax now.

In a few minutes, he would be back on a plane and away from all those vexing doofuses. Let them take care of their own problems, now that he wasn't a part of it anymore.

"Sir." The Boss's only loyal henchman motioned him forward in the line.

The Boss presented his ticket and identification to the guard before him. "Beautiful weather for this time of year, isn't it?"

The security guard glanced up, then back down. "If you will wait right over here, sir." He motioned to the spot beside himself.

The Boss hesitated. Something didn't feel right about this. He had never been pulled out of line at the airport. Not once in his life. What idiot dared to interrupt his schedule now? The guard didn't even return his identification. Who dared to hold him hostage?

"Sir?" His henchmen uttered the question in a tone devoid of sympathy, but full of concern.

The Boss pasted his smile on and took a step to the side.

The guard inclined his head in thanks. He directed his next question toward the henchman. "Are you with him?"

The henchman gave a nod.

"You step aside, too."

The Boss's spine stiffened. The hairs on the back of his neck tingled, warning him that something felt very, very wrong. He should escape. Get away before something happened. He hesitated a moment too long.

A small platoon of men marched straight to the security desk. The Boss recognized a few of them. They had been patrolling the brat's dance party the other night. This could mean good things or bad things. His gut instinct leaned toward the bad.

"Senator Ron Lenley?" The man at the front of the group stepped forward. "The Prince-Regent would like a word before you leave. If you would accompany me back to Vitromont Palace."

The words were meant to be diplomatic and mannered. The tone with which they were delivered depicted anything but pleasantries. They knew something.

The henchman must have felt the same odd energy. He launched forward, aiming for the man who had spoken.

The royal guard caught and twisted the henchman until he had trapped him on his knees.

The guard looked up at Ron with vengeance in his gaze. "I would suggest you do not make it any harder on yourself or your subordinate. The Prince-Regent would like a word."

Ron chuckled, a haughty sound even he disliked. "I'm not a Veldorian citizen."

"Would you like me to arrest you as an international criminal? I brought the police." The guard arched a brow, daring Ron to argue.

"I would like to see you try."

"Come back with me and we'll discuss it civilly, away from the ears of a multitude of civilians. You wouldn't want your dirty secrets getting out, would you?"

Ron hated that he had a point. It would be easier to contain any possible evidence if they didn't talk where rumors might begin. "I suppose I don't have a choice, do I? I'm disappointed in how your Prince-Regent handles matters."

The man in charge handed the henchman off to another guard and took a step closer to Ron. "He wouldn't have to handle it this way if you didn't get involved. It was a mistake, to upset him by using lady Alissa."

"Who?" Ron grinned. Plausible deniability would get one everywhere. No one knew he had been part of that woman's abduction. No one needed to know. He would get off Scot-free, in the end.

The guard grinned right back at him. "There's a car waiting. Let's go."

With his henchman out of the way and his passport confiscated, Ron didn't have much of a choice. With a resigned nod of his head, Ron stepped forward to go with the palace security. He would figure a way out of it later.

A feat which felt a little more hopeless with each guard that fell in line around him.

"May I ask your name?" Ron gave the sturdy, in-charge guard a once-over. He looked more brawn than brains.

The man didn't even bother to look back. "Guillaume. I'm head of security and the Prince-Regent's personal bodyguard."

"No last name?" If he could keep the conversation rolling, maybe he could find a weak spot.

Guillaume chuckled. "My last name isn't for you to know. I already gave you enough information."

Well. He seemed upset. Ron couldn't quite understand why. Guillaume had no personal relations to the missing woman, and surely he only served the palace for money. Men could be bought and sold easier than anything else. Guillaume wouldn't be an exception, right?

"You sound angry. Why is that?"

Guillaume stepped out the automatic doors and marched to the curb. He yanked at the back door to a black car. "Get in."

"Answer my question."

"You toyed with The Crown's emotions." Guillaume finally met Ron's gaze. "And you assisted the most vicious criminal organization in Veldoria. Now, get in the car. We'll talk more at Vitromont."

With that small piece of anger, Ron knew the source of his exposure. That deceitful woman had really done it. She had sent her evidence up the food chain, leaving Ron to be devoured by the carnivores.

Ron settled into the vehicle, but his heart didn't settle. He would make her pay, one day soon. For double-crossing him and causing his downfall, Lady Estrella Hilmar would pay dearly.

Chapter 31

"Thirty-seven cameras and this is all they caught?" Violet spun the computer screen around to face Jonathan. "I'm beginning to think everyone has been paid off."

"It's possible, knowing how the Anti-Monarchists usually work." Frederick rolled his chair down the length of the table to take a closer look at the screen. "If they can't buy it with money, they blackmail emotions."

Jonathan loosened his tie and ran his fingers back through his hair. "A single glimpse of Alissa being dragged into the crowd. No way to tell who pulled her over the gate. Brilliant."

Violet rolled her eyes. "You would think in this day and age of technical advancement, someone would have snapped a picture or a video."

"Yet, here we sit." Jonathan leaned his head back, wishing that the headache forming along his temples would go away.

"It's been a day and a half." Violet turned the computer back around. "If we don't find her overnight... her chances..."

Jonathan and Frederick exchanged a knowing glance. They couldn't get Violet's hopes up, but it was hard to see them wither away. The longer she searched, the more negative she became.

"I've made my plea to the people. Someone will provide information. We simply have to wait." Jonathan did his best to console Violet, but it was hard on him, too. Alissa had been so frightened after the attack at the restaurant. How must she feel now? He could do nothing to ease her suffering. That hurt the most.

"If only we could convince Joffrey to talk." Frederick reached for his own laptop. "My sources don't have much. It's been eerily quiet."

"The calm before the storm, huh?" Violet stretched her arms up over her head. "Maybe we should bring the storm first."

"You're not going to the media," Frederick shot her a glare.

Violet stuck her tongue out at him. "That wasn't the storm I had in mind."

"I'm not giving you a weapon, either." Jonathan shook his head at her. "Keep watching videos until you have something solid. That's the best you can do."

"It sucks," Violet pouted.

"Not to bring the mood down any further, but..." Frederick sank back in his chair. "I finished trailing the source of the video. The one with the weapons."

"And?" Jonathan prodded.

Frederick shook his head. "The account belongs to Estrella Hilmar."

"Estrella?" Jonathan couldn't fathom it. Estrella may have her own way of dealing with situations, but she had never been anything but loyal to The Crown.

"It isn't a mistake." Frederick shrugged his shoulders. "I don't understand how she acquired the video, but Estrella sent it."

Yet another aspect of this whole situation that didn't make any sense. "Why send it when she could come hand it over herself?"

Guillaume rapped his knuckles on the open door. "Sire."

Jonathan turned his full attention to Guillaume. "Oh, you've returned."

"The senator has been taken into police custody. He confessed to selling the weapons and named the middle-man who arranged the meeting."

Finally, progress. Jonathan stood to his feet. Out of all the things that had happened, he could at least avenge the restaurant attack. Now that he knew the supplier behind the Anti-Monarchist's weapons. "Have we apprehended the man responsible?"

"It's a woman." Guillaume lowered his eyes to his feet. "A woman you know."

"Surely he didn't implicate Alissa in such a weak defense." Jonathan huffed a humorless laugh.

Guillaume shook his head. "Not Alissa. Estrella."

Jonathan didn't know how to react. Estrella had been a good friend these many years. Why now? When did she begin to work with those who opposed everything Jonathan stood for? Furthermore, did she have something to do with Alissa's abduction? Questions swarmed in Jonathan's head like bees itching to sting.

"When you say 'Estrella', do you mean that blonde witch lady with a stuck-up nose?" Violet slammed her laptop shut. "Because I've never officially met her, but I would like to punch her lights out."

"I've never liked her, either," Frederick piped up.

Violet pointed a finger at him. "Finally, something Freddie and I can agree on."

"Would you stop calling me Freddie?"

"Not likely to happen."

"Both of you shut up. I need to think." Jonathan leaned forward to rest his elbows on his knees. He didn't mind his brother or

Violet, but sometimes one needed a quiet space to collect his thoughts.

"There are two more matters to deal with, as well." Guillaume folded his hands behind his back. "Alissa's family has arrived, for one. Secondly, I'm told there is a young mother and her daughter who have visited the palace these past two days asking for an audience. They say it is related to lady Alissa. I can apprehend Estrella myself, but these two matters should be attended to personally."

Jonathan nodded. He couldn't argue with anything that Guillaume said. Everything needed tending to, and Jonathan was stretched too thin to do much about it.

"Violet, will you greet her family? Frederick can go with you, as well, to extend my apologies." Jonathan stood to his feet. "I will meet the mother and daughter. Please bring them to my office posthaste."

"Yes, sire." Guillaume bent in a quick bow before he went to carry out the orders.

Violet jumped to her feet and gave a salute. "Sir, yes sir!"

"He's not a general." Frederick sighed and waved a hand at Jonathan. "Go see to your guests. Perhaps they know more than we can find. I'll watch the loon."

Violet planted her hands on her hips. "Did you just call me crazy?"

"Think what you will."

Jonathan didn't have time to think about or read into their banter. With a thousand different things to accomplish, he couldn't afford time even to eat, let alone play nanny to his brother.

He left Violet and Frederick to sort out their own affairs. His office sat a good distance from the Security Hub, but thankfully Jonathan had long legs. He covered the distance in as short a time as he could manage.

Minutes after he made it back to his office, a knock sounded on Jonathan's door.

Jonathan took a steadying breath, fixed his tie, and rose to his feet. "Come in."

The door swung open boldly, but the visitors were more timid about their approach. Markum, who had opened the door himself, waited patiently for them to gather their wits.

When Guillaume had said a mother and daughter, Jonathan hadn't expected the sight that greeted him. A woman who couldn't be any older than Alissa and a girl so small she didn't even reach the doorknob. He had been curious before. Now, he couldn't help his desperate desire to know what they knew.

"Please, do come in." Jonathan stepped out from behind his desk. It seemed much too intimidating to remain there. Instead, he motioned toward a small table at the side of the room. "Markum, have the staff bring some tea and scones, would you?"

Markum dipped a bow. "As your highness wishes."

"Have a seat, if you will." Jonathan pulled a chair out from the table.

The young mother cautiously dipped a curtsy as she ventured across the room. "Thank you, Your Highness. You are too kind."

"I heard you came specifically to talk to me." Jonathan helped the mother into the chair, then watched as the daughter climbed into her lap. "Your child is lovely."

"Thank you, Your Highness."

"May I ask what your name is?" Jonathan took a seat across the table from the mother-daughter duo.

The mother dipped her head respectfully. "I am Jacqueline Garsonne, Your Highness."

"And your daughter?"

"Angelique."

Jonathan nodded thoughtfully. They seemed harmless enough. Perhaps they really did have something to tell him, but Jacqueline seemed extremely timid. He might be, too, if he sat as a commoner in the presence of a king.

Markum ushered a maid and a cart through the door. The maid quickly set out tea and scones on the table, along with a small plate of treats for the child.

Jonathan nodded his thanks. "I hope it is all to your satisfaction."

"Thank you, Your Highness." Jacqueline gingerly accepted a scone as the maid poured the tea.

Jonathan took a small sip of his drink before he dove in to the real reason for their meeting. "I've been told you came looking for me yesterday, as well."

"Yes, Your Highness." Jacqueline broke off the tip of her scone, but didn't eat it.

"What is your purpose?" Jonathan remained cordial, but he didn't like beating around the bush. He would get the information as quickly as possible. They didn't have time to spare.

Jacqueline settled her scone onto a dessert plate. "Lady Alissa was very kind to my daughter and I at the parade."

"Alissa is always kind." Jonathan fought to keep his voice steady and calm. He couldn't think about the current situation without emotion warring within him.

Jacqueline gave a solemn nod. "We... I... saw something happen."

"You were close by when Alissa was taken, then?"

"I didn't think it appropriate to discuss what I thought I saw. She had gone far down the fence-line, but... it was a man in the attire of a Royal Guard who ran after her and lifted her over the gate. Of this, I am certain." Jacqueline twisted her hands together atop the table, while Angelique focused solely on the treat in her pudgy little hands.

Jonathan let the silence hang. Deep down, he had known this would happen. Had known that, somehow, there was someone inside the palace who would betray him. After the accusation of Estrella earlier, it seemed only fitting to hear this news now.

"If I provide photographs of our palace staff, would you be able to recognize him?" Jonathan kept his voice low. If he let himself think too much, he would either give up or scream in anger.

Jacqueline nodded her head again. "I would, Your Highness. I apologize it has taken me so long to bring this information to you."

"You were denied audience yesterday. The fault does not lie entirely in your hands." Jonathan motioned to Markum. "Your tablet."

Markum extended the piece of technology to Jonathan. It took less than a minute to sign in to the personnel files.

Jonathan set the tablet in front of Jacqueline. "Please, take your time."

Jacqueline scrolled through the pictures, file by file, taking her time to examine each one. Sometimes, Jacqueline tilted her head like a bird, as if she might recognize the face. Jonathan settled on the edge of his seat, anxious to hear her final answer.

After a dozen false alarms, Jacqueline set the tablet down on the table. "This is the man."

Angelique looked up from her crumb-covered hands. "The bad man who hurt the princess. I didn't like him."

Jonathan picked up the tablet and glanced at the picture. He had known, deep down, who it would be. Anger wouldn't even come any more. All Jonathan felt was a resigned numbness. Even if they did manage to get Alissa back alive, those whom he trusted had betrayed him in the worst of ways.

Markum retrieved the tablet from Jonathan's hands. "Sire, should I take action?"

"Tell Guillaume to talk to him first. I will conclude my meeting with my guests." Jonathan subtly dismissed Markum from the room.

Markum left jogging.

"My apologies, Your Highness." Jacqueline bowed her head respectfully.

Jonathan shook his head. "Do not apologize. This is the kind of thing we have been in search of. I do not know how to repay your great kindness."

"It is my duty to serve my nation's leaders."

Angelique finished her snack. "Mama, I wanna see the princess."

"She isn't here today." Jacqueline cleared her throat uncomfortably.

Jonathan leaned forward against his knees. He caught Angelique's attention with a serious stare. "You should visit again. We would love to host you. Perhaps you can attend the next royal party at the palace, would you like that?"

"Can I wear a pretty dress?" Angelique tipped her head in a fashion similar to her mother.

Jonathan smiled gently. "Of course."

"I would love to come." And with that, Angelique lost her interest in requesting an audience with the princess.

Jacqueline set Angelique on her feet. "We have taken enough of your time. We should go."

"Allow me to send a reward for this information." Jonathan stood to his feet. "Something such as this shouldn't go unrewarded."

Jacqueline paused, then bent in deference. "If Your Highness so wishes."

"Please leave your names and address with the secretary on your way out." Jonathan walked Jacqueline and Angelique to the door. "I hope to see you soon."

Jacqueline bent another bow. "Yes, Your Highness. Our deepest sympathies for what you are going through."

"Thank you for your concern." Jonathan remained at the door until he saw the secretary taking their information. He refused to leave them without some sort of recompense for their valuable information.

With this, Jonathan finally had some of the upper hand. At the very least, he had a card he could play. Just in time. No one had a minute to spare anymore.

Chapter 32

Frederick rested a hand against Jonathan's shoulder. "Are you sure you want to do this alone?"

"Who else would we allow to question him? Violet?" Jonathan shrugged Frederick's hand off. "That's not a valid idea."

"I don't think Alissa's family will allow Violet to leave their side, anyway." Frederick shoved his hands into his pockets. "I barely managed to placate any of them after we broke the news. Her parents seem to believe it isn't our fault. Her brother is... less cooperative."

"I can put no fault on him for that." Jonathan shuffled through the folder in his hands. "If Joffrey manages to get free of his bonds, feel free to rush in and help."

"Trust me, it would be my pleasure." Frederick ground his teeth together. "Make it snappy. I should return to our guests soon."

"Sire." Guillaume opened the interview room door. "The police are on their way. We should begin now."

"Good luck." Frederick shot a devilish grin at his brother. As if he knew more than he let on.

Jonathan marched through the door and settled in the chair across from Joffrey. "I hear you handed your charge over to her abductors."

"Oh, did I?" Joffrey shrugged a shoulder. "I don't remember doing such a thing."

"We have witnesses." Jonathan leaned back in his chair and folded his arms across his chest. "Do you have an explanation for your behavior?"

"Do you have an explanation for yours? I returned to tell about Alissa's abduction. I escaped from those beating me. And this is how you treat me?" Joffrey rolled his eyes. "Yes, our monarch is quite hospitable."

"You didn't escape from anyone. *If* anyone beat you, you allowed it."

Joffrey blinked, as if he hadn't expected that deduction from the Prince-Regent. "What makes you say that?"

Finally, a break in the dam. Joffrey must have thought his story would hold up. He underestimated the intelligence of those working in the palace.

Jonathan nodded to Joffrey's cuffed hands. "Your hands are immaculate. No defensive wounds, which means you didn't fight back. Had it been a situation such as the one you describe, you should have wounds on your hands. Don't you know that?"

Joffrey remained silent, but his eyes darted to and fro. He must not know how to handle this turn of events.

Jonathan flipped open the printed file and spread the pages out. "I would think your brother would have taught you something so simple. He served alongside Adison Cebon in the Black Forces, yes?"

A muscle ticked in the side of Joffrey's jaw. "Don't speak of him."

"Adison? Or your brother?" Jonathan leaned his elbows on the table. Most unmannerly, but he wanted intimidation instead.

Joffrey glared at Jonathan. "My brother. Your foul mouth doesn't deserve to speak of his existence."

"That's quite the way to speak to your superior. Let alone your Sovereign." Jonathan clucked his tongue. "Your brother was honorable. I hear he gave his life in the pursuit of our nation's interests."

"Stop."

"I'm sure he served quite well. Adison had many good things to say about him. That's why he recommended you for Lady Alissa's detail. He thought you would have the same loyalty as your brother."

"I said stop."

"What was your brother's name? Oh, yes, here it is. Jordan. A fine name."

"SHUT UP!" Chains rattled as Joffrey yanked at his restraints. His chest heaved with the exertion of his emotions. "Don't say another word about Jordan."

Jonathan knew a breaking man when he saw one. He had chosen the correct card to play in this fierce game. "Why?"

"I told you, you don't deserve to utter his name. Jordan was too good for such an end." Joffrey dropped his chin to his chest. "Shut up about him."

"We could always talk about the Anti-Monarchists instead." Jonathan flipped to a different page. "You've been in touch with them. Often. I don't think your brother would approve."

"He would approve more than anyone," Joffrey muttered.

Jonathan arched his brows, surprised at the certainty with which Joffrey defended his own actions. "Why would he approve? You're going against the very thing that he devoted his life to protect."

"This country *took* his life. Don't make it a pretty picture to suit your whims."

"He was a hero. He died a hero's death."

"He was a pitiful man who died in a place no one can speak of and will never be remembered by the country he thought he loved," Joffrey growled.

"Ah." Jonathan nodded slowly. "So that's why you betrayed your country. A false sense of justice." He should have known. The Anti-Monarchists were brilliant at manipulating people into thinking they were doing the right thing. Joffrey, of course, would never be an exception.

"I'm done talking about Jordan."

"That's fine." Jonathan snagged a piece of paper he had scoured well. Joffrey's financial statements. "The police will be here soon to arrest you on charges of conspiracy, accepting bribes, and various other things. You could reduce your sentence if you tell us where Lady Alissa is."

Joffrey snorted. "As if I know."

"Why wouldn't you? They paid you handsomely enough." Jonathan waved the paper. "This is your last chance to fulfill the oath you took upon entering the palace."

"I don't believe in that oath." Joffrey looked away. "Even if I did, they segmented the whole plan. I did my part. Just wait and see what happens."

"I know what's going to happen." Jonathan dropped the paper back onto the table. "I am truly sorry you do not wish to take part in the winning side's victory."

Joffrey's laugh started as a scoff, then built to an outcry of mockery.

Jonathan sat and took each loud bellow as it fell from Joffrey's wide mouth. He could allow a broken man time to laugh. In a few hours, Joffrey would sit behind bars. Jonathan had certainty that

Joffrey wouldn't laugh, then. For now, they had the evidence they needed to put him away. They would start with that.

Jonathan refused to offer any tidings of good will. He stood to his feet and took the papers with him when he exited. Something inside of Joffrey had twisted long ago. Even a king couldn't untwist it.

Guillaume and Markum met Jonathan outside the door.

Markum shoved his glasses up on his nose. "We have word from parliament."

"Did the bill pass?" Jonathan handed the security file off to Guillaume.

Markum nodded. "It will arrive on your desk tomorrow morning."

"The Prime Minister called, as well." Frederick appeared through the doorway of the Viewing Room. "Estrella is set to be released during the night. He has a location for pickup."

Good. The timeline had moved at a speed Jonathan could accept. Nervousness, fear, and relief all warred inside his chest. A thousand things could happen in the next twelve hours. Jonathan dreaded most of them.

"Make sure no one tells Estrella we know what she's been up to." Jonathan squared his shoulders and tried to shut off the part of his brain where emotions thrived. "In the meantime, we have things to prepare."

"Yes, sir," Markum and Guillaume answered in unison.

Frederick pocketed his cell phone. A brief glimmer of something sad passed over his face, but Jonathan didn't have the heart to ask about it. For now, they would prepare for the worst. Tomorrow, they would discover what horrible future awaited them.

ഓരുള

Alissa didn't like any of the ways her body felt. Her ankle throbbed too hard to stand. Her ribs ached. Her breathing still hadn't returned to normal, causing dizziness and occasional nausea. On top of all that, her wrists hurt every time she moved them and she didn't know how long she had been in this stupid room.

No one had come to offer first aid, but they hadn't come to shoot her, either. They must need her alive for something. At least, that's what her creative brain assumed. Should she survive this ordeal, it would make a great chapter in a novel.

Then again, her whole life had been novel as of late.

Why did she ever think things would turn out well for a prince and a commoner? Fairytales didn't exist in real life.

Another contrived breath rattled in her chest. Alissa leaned her head back against the wall. She had to remain calm. If she panicked, it wouldn't help anything. There had to be a way out of this. Somehow, she could survive whatever they threw at her.

Lord, let me survive this.

The thought brought with it a rush of tears. Perhaps because the pain radiated so strongly through her body, weakening her defenses, Alissa let them flow. What use was it to hold them in?

Still, Alissa didn't allow them to fall for long. It wouldn't help for Estrella or someone to see them and use Alissa's weak state to their advantage. *Mentally strong. I can be mentally strong.*

Like Violet, Alissa would press through to the bitter end. Or so she told herself.

A shuffle of feet outside the door sounded far more frantic than Alissa had heard them before. A few shouted commands seemed to thrust everyone into hurry-mode.

Alissa attempted to sit straighter, but immediately gave up on the idea. Moving around hurt more than staying still.

The door crashed open. The man from before stormed his way inside.

Alissa lifted her chin defiantly, despite her sorry state. She wouldn't go down without a fight.

"Get up, we're leaving."

How rude. He didn't even bother to scoff at Alissa's attempt to keep her head up. Something must be going on, or else he wouldn't be here.

Alissa didn't budge an inch. Why would she? She may be his prisoner, but she wasn't his subordinate. Even in this situation, she didn't have to do what he said. Besides, it felt good to resist his demands.

The man didn't say another word. He simply reached out and hefted Alissa to her feet.

A squeaky cry left Alissa's lips. Her ankle nearly gave out again. Her breathing went sporadic and shallow. Vertigo tilted the world around her.

The man latched a hand around her arm and toted her along beside him, despite her discomfort and ill stomach.

Alissa wanted to ask where they were headed. She wanted to spew insults and demand answers. Instead, she kept quiet. It took enough effort to breathe, she couldn't spare any to speak.

The man dragged her down a few hallways before a van loomed in front of them. With little ceremony, he shoved Alissa to the floor in the back.

Alissa glanced up to find four of her original captors sitting around the benches. So much for an escape attempt. She couldn't even keep her eyes open unless she wanted to puke.

Alissa dropped her head back against the nearest panel and shut her eyes. She would need her strength for anything they planned. If only she could catch a breath.

Chapter 33

The last person Jonathan expected to see in his office at nine o'clock in the morning was Estrella. Yet, upon entering his office, there she sat. Alongside her father the Prime Minister, of course. Jonathan hadn't expected her to be stupid enough to show up on her own.

As soon as the door clicked shut, Estrella stumbled to her feet. "Jean!"

Oh, heavens. Jonathan tried his best not to roll his eyes. Estrella had always been dramatic. Why had he never seen the act before? Because he had grown used to it? Because he wanted to believe her sincerity from their childhood? Jonathan didn't know anymore.

"Jean, it was terrible." Estrella rushed her way across the office floor and threw her arms around Jonathan's torso. "I thought I was going to die!"

Jonathan carefully extricated himself from Estrella's lethal grip. "Are you injured anywhere?"

"No, they didn't hurt me." Estrella reached up to swipe at a crocodile tear. "But they frightened me."

Jonathan hadn't expected her to come back injured. If she had helped the Anti-Monarchists, they wouldn't lay a finger on her. She was a valuable connection to them. Thus, it made sense that she would stand here unscathed and spew lies about how terrified she had been. Estrella simply didn't get scared. She never had.

Estrella tipped up her face to pout. "Aren't you going to say anything?"

There were a thousand things Jonathan wanted to say, but he couldn't afford for the Anti-Monarchists to find out that he knew their plan. So, he settled for the one question that would determine the level of his leniency on Estrella.

"Did you happen to see Alissa there? Is she alright?"

Estrella looked down and shook her head slowly. Her blonde hair quivered in the cold breeze the action emitted. "I didn't know she was missing, as well. My sincerest apologies, Jean. You must be hurting."

"More than you know." Jonathan barely contained the sneer he wanted to throw in her direction. Where had she gone wrong? Why would Estrella set things up like this and then lie to him about it? She used to be upright and righteous. When did she change?

Estrella glanced up again.

Jonathan stepped around her and headed for his desk. He couldn't look her in the eye and pretend she hadn't betrayed him. "Did you discuss what happened with the police? I presume they would covet any information you could provide."

"I spent hours with them last night." Estrella turned and followed Jonathan.

Jonathan nodded once. "Prime Minister, are you feeling better this morning?"

"My daughter has returned. I feel relieved." The Prime Minister seemed to watch Jonathan and Estrella a little too closely.

Jonathan didn't know if it was suspicion or concern that clouded the Prime Minister's face. He hated to have to tell a father that his daughter had taken a dark and dangerous path. It couldn't be avoided. If all went according to plan, he would have to shatter Estrella's father's world in mere hours.

"Aren't you even the least bit relieved that I came back safely?" Estrella planted her palms on the far side of Jonathan's desk.

Jonathan didn't look up from the papers in front of him. If he did, he might snap. "I never wish for any of my acquaintances to die, so I am relieved you are well."

"Then you should treat us to breakfast. Tea, at the least."

"Apologies, but in your absence I've been named Prince-Regent. I am busy." Jonathan flipped a page, Perhaps a little too violently.

Estrella frowned. "Are you angry with me over something?"

"My girlfriend has been abducted and I don't know the demands. It's stress." Half a truth. Not entirely a lie. Jonathan was stressed, but it didn't entirely rest in the fact that Alissa had gone missing. Anger and distrust simmered, too.

"It feels like anger."

Jonathan set the papers down on his desk and pasted a half-hearted smile on his face. "Considering we believe that the men who took Alissa may be the same men who abducted you, security has asked for a personal statement from you. Markum can see you and your father to the Hub. Try to avoid the small brunette if you want to continue living. She doesn't seem to like you."

"What about breakfast?"

"I'm sure the palace staff can provide you with something. The guards wouldn't let a lady like yourself starve." Jonathan hated the words coming out of his own mouth. He wanted to scream at her, to make Estrella come to her senses, but the timing hadn't come yet.

"I suppose you're too busy to come with me."

Jonathan nodded and pressed the intercom button. "Markum, please escort Prime Minister and his daughter to security." He didn't wait for an answer. Another minute in Estrella's presence and Jonathan wouldn't be able to take any more.

Markum cracked the door and poked his head inside. "Um..."

Jonathan stood to his feet. Markum didn't hesitate in his speech. Something seemed wrong. Very, very wrong. "What is it?"

"Your highness. That is..." Markum shoved his glasses up his nose. "There's... a disturbance..."

"What kind of disturbance?" Jonathan brushed past Estrella's shoulder as he rushed for the door. "What's going on?"

Markum hesitated again.

The door jerked all the way open. Guillaume stepped inside and held out a tablet with video already cued. "This van circled the palace seven times since early this morning. Five minutes ago, it parked."

"Oh. Is that all?" Jonathan had been hoping for more. Incidences of this kind were hardly rare.

Guillaume opened his mouth to speak, but it was Frederick's voice that rose from the hall.

"Alissa is in the State Rooms entrance and the man holding her has a gun."

Jonathan didn't wait for a further explanation. He sprinted for the door.

Guillaume reached out to yank him back. "I don't think it's a wise decision, sire."

"I don't care if it's a wise decision or not. Isn't he asking for me? And the bill passed in parliament?" Jonathan jerked his arm away from Guillaume's hold. "If you're concerned, come with me. I won't sit idly by."

Jonathan didn't understand where he got the courage to spew such nonsense, but he didn't regret a word of it. If a king couldn't take action, himself, then why should he be allowed to rule a nation?

Guillaume inclined his head in a single nod. "Let's go."

"Thank you." Jonathan stepped into the hall.

Frederick fell in line beside him.

Neither brother spoke a word on the march to the State Rooms. Guillaume, behind them, spit commands and demands into his comm. Markum protested this course of action. No one listened to him.

Guillaume stepped in front of the princes as they reached the State Rooms' door. "As you predicted, he's demanding to see you with the bill in hand."

"Markum?"

"I'll go retrieve it, if your highness so wishes, but I must advise against this, as well."

Jonathan shook his head. "It doesn't matter as long as Alissa is safe. What about snipers?"

"He positioned himself well. We're working on it. Right now, there are too many civilians still inside. We've sent as much security as we can spare." Guillaume glanced to his feet. "The picture inside isn't pretty, sire."

"I'll see it for myself." Jonathan straightened his suit jacket and adjusted his tie. If he was going in to such a situation, he would do so with the presence of a Ruler.

Guillaume pressed a finger to his ear. "His highness and I are entering now."

Jonathan glanced to his brother beside him. Frederick nodded his own unspoken assurances. Both brothers shoved open one of the double doors.

Dress shoes clicked against ancient stone as the brothers made their way onto the balcony overlooking the State Rooms' lobby.

Scattered civilians cowered in corners, while others stood proudly with their phones clicking pictures or recording videos. All the better for evidence later.

The double staircase descending either side of the balcony held a regiment of security. Even more lined the room below. All held weapons pointing at one focal point.

Jonathan peered over the closest security guard's shoulder. His fists clenched at the sight before him.

Alissa didn't look uninjured in the slightest. Even at this distance, Jonathan could see problems. Wrists and fingers stained brown with her own blood, now caked and dried. Her shoulders heaving with each shallow breath. The tint of blue around her lips, and the daze in her eyes.

Behind her, like a coward, a single man hid. Guillaume had a point. The man had positioned himself well. With the wall at his back and Alissa positioned in front of his slouched body, he could remain unharmed for now.

It was the black gun pressed against Alissa's head that concerned Jonathan the most.

"I've come," Jonathan projected his voice rather than shouting.

Alissa's gaze shot up to the balcony. Jonathan didn't know if the expression on her face meant hope or sorrow.

The man didn't make any move that would give way for one of the guards to shoot. "Did you bring the bill?"

"It's on its way."

Guillaume leaned to Jonathan's ear. "Her family heard. They're almost here."

Jonathan nodded. He couldn't do anything about it. They deserved to see what was going on, as much as Jonathan deserved to be here.

"If the bill isn't here, what are you doing here? Trying to stall me? It won't work."

That didn't sound promising. Either the man holding Alissa had too much courage, or he was a true and genuine coward. If the first, he would never settle. If the second, Jonathan worried about a twitchy trigger finger.

A clatter of various feet filed onto the balcony behind Jonathan and Frederick. Both princes turned to look.

Alissa's stone-faced father and weeping mother stared back at them.

A piece of Jonathan's heart tore at their heartbreak. It mirrored his own, only so much more expressive.

Violet marched forward, away from the family, and poked her head between two guards' arms. "He's got a gun? Pointed at *my* bestie?"

Fuming, Violet spun and started for the stairs.

Frederick made a move to stop her, but Alissa's brother moved faster.

Cody snagged Violet's arm and hauled her backward. "Oh, no, you don't. She doesn't need you messing everything up right now. Stay still and let the pros handle this."

"Who says I'm not a pro?" Violet hissed.

Jonathan threw up a hand to stop her. "Not now, Violet. Stay with the family. No one descends this balcony."

"Stop talking up there!" the man behind Alissa shouted. The tremor in his voice didn't bode well for the situation at hand.

Jonathan moved back to the line of guards at the railing. "Okay, we'll stop. We'll stop. Calm down."

"I am calm."

The twitch and shake of the man's hand said otherwise. Jonathan tapped his fingers against his leg. It worried him that Alissa hadn't said a word. In fact, she seemed to sway on her feet. As if she might collapse at any moment.

Markum pushed through the throng of people behind Jonathan and held out a folder. "The bill."

"The document just arrived." Jonathan snatched the folder before Markum could attempt to dissuade him. "What shall I do now?"

"Move the guards so I can see you."

"I can barely see your face, either." Jonathan tried his best to remain calm, not sarcastic. "Shouldn't this favor go both ways?"

"They'll shoot me if I come out."

"And you won't shoot me? You've done quite a lot to overthrow the monarchy."

"I won't shoot you. It defeats the purpose if I shoot you. Then your signature won't be valid. You won't be the reigning sovereign anymore."

"Ironically, I won't be the reigning sovereign anymore if I sign the papers, either."

The gun rattled as the man shook it at Alissa's head. "Do what you're told! Don't try to play this cleverly."

Alissa's fragile whimper echoed in the grand hall.

Jonathan dug his fingers into the folder. Only by doing so could he keep his face stoic. "Move." He wouldn't stand for this, but he would play along until his chance came.

The guards moved just enough to allow Jonathan to stand at the banister. Even so, Jonathan heard Guillaume's quiet grumbling behind him.

"Show me the document," the man below demanded.

Jonathan held up the folder. "It's here."

"Open it and show me."

With a sigh, Jonathan flipped open the cover and held it up.

The man shook the gun at Alissa's head again. "Come down here so I can see it."

"That's a ridiculous breach of security," Guillaume instantly piped up.

Jonathan shook his head. The man behind Alissa didn't seem stable enough to argue logically. "Do it. You come with me."

"Take me with you, too!" Violet demanded.

Both Frederick and Cody shot her a glare. "No."

Jonathan didn't pay attention to the insults she spewed at them in the next few moments. All that mattered was keeping Alissa safe. Responding to the demands made so they could end the negotiation on good terms. The Anti-Monarchists could pay for this later, in a myriad of ways.

Without bothering to argue with anyone, Jonathan jogged his way down the stairs and to the middle of the lobby. He held open the folder again. "This is the document."

"Sign it."

"If I sign it, will you let her go?"

The man's pause could have been for thinking, but Jonathan had other hunches. In the end, the man pressed the gun closer to Alissa's head.

She lost her balance and stumbled sideways.

It should have been the perfect opportunity, except the man managed to move with her.

Jonathan scowled at the misfortune. "Will you release her?"

"Yeah, sure, whatever." The man shook the gun again. "Just sign it."

Alissa winced this time.

Jonathan reached a hand back to Guillaume. "Give me a pen."

"Sire."

"A pen!" Jonathan could no longer hold back his rage or despair. Not when Alissa stood mere feet in front of him, waiting for someone to save her.

Guillaume kept one hand on his weapon and extended a pen with the other.

Jonathan quickly scribbled on the page and held it up again. "It's signed. I signed it. Let her go now."

"Toss the document to me."

"Not until you release Alissa." Jonathan knew better than to obey every whim of someone like that. If he handed over the document now, Alissa would never go free.

"You'll just shoot me if I do."

"I won't. You have my word. Hand over Alissa and you can leave here unharmed." Jonathan held the folder out toward the man. "Take it with you, I don't mind. Just let her go."

"Sire."

"Here's how we do this." The man's voice became suspiciously calm. "You toss the document this way. I use her as my shield until we reach the main gate, and then I'll let her go. When I'm sure there's not any security that can shoot me."

"Alright. Let's do that."

"Sire!"

"Shut up." Jonathan shot a glare in Guillaume's direction.

Guillaume nodded once, but he lifted his weapon higher.

Jonathan turned back to the scene before him. They were so close. So close to recovering Alissa from the clutches of madmen. "You move first. We will follow." Jonathan glanced to Guillaume. "Tell the men to stand down."

"Yes, sir," Guillaume bit out. If looks could kill, Guillaume would have slain a good portion of the people inside the hall.

The man pulled Alissa flush against him and took a sideways step. His back remained against the wall, always guarded.

Jonathan gave Alissa another once-over as she started moving. She limped, which meant a foot, ankle, or knee must be hurting. "Alissa, are you alright?"

The soft-spoken answer Jonathan wanted never came. Alissa merely shook her head once.

"Stop talking. Just move." The man moved the gun down to Alissa's shoulder, somewhere near her heart.

It would, of course, be easier to move around that way. Jonathan could commend his thoughtfulness, but he couldn't commend his actions.

Bit by cautious bit, the four of them stalked to the entrance, then out into the open air. The public courtyard held even more spectators, none of them oblivious to the situation. The whole ordeal would be on the nightly news, thanks in part to the videos shot by Jonathan's own subjects.

He didn't care, as long as the man released Alissa.

"Stop here," The man commanded Alissa. He stood to his full height and took a step back. "Toss me the document."

Jonathan set the folder on the cobblestones and kicked it. Hard. It ended up by the man's feet.

The man bent to pick it up, always keeping his gun leveled at Alissa. Twitchy, he may be, but he obviously knew how to use the weapon.

"I'm leaving now. Don't try to stop me or I'll shoot."

"Go." Jonathan couldn't force more than the one word out of his mouth. He wanted to beg, but he couldn't. Not on camera and not with Alissa's life on the line.

Alissa swayed on her feet again, staggering to one side.

The man jogged backward until he reached the main gates.

A shot rang out.

Alissa collapsed.

"No!" Jonathan cried at the same moment Guillaume tackled him to the ground.

A dozen more shots echoed in the courtyard. Jonathan knew who the other shots had been aimed at. He didn't care. Only one thing mattered.

Guillaume tried to haul Jonathan to his feet, but Jonathan refused to give in and go inside.

"Alissa." Jonathan looked around, trying to regain his bearings. Where had she fallen? "Alissa?"

A sea of black-clad security personnel invaded the courtyard. Civilian visitors raced for cover, even though the shooting had stopped.

Jonathan finally spotted her, laying still against the cobble-stones. "Alissa!"

Try as he might to scramble to his feet, Jonathan couldn't. Instead, he half-crawled, half-ran to her side. Nevermind the men swarming around them. Nevermind the man at the main gates, bleeding out onto the stone. All that mattered was the woman before him.

Red blossomed from Alissa's shoulder, across the white dress she wore.

Jonathan wrapped his arms around her and lifted, cradling her close to his chest. "Alissa, wake up. Look at me."

Those long eyelashes fluttered. Open. Closed. Open again.

"Stay with me, hmm?" Jonathan pressed a hand to her shoulder. He didn't like the rasp in her breaths, nor the blue tint still around her lips. "Just stay awake. Help is coming. You'll be alright."

Alissa shook her head, slowly from one side to the other.

"No, don't be like that. You'll be alright." She had to believe it so that Jonathan could believe it. "You're going to be fine."

Alissa opened her mouth as if to say something, but all that came out was a desperate cough and a small trail of crimson. Her eyes fluttered shut again.

"No. Alissa, no. Don't do this." Jonathan pressed a hand to her cheek, wishing he knew how to make her better. Wishing he could make her hold on. "You can't."

Alissa's trembling fingers closed over Jonathan's. Inch by inch, she tugged, until she could force her dangling earring into Jonathan's palm.

Jonathan frowned. What was she trying to say? He didn't understand why any woman would give her earring as a parting gift. It was only when he looked at the flower shimmering on the end of the chain that he understood. One perfect azalea.

Take care of yourself for me.

Jonathan moved his attention back to Alissa's face just in time to see her eyes shut fully. Her fingers slipped from his and landed against her stomach, then the cobblestones.

"Alissa!" A shout of her name came from her family as they rushed into the courtyard.

Jonathan shut his eyes in an attempt to block the tears, but they escaped anyway. Along with a cry that echoed back and forth across the courtyard. One uncontainable wail that held all the anger, contempt, and sorrow built up inside.

Chapter 34

A draft blew across Alissa's cheek, a puff of warm air that drew her back to consciousness. The consistent ping of heartbeats and oxygen levels created a distracting white noise in the quiet room. Something soft and cozy covered her now, instead of only dank coldness in her prison.

Alissa let her eyes adjust to the light before she dared move. Surprisingly, it seemed she could breathe better here. Her ankle didn't throb quite as much. Her shoulder, on the other hand, ached ferociously.

That same huff of warm air crossed Alissa's cheek again. She turned her head to find its source.

Jonathan's face lay too close, but the sight of it washed relief over Alissa's heart and mind. They had survived. Both of them. And they were finally together again.

Upon closer inspection, it appeared that Jonathan had fallen asleep sitting up, then slumped sideways. That action must have landed his head on the far side of her pillows. With his eyes closed, he seemed so peaceful. So serene.

Jonathan's nose and brow crinkled briefly. He blinked his eyes open. A slow smile spread over his lips. "You're awake."

"So are you." Alissa didn't know where else to begin. There were so many things she should probably say, but she couldn't focus on any of them.

"How do you feel? Better?" Jonathan didn't move from his spot, but Alissa didn't mind.

"Some." Alissa braced her arm to push herself upright.

Jonathan quickly reached out to help. "Careful, you've a tube in your chest."

"Why?" Alissa realized this was a hospital room, but she didn't know the extent of her own injuries.

Jonathan stroked a hand over her hair to smooth it. "You had a deflated lung. It seems you somehow managed to break a rib, which caused this. You also had infected wounds on both wrists and a hairline fracture in your ankle."

"So you're saying I'm going to be here for a while." Alissa groaned and leaned her head back. Just what she wanted. Hospital confinement.

"Adison is two doors down. I'm certain he would enjoy keeping you company. If not, I'll send your family or Frederick."

Alissa smiled softly, as close to a laugh as she could manage at the moment. "Why does my shoulder hurt?"

"That is from the bullet wound. They've stitched you up and it wasn't too serious."

"The guy that shot me?" Alissa didn't know what else to ask. There were too many things that had happened in the last few days. How did she know where to start her inquiries?

Jonathan took her hand in both of his. "He made it through surgery. Barely. We'll see if he wakes up."

"Estrella was there, with me." Even if Jonathan and Estrella had been childhood friends—perhaps *because* they had been childhood friends—Alissa felt the need to tell him about everything. "Not *with* me, with me. Just there. She got to walk around freely."

"I know." Jonathan gave Alissa's hand a squeeze. "Frederick found evidence of her involvement with the Anti-Monarchists. She will be prosecuted according to our laws."

"I'm sorry." Alissa couldn't imagine what it must feel like, for someone that had once been so close to betray like that.

"Don't be sorry. You're alive." Jonathan lifted Alissa's fingers to his lips. "Thank you for enduring. You never should have had to go through that."

"Joffrey..."

"I know about that, as well. We've taken care of it. Don't worry. Just rest."

A door slammed against the wall. Jonathan and Alissa both turned to look.

"My precious little angel!" Violet raced into the room and landed on the other side of Alissa's bed. "What happened to you? Are you okay? Because I would totally go find that jerk-face idiot and beat him up."

"He already got shot, I think you're in the clear." Alissa closed her eyes, hoping someone would come to calm Violet down. She couldn't handle many more threats on the men who abducted her. Listening to Violet rant gave Alissa a headache.

"Queen Bee, leave her alone. She's working on reinflating a lung."

Alissa peeked open one eye at the sound of her brother's voice

Cody strode into the room, hands in his pockets. "You doing okay, little sis?"

"Better than before." Alissa tried to sneak a peek behind Cody, in case there were any more surprise guests. "I don't remember you being here before I was taken. Were you?"

"Nah, Prince Charming over there flew us in after that whole mess. We've been here a few days." Cody shrugged his shoulders. "Before you ask, I convinced your parental units to stay in the waiting room. I didn't figure you could take too many visitors and you know how mom gets when one of us is hurt."

"Thanks, Codester." Alissa let her eyes close again. "I appreciate it."

"She should rest for now." Jonathan released Alissa's hand, like a sloth releasing his favorite branch. "We should all give her time to recuperate."

"I exercise my rights as best friend forever!" Violet's weight lifted from the bed. "I'll stay, you go. Talk to you later."

"Like that's going to happen." Cody's voice. "Get your butt out that door, young lady."

"You're not the boss of me."

"Everyone, *please*," Jonathan interrupted. "We can discuss this in the hall."

"Not if I'm staying here!"

The argument continued, with Violet and Cody in the center. Like always. Alissa couldn't help but smile at the warm, homey feeling it presented her. Finally, things felt right again. With her brother, her best friend, and her boyfriend as background noise, Alissa slipped to sleep.

Chapter 35

Two weeks after the incident, Jonathan had barely caught up on any of the work assigned to him. Of course, he had taken time off more often than not, in order to visit Alissa in the hospital. She should be discharged today and, if all went according to plan, she would move into her suite in the palace. This one closer to the royal residences than her guest room.

Only one crucial detail remained. Jonathan glanced at his watch and stood from his desk. He should be here any moment.

On cue, Jonathan's intercom buzzed. The secretary's voice rang over the speaker. "Lady Alissa's father is here to see you."

"Send him in." Jonathan circled the desk and waited, instead, by the tea table. How could he be more nervous now than he had been when he asked to date the woman?

Alissa's father stepped through the doors like he owned the place, scowl firmly set on his face. Jonathan couldn't blame him. If he had trusted his daughter to Jonathan, he should expect better results than these.

"Mr. Cassidy."

"Jonathan."

Jonathan winced. Part of him hated being just a man in front of Alissa's father. The other part of him respected that Mr. Cassidy overlooked the royal bloodline flowing through Jonathan's veins.

"Please have a seat." Jonathan motioned to the table. "One of the maids is bringing up tea and coffee, if you are interested."

Mr. Cassidy did take a seat, but not at the table. Instead, he chose the sofa near the door. "Let's get straight to the point of why you called me in here."

"Alissa is supposed to be discharged today." He couldn't beat around the bush with her father. Mr. Cassidy wasn't that kind of man.

"Cody already went to pick her up. What of it?" Mr. Cassidy folded his arms.

Jonathan glanced heavenward to silently plead for help. "If you consent to it, I would like it if Alissa could stay on, here in the palace."

"Why should I let her do that? You're nothing more than a boyfriend."

"I intend to marry her, as soon as she'll have me, but there are protocols that need to be completed first." Jonathan knew he would ramble if he continued on, but at this juncture he didn't care. "It's dangerous to send her home with her injuries and with the Anti-Monarchists still on the hunt—"

"Oh, yeah. Those idiots. I thought they got your signature on some bill overthrowing the monarchy? And what about that Estrella lady?"

"Estrella is going to prison, and I didn't actually sign the bill. I'm not foolish." Jonathan pressed a fist to his lips and coughed. He hadn't meant to say that out loud. "That aside, I believe she would be safer staying in a residence internally. Here."

"Her mother and I can't leave our business indefinitely. Why should I leave my daughter half a world away?"

"I love her." Jonathan took a step forward, as if proximity would convince Mr. Cassidy of his sincerity. "She'll have people around her twenty-four hours a day here. She'll have things to learn and people to meet. I won't misbehave."

"I wasn't worried about you misbehaving." Mr. Cassidy shrugged a shoulder. "I'm only concerned about what Alissa wants right now, so if she agrees to stay here, I'll give consent. But I have conditions."

"Of course. Anything you desire."

"Those conditions are for Alissa, not you. I'm sure you'll protect her like you've been doing." Mr. Cassidy stood to his feet. "If that's all, I'm going to finish packing. We have a flight to catch."

"Are you taking Violet with you?"

Mr. Cassidy chuckled. "At Alissa's insistence. Take care of my girl."

"Yes, sir."

Jonathan had never felt such relief in his entire life. It felt like he had won the jackpot. Like Christmas and his birthday all in one. From now on, he could earnestly plan his future with Alissa, and with her father's blessing at that. It meant everything to him.

With a light heart, Jonathan returned to his work.

Anticipation of Alissa's arrival got the better of him after a good hour. Jonathan found himself wandering the halls, waiting. Wondering. How would the next chapter of their lives pan out for them? Would things always be dangerous, or would he and Alissa find their happily ever after?

It was Guillaume's number that dialed Jonathan's cell phone to announce Alissa's arrival. Jonathan hadn't bothered to try and find someone else who could be trusted to get her from the hospital to the palace. Guillaume had volunteered.

Jonathan met the car at the private entrance. He personally opened the back door and offered Alissa a hand.

Alissa smiled up at him, her eyes finally bright again after all she had been through.

Cody shot out the other side of the car and jogged around. "Hey, what's going on? You come to greet your guests now?"

"I have something to show Alissa." Jonathan reached for Alissa's hand again. "Shall we?"

Alissa didn't hesitate to accept Jonathan's generous offer.

Their trip through the halls went slower than normal, thanks to Alissa's crutches and rib-bracing bandages. Jonathan didn't mind. He enjoyed being able to help her.

Alissa seemed too focused on breathing to ask where they were going, or she didn't notice that they had taken a different route. She only stopped when Jonathan did, outside a door fit with both a traditional and modern locking mechanism.

"You'll have to set the code," Jonathan instructed as he opened the door.

"Are you going to help me in?" Alissa lifted that all-knowing gaze to him again.

Jonathan shook his head. "These apartments are yours. I will not be entering. Not alone."

"Why?"

"Because I promised your father I would take care of you. Your ladies' maids will be up here to introduce themselves later. Rest for now."

Alissa nodded once and took a step forward. She immediately wobbled.

Jonathan reached out to steady her.

"Are you sure you're not going to help me?" Alissa asked again

Jonathan couldn't help himself. With those eyes staring at him and those lips pouting, who could? He bent his head and pressed a kiss to her lips. Not long, but firm.

He smiled when he pulled back. One woman shouldn't look so satisfied with such a kiss. "I told you. Not alone."

"I'll respect that." Alissa's eyes fluttered open. As soon as Jonathan caught a hint of a blush against her cheeks, she scrambled to limp through the door. "Bye, I'll see you later." The door clicked shut behind her.

Jonathan smiled to himself, his fingers brushing his lips. She would be safe here, even from him. That was a thought that Jonathan treasured, since he cherished Alissa more than anything else. One day, their relationship would progress. They would marry, have a future and a family.

For today, Jonathan turned away from the door and headed for his office. There was much work to be done before happily ever after began.

ACKNOWLEDGEMENTS

First of all, to my Lord and Savior Jesus the Christ – without His guidance and inspiration, I never could have started or finished this story. My creativity is merely an extension of His.

As always, a huge thanks to my family – you all know how much I appreciate your support. It's a huge job to put up with me while I'm putting together a new release and you've all been so patient with me. I love you guys!

To my Beta Readers – you know who you are. I appreciate all the positive and constructive feedback. This book wouldn't be as good without your comments.

All of my social media followers – it always amazes me that you still follow me! Thank you all for being there every time I publish a book.

My readers – it's weird to think I have fans out there, but you keep buying my books so... (insert laughing emoji here). I am so thankful for all of you, new and old. Without you I wouldn't have a job.

Author's Note

Here we are, starting another journey together. This particular book (and the rest of this trilogy) are near and dear to my heart for so many reasons. Without going into an hours-long diatribe about it, these books have been a long time in coming and contain some of my favorite things.

Exploring Jonathan and Alissa's story began as an exploration of a personal "what-if" and blossomed from there. Some parts were easy to write, others difficult to express in words. I hope it comes across as I intended it, and that you love them as much as I do.

The rest of the trilogy is sure to have other things in store for you, but I certainly hope that you remember Jonathan and Alissa as the epic love story they were meant to be.

All my love and respect to my readers,

Megan